Coming Home

A Windsor Peak Novel

Denise Latham

Dedication

To Camden and Calum, my everything and my reason for everything I do. I love you both forever and always, and am so proud to be your mom.   To my husband, Tom, who served our country fearlessly with the U.S. Army prior to retirement, giving up time with his family and away from home. We are proud of you and love you.

To Brendan, Conor, Timmy, Tessa and Emmy, I love you all more than words could say.

In loving memory of Jen Kane, who was stolen from the world on 9/11.

She will never be forgotten.

Chapter 1

"Stay with me, Chris. Medics will be here any minute now." The heat of the desert sun beat down on his back. The sounds of bullets flying surrounded him, his team in action at his command, doing as they had been trained. Sand blew into his eyes and mouth, making them gritty.

"Sarge, I want to go home." His face grew paler by the second, and tears tracked down his dirty cheeks.

"You're going home. As soon as we can get you on a chopper, you're on the way home. Don't close your eyes, Chris." He pressed down harder on the wound on the teenager's abdomen, trying to stop the pulsating flow of blood.

Jake hung his head, letting his own tears rain down to mix with the ones on Chris's face. It should have been me, he thought, looking down at the innocence and youth that lay dead in his arms.

***

Shaking his head, taking a few deep breaths, and loosening his iron grip on the steering wheel, Jake Burrows focused on the road in front of him. The lone stop sign at the entrance to the downtown area of Windsor Peak, Vermont, gave him a chance to take his first deep breath in weeks. Main Street looked the same, with some trees just starting to turn their bright colors that would draw in the tourists. The mountain looming over the town was free from snow for a few more weeks at least. This time of year was usually his favorite, and he was grateful that this one little piece of the planet had remained mostly unchanged.

A country singer was praising the virtues of a cold beer before Jake silenced him with the power button and forced himself to switch into stoic mode. It had kept him alive for many years, and he needed to rely on it now. Falling apart as soon as he set foot in the farmhouse would set off his entire family, and he couldn't handle their worry on top of what he was already dealing with. He needed to get through the door, face his son for the first time in over a year, and hold it together.

Once his head hit the pillow tonight, the nightmares would come, and he would deal with them in the privacy of his room.

He parked his SUV in the driveway, happy to see two yellow Labrador retrievers, Twix and Reese, come bounding off the porch to greet him. His entire body groaned as he got out of the car, but his left shoulder screamed in outrage. The sling holding his arm in place provided support, but not pain relief, and every bump up the country roads from the highway had woken his nerve endings. Doing the drive straight through from Virginia with only a few stops had seemed a good idea when he set out, but now he realized it was a mistake.

As he stood waiting for his body to adjust, petting the dogs, the front door opened, and a welcome sight appeared. Stella St. Claire, with her hair pinned up and an apron on, stepped out of the front door. She was no more than five feet tall and was light enough that he and his brothers had regularly picked her up in a hug. Her hair was grayer now than the last time he had seen her, but her blue eyes were bright and shining with some unshed tears at the sight of Jake.

"Jake! You're here! I can't believe it; we had no idea you were coming. What an amazing surprise!" She rushed down the porch steps and crossed to him with outstretched arms. "What happened to you?"

"Hi, Stella." He hugged her, then reached into the open back of his SUV to sling a guitar over his shoulder. "I just started driving and never quite got the nerve up to call ahead. The shoulder met a bullet it didn't like, so I need some recovery time. I hope it's okay that I came without notice."

"Of course, it's fine, this is your home, no need to call ahead. I'm so glad you're here, and well enough to drive yourself." Stella patted his good arm. "Let me help you with your stuff."

He waved her away, grabbing a duffel bag. "I only have this, so I can get it if you don't mind hitting the button to close the back. Who else is here?"

She turned to walk back into the house, opening the door for him to pass through. "Your dad is out but should be back soon. He had a meeting downtown about the Harvest Festival that should be wrapping up about now. Charlie is up in his room."

Feeling a tightness in his chest at the knowledge that his son was in the house, he turned to Stella as he placed his gear at the base of the stairs. "How has everything been around here?"

"Same old thing, Jake. We worry about you, and we see your brothers once in a while." She looked up the stairs. "Charlie is doing well, but I'll let him fill you in on his life."

"Not so sure he'll want to do that. Most of my emails and texts only get brief responses, if any." Jake wiped a hand over his face. "And he never answers when I try to call him."

"He's a teenager, Jake. He feels a little lost and unsure of his place in life, and what he wants the future to hold." She paused and studied Jake, making him feel as though she could see right into his soul. "Very much like his father, I think. Are you hungry? Do you want to sit and chat for a few minutes before anyone else knows you're here?"

He ached for the offered comfort more than he needed air in his lungs. Throughout his life, all the sicknesses, the times he got in trouble with his father, fights with his brothers, and minor things like bee stings, Stella had been the one making it all better. She was the mother he had needed then and now, the only mother figure he had ever known, and letting out all his worries would unburden him in so many ways.

As quickly as the thought came, the reminder that he was a father himself, with a son who needed his attention, brought him back to reality. First, he would focus on his relationship with Charlie, then he could spend time working through the memories that haunted him.

Stella grabbed him around the waist and hugged him with every bit of strength in her small frame, and he soaked it in as long as he could. Even without him saying anything, of course, she knew how badly he needed it. After all, she had moved in and helped to raise him after his own mother had died, and probably knew him better than almost anyone.

"I think I'll just put my stuff upstairs and say hi to Charlie," he said as he backed away from her. He took the stairs slowly, stopping at the top as he heard a bedroom door open.

His son stood at the open door, looking at the phone in his hand. Just a bit taller than Jake now, at least six foot two, he had put on muscle in the last year. His sandy-colored hair was just a little too long, falling to cover his blue eyes as he looked down. Jake drank in the sight of him, his heart aching at how his baby had grown up so fast. Charlie was about to turn fifteen, and he couldn't take credit for how good he was turning out.

"Grandpa, I forgot to tell you…" Charlie's voice trailed off as he saw his father standing in the hall. "What are you doing here?" His cheeks reddened slightly, his expression quickly switching from open and friendly to angry.

"Hi, Charlie," Jake tried to hide his disappointment in his son's reaction to seeing him after a year. The hug he had been thinking about for days wasn't going to happen, so he tucked his hand into his pocket to resist the urge. "I came to see you, and to spend some time up here while I recover."

"Nice of you to squeeze it in. I'll try to stay out of your way." Charlie stepped back into his room and slammed the door.

Not the homecoming he wanted, but certainly what he expected. It had been over a year since he had seen Charlie before his last tour started in Afghanistan. Every time he came home and left again when his leave ended, the divide grew bigger between them. He knew he wasn't the father Charlie wanted, but he didn't know how to be that man. He moved down the hall and opened the door to his bedroom, dropping his bag by the bed and propping the guitar up by the closet. Resisting the urge to lie down and sleep for a few days, he instead sat in the chair by his desk, trying to adjust his mind and heart to being home again.

Chapter 2

Charlie paced the floor of his room, debating the merits of punching the wall versus crossing the hall to hit his father. Why was he here? He always let them know when he was taking leave, he never just showed up. And the last time he was home was so awful, he couldn't even think about it. All these years, they had a routine that Charlie was used to, and this did not fit into the way things should go. Usually, his dad timed it to visit during hockey playoffs, or the end of the school year, a time when Charlie was so busy, he barely had time to see his father. And now he was here, injured, and obviously expecting to be welcomed with open arms.

The last time he was here, they had a huge blowout fight over something Charlie couldn't even remember. All he could recall was that when he woke up the next morning, knowing he owed his dad an apology, his dad had left without a word in the middle of the night. No goodbye, no note, nothing. It was a month before Charlie heard from his dad, and when he did, it was a phone call from Afghanistan. Sure, he had apologized for disappearing and explained why he was called back overseas, and told Charlie how difficult it had been, but the rift was there.

As a kid he'd tried hard to be the perfect son, so his dad would want to spend time with him. Now that he was a teenager, he was just mad that he even had to pretend to have a relationship. Clearly, his dad only wanted one when it was convenient for him, so why should he have to try?

This was the home he had known for as long as he could remember, and his grandfather and Stella were the ones who had raised him. His father was off fighting wars, and while Charlie knew that was important, it sucked to feel second best to anything else. His mom had died when he was just a baby, and people rarely talked about her around him. It was as if his very existence made everyone sad because they had to think about his mom. If his dad was going to leave him anyway, maybe it would have been easier for everyone if Jake had just given him up for adoption.

A picture of his mom holding him as a baby, with his father sitting right behind her, was perched on a shelf in his room. There were other pictures of her throughout the house, but this one was his favorite. She was smiling right at the camera, looking as though she had been caught mid-laugh. Even his dad had a big grin on his face, more relaxed than Charlie had ever seen him. His mom's golden hair was pulled back into a ponytail, with a few curls hanging around her face. The blue eyes that shone in the picture were the same as the ones that stared out at him from the mirror, and he recognized his smile in her as well. He didn't know much else that he could have inherited from her but looking at the picture and seeing the small similarities had given him comfort as a kid.

He flopped backward on his bed, pulling his cell phone out of his pocket. Sending a few quick texts, asking what his friends were up to and if someone would give him an excuse to get out of this house before his head exploded. A quick reply came in from a hockey teammate, telling him to meet up with a group of them at the driving range and then for burgers.

Hearing a car door close in the driveway, he rushed to the window to see if maybe his father had changed his mind and headed right back out. Instead, it was his grandfather, climbing out of the pickup truck he took to town when he had to bring back chicken feed or supplies for the horses. He watched as his grandfather examined the SUV with out-of-state plates before starting to walk into the house. After hearing the front door close, he snuck out to the landing, guiltily eavesdropping.

"Is that Jake's car outside?" His grandfather questioned Stella as he walked into the kitchen.

"Well, hello to you too, Ben."

"Stella, I only left two hours ago, it's not like I've been gone for months. We had lunch together before I left!"

"Doesn't mean you can't be friendly before you start firing questions at me." Stella wiped her hands on a small towel. "Yes, that is Jake's car. He looks banged up, and I don't just mean the sling on his arm. Take it easy on him, Benny."

"He has a sling? What happened?"

"All I know right now is that he was shot and that he needs some time to recover, both physically and mentally." Charlie could hear ice hitting a glass and knew she would be pouring whiskey for his grandfather. She usually allowed him one per night, so if he was being given one this early, she must be worried. "Sit for a minute and relax."

"I need more than this little sip if you want me to relax," Ben grumbled. "Where is Charlie?"

"He's up in his room. I know they saw each other, but other than a door slam I haven't heard a peep since Jake went up."

A chair scraped as if he was standing up. "Maybe I should…"

"Sit here and have a drink with your old friend? Yes, that's a great plan," Stella's voice was gentle. "We can't fix everything, let's just wait and see what happens between them. I'm sure they both heard you come in and will be down any minute, so let them come to you."

"How bad does Jake look?" Ben asked Stella, and Charlie could almost hear the unspoken words as well, feeling how uneasy his grandfather was.

"Bad enough to call the boys home, which I think you should do right now," Stella's voice dropped lower, so Charlie had to really strain to hear. "There is something in his eyes that I can't put my finger on, but it's more than sadness. He's been carrying the weight of grief for so long he is accustomed to it, but he looks haunted today. That's the best way I can describe it. He looked beat up and haunted."

"Well shit," Ben said, and Charlie heard the glass hit the table a moment later, the tinkling sound of the ice hitting the glass resounding in the silence.

He snuck back into his room, closing the door quietly. Charlie hadn't looked too closely at his father when he came to the door, he had been so shaken up just realizing it was him. He had looked the same to him, maybe a little rougher. His hair had been a little longer than he usually had it, and maybe his eyes had some more lines around them. Did he look beat up? Should he care?

A part of him was grateful that his dad was here and alive, but was he supposed to drop everything and pretend all was fine? He would let his grandfather and Stella worry about his dad, and his uncles who would likely show up any minute. He was going to stay put in his room until it was time to go off with his friends and avoid his dad as much as possible. Hearing his dad's bedroom door open, he held his breath until he heard his feet hit the stairs. Resisting the temptation to sneak out and listen, he stuck in his air pods and tried to forget that his dad was home.

<h1 style="text-align:center">Chapter 3</h1>

Jake made his way to the kitchen, his stomach grumbling at all the heavenly smells in the air. He spotted his father before he saw him and had a second to take in how his dad had aged. Whiter hair, his shoulders a little more rounded than a few years prior. Same bright eyes that seemed to catch everything, he noted as his dad turned at his footsteps.

"Jake." Ben stood to embrace his son. "I can't believe you're here. What happened?"

"It's nothing, Dad. Don't worry." He held onto his dad a little longer than he could remember having done in a long time.

"I'm your father. My entire job is to worry." Ben pushed out the chair next to him. "Sit."

"First let me see if there's any more of that whiskey hidden around here."

Stella stood before he could start looking. "I'll get it for you, why don't you sit with your dad?"

"How long are you here for?" Ben asked.

"A couple weeks at least, could be longer." He sat heavily in the chair his father had pushed out for him. "I need to do a lot of physical therapy, which I can do here at the VA in Burlington. Things got pretty bad on the last tour, and the one before that. I need some time to recover, and I need to see if the shoulder will ever be good enough to continue in the military."

"Tell me about the shoulder," Ben requested.

"I was shot. Got me from the side so a few inches the other way and my vest would have stopped it. Instead, it went in and wreaked some havoc on my rotator cuff, bicep, and tendons. The doctor was able to piece it back together and I'm grateful, but it's not likely to ever be the same again." Jake paused before continuing. "Got my bell rung pretty bad too, so a lot of the actual incident isn't in my memory, which might be for the best."

"How many concussions does that make?" Ben asked.

"Lost count back in my hockey days, but I know —" Jake looked at his father, "-probably one too many."

"You are getting some help for that as well?" Jake knew Ben wasn't asking about his concussions, it was his father's way of asking about his mental health.

"Yeah." Jake sipped his drink. "My doctor in Germany sent over some orders, got the ball rolling on appointments for me for the physical aspect. I'll make some calls on Monday to find someone who can squeeze me in for the rest."

"Good. I know you encourage your men to do it as soon as they get home. It's about time you took your own advice."

"They are kids most of the time, Dad. The first time in battle is rough."

"Well, I can only imagine what the twentieth time is like then." Ben reached out and put his hand on the back of Jake's neck, pulling him into a rough hug. "I'm just so damn glad you are here."

"Me too, Dad." Jake choked back the emotion and glanced at the stairs as his father released him. "Hoping to reconnect with Charlie and get in a better place."

"Got your work cut out for you there. Picking up the phone occasionally would have helped." Ben was never one to bite his tongue, especially when it came to his boys.

"Hard to do when you're overseas and barely know what day it is," Jake's voice, always raspy, seemed to drop even lower, knowing his father was right.

Jake's façade slipped for a second, allowing a dark thought to cross his mind, but covered it up as quickly as possible. Glancing at his father, he knew that he had caught it, so he took a healthy sip of whiskey, trying to look relaxed.

"Was anyone else hurt when you were?" Stella asked gently as she sat on Jake's other side.

"Yes. I'm one of the lucky ones. And I really don't want to talk about it right now."

Ben leveled him with a look. "Just need to know what we are dealing with here."

"*We* aren't dealing with anything. I am. And I'm fine."

"Sure, looks it." Ben leaned back in his chair, not ready to back down. "You bring your problems to me, that's fine. That's why I'm here. That boy upstairs has already been through the wringer, and he doesn't need you coming in, raising havoc, and disappearing in the middle of the night again."

"If all goes well with my physical therapy, I'll be gone in a few weeks." Jake tamped down his temper again. "And I will try not to make things worse for anyone while I'm here."

"It's not when you're here, Jake," Ben paused to let it sink in. "It's what's left behind when you leave. It breaks that boy's heart every single time, whether he admits it or not."

They both turned as they heard the bedroom door upstairs open and heard Charlie jog down the stairs. "Couple of the guys are going to hit some balls at the driving range and then go to White's for burgers, thought I would go with them."

"Stella cooked dinner here —" Ben started to say.

Stella cut him off with a look. "Go on, Charlie. Enjoy your time with your friends." She rushed forward to fuss over him as he opened the door, trying to convince him to wear a jacket or a hat before he laughed, kissed her on the cheek, and ran out the door.

"Well, I guess we know how Charlie feels," Ben said to the closing door.

"Guess we do." Jake sighed, then refilled his whiskey.

Chapter 4

Jake relocated to the porch after dinner, settling into a rocking chair with his feet up on the railing. This had always been a favorite spot for him, especially on nights like this, where the sounds of the crickets and frogs settling in for the night were just enough noise to keep the thoughts in his head from overwhelming him. This exact spot was the one he pictured when holding a dying soldier or packing up the belongings of someone injured badly enough to never return to battle. It had kept him sane, being able to move his thoughts to this porch when dealing with the worst parts of war.

Stella joined him, sitting with a sigh. "Your dad is making sure all is ready for your brothers; they are on the way home now."

"I figured you probably called them."

"Your dad did. Texted them to come home, so you know they have no idea what is happening." They both laughed at the short, all-caps texts Ben was known for sending. "It will be so nice to have you three under the same roof again."

"You sure about that?"

"Well, my 'Burrows boys', as the people in town liked to call you three, always kept me on my toes. But I can't say I didn't love every second of it." Stella's eyes shone as she talked about them. "Watching you all compete with each other, but never breaking the closeness you had, was amazing."

"What have they been up to? Last I heard, Patrick was on Broadway? And Dan made partner." Jake thought back a few weeks to the last time he had spoken to each of his brothers.

"Yes," Stella said. "Patrick was phenomenal in his show, we drove down and spent a couple nights with him to see it. Charlie really enjoyed being in the city with Patrick. We didn't see Dan but for a minute, he was so busy."

"Always seems to be," Jake murmured. "I envy them a little, but don't ever tell them I said that."

"Why?"
He knew she wasn't asking about the need for secrecy. "They are both happy in their lives, doing what they love."

"And you aren't?"

He sighed, unsure how to respond. "It's not that I'm unhappy. I'm discontent." He glanced over, saw her sympathetic gaze. "I have it better than so many, I can't complain. Lying in that hospital in Germany, I saw the worst of what the war can do to a person. I know I'm lucky. But sometimes I think it would be so nice to just be able to do something simple, like go out to dinner, and enjoy it without worry."

"Oh, honey." She reached over for his hand. "Maybe this is a sign it's time to leave the military."

She said it so easily, as if that decision could just be made on a whim. Thinking of the soldiers who depended on him, the stability his life offered, he shook his head. "It's not that simple."

"It's also not that hard, Jake." They both heard Ben yell from inside the house, and she stood up. "I should go help him; you know he can't find anything without me. We can continue this later."

Jake heard the door close behind him and closed his eyes, waking suddenly when he heard tires on the driveway. He watched as a luxury SUV pulled in, with Dan behind the wheel.

Not surprising that control freak Dan had driven them from the city, or that Patrick jumped out before the wheels had come to a complete stop.

"Jake." Patrick bounded up the stairs to embrace his older brother, careful to avoid the sling on his left arm. "I can't believe you're here. It's so good to see you. What happened to your arm?"

Jake smiled and allowed himself to be warmed by his brother's enthusiastic embrace. Dan stepped in next, a quicker but no less firm hug from his older brother, along with a thump on the back.

"So glad to see you home," Dan said quietly as they stepped apart.

Jake sat back down in his chair, indicating the empty seats next to him and the open bottle of whiskey on the low table. "Dad will be out in a few minutes. He had Stella fussing over the rooms for you two princes."

"Us?" Scoffed Dan. "The prodigal son has returned, and we have only been summoned to greet him."

Patrick groaned. "Please don't start already. Jake, why are you home? Are you okay?"

Jake nodded. "I had an incident overseas. I spent some time in the hospital in Germany but need more time to recover."

The words were met with silence, only the sounds of a country night could be heard. Patrick and Dan exchanged glances, clearly wanting the other to ask the question on their minds.

"What happened?" Patrick finally asked gently.

"Bullet met shoulder." Jake took a sip of his scotch. "Plus, a bit of a concussion from an explosion."

The words hit the quiet of the night, making it seem even more stiller before the frogs and crickets returned to their nightly songs. Patrick and Dan turned to stare at each other, both starting to speak before closing their mouths again.

"You were shot, and we're just hearing about it?" Dan sounded angry.

"Sorry." Jake shrugged, not feeling very remorseful. "What good would it have done to have you all worried here? I was in good hands, and it made sense to wait until I could tell everyone in person."

Patrick and Dan exchanged looks again, and Jake couldn't help but feel like the left-out middle child all over again. Growing up they had rotated who teamed up against the other, although he and Dan being competitive with each other meant they rarely went together against the gentler Patrick. Only when faced with an outsider would they be united, because neither would allow someone else to treat their brother poorly. As adults their lives were so different, it only made sense that Dan and Patrick would be more in tune with each other, but it still grated on Jake's raw nerves.

"Don't be mad," Jake insisted. "Yes, of course I knew one or both of you would fly over, or Dad would have. I needed the time alone, to decompress, before I saw anyone."

"Still, a phone call would be nice. We assume you are in danger all the time, so a quick call or text to say you're safe in Germany and all is fine would have worked." Dan was always reasonable, and Jake heard the truth in the words.

"You're right," Jake conceded. "I should have let someone know. I just thought it would cause more worry, and no one would listen if I asked them not to come. Plus, I had a pretty severe concussion, so it was hard to use a phone or send an email until I was ready to come back to the States. And by then, I figured it was easier just to come home."

"Have you seen Charlie?" Patrick dared to ask.

"Yes. I got here a few hours ago."

"How did that go?" Patrick asked.

"About as well as expected," Jake sighed. "I've been a shit father and we all know it."

Patrick moved closer and clapped a hand on Jake's good shoulder. "You did what you thought was best for him. He was always surrounded by love. Moving him with you every few years would have been traumatic enough, never mind you disappearing for months at a time. You tried when he was young, and everyone knew it wouldn't work. Hard to go poof in the night when you have a baby in the next room."

"All true but try telling that to Charlie." The brothers were quiet for once. "So why are you two here, really?"

Patrick shrugged. "Dad texted, so we came. We do love you, shocking as that may be."

"You, I believe. Dan, on the other hand…"

Dan hit Jake on the arm. "Take that back. You know I do."

"Yes, you always show your emotions so well."

"Pot, meet kettle."

"We had to call Stella to make sense of Dad's text. She made it sound like you were a total train wreck, and I don't think she was wrong." Dan sipped his whiskey. "You would show up if I were having a hard time, and you have done your best to be there for us, even from far away. It's only fair we return the favor."

"You already have, ten times over, just by being here for Charlie over the years. I know how much time you've both spent here with him, and I appreciate it."

"He's a lot easier to deal with, if we're being honest." Patrick sipped his drink. "He doesn't get all shot up and not tell anyone."

"Let's hope not," Jake responded. "I know this life isn't what any of us pictured for me when we were kids. But after what happened to Jenna, I had to enlist."

They both nodded. "We get it. I think Charlie would too if you really told him everything. He had no idea you were about to start working in construction and trying to take college classes when she was killed. Maybe if he knew the whole story…" Patrick looked to Jake, gauging his response.

"I know. I keep gearing myself up to talk about her with him, and I get in my own way." Jake hung his head, thinking of Jenna's gentle way of helping anyone who was in trouble, knowing she would have been able to navigate this way easier than he could. "It's not easy."

"We know. We loved her too, not like you, but like a sister," Patrick commiserated.

"I hope you didn't love her like I did," Jake choked out a laugh.

Dan refilled everyone's glasses of whiskey and handed them out before sitting back down next to Jake. "Let's switch topics for a minute and look at what we're dealing with first. Where were you and what happened?"

"Afghanistan." Jake sipped his drink. "Truck in front of us hit a bomb, the impact flipped us right over. We came under fire while we were trying to get out and regroup. I don't remember a lot of it, head injuries can do that to you."

"That sounds awful." Patrick paled at his brother's words.

"Well, it's no show on Broadway, I can tell you that."

"That's not fair," Dan cut in. "You chose what you do, and you're good at it. Same for Patrick. Don't throw it in his face that his job doesn't come with bullets."

"You're right. I'm sorry, Patrick. I was trying to lighten the mood." Jake sighed and ran a hand through his dark hair. "I'm exhausted and sore. But you don't deserve that."

"You think I can't take it after growing up with you two?" Patrick punched Jake lightly in his right arm. "I'm just glad you're alive to give me shit."

"This may be the whiskey talking, but I really am glad you guys are here," Jake stated. "How long are you home for?"

"Well, my stretch on Broadway ended a week ago, so I'm doing virtually nothing for a few months. Might as well hang here with you, at least for a few weeks." Patrick pointed at Dan. "Workaholic over there thinks he's heading back to the city on Sunday, but I'm sure we can talk him out of it."

"Doubtful. I have a lot on my plate," Dan replied.

"I'm sure you can manage from here. And I happen to have a couple endorsement contracts I need you to look at, so as my lawyer you can stay right here and take care of your number one client." Patrick looked at Jake. "It's nice when I have the upper hand over either of my older brothers."

"We'll discuss it later," Dan stated, causing a smug smile from Patrick. "I didn't realize your show ended."

"The show didn't end, my guest spot did. They rotate us through there every eight weeks or so. I sent tickets to the final night to your office." Patrick shot a look at Dan.

"Shit, you did. I'm sorry. I meant to be there." Dan ran a hand through his hair. "I don't know how that slipped my mind."

"You two couldn't have hashed out your issues on the three-hour drive?" Jake asked, half joking.

"Yes, let's focus on you." Dan turned an intense gaze on Jake. "Exactly how fucked up are you right now?"

"Wow," Jake was stunned. "That's —"

"What he means," Patrick said, "is how can we help?"

"No, what he means is how bad is it? Could this really be it for you and the Army? Where are you mentally?" Dan was leaning forward now, unrelenting gaze on Jake. "Be honest with us."

"Honestly?" Jake sipped his whiskey. "I wish I knew. I'm a mess physically. Career could be over. Most of it I don't want to talk about or think about."

"You have to. It would be too easy to get lost in the bad stuff," Dan wasn't letting up.

"But we won't let you," Patrick stated, giving Dan a look that clearly said to shut up.

"I don't know what I need right now, but I know you already did one of the things I needed. You showed up." Jake swallowed the lump in his throat. "You just have to give me some time to work through it. I know I've talked about how rough some people have it when they go home. I can't promise I won't make this hard or have my moments. But I will take my own advice and seek the help that I need, you have my word."

"We're here for whatever you need. Even Dan's clients aren't as important as you." Patrick shot a look at Dan.

"Right, because you would have been able to walk away from a shoot so easily." Dan rolled his eyes.

"Totally different things, but I would have figured it out. My lawyer is smart enough to make these things happen for me." Patrick leaned back in his chair, holding his glass up to toast his brothers.

The three brothers settled into an easy conversation, letting Patrick entertain as usual, with bits of Dan's dry humor thrown in as they told stories about life in the city. He'd always been close to his brothers, with not even two years in age between each of them, and he realized how much he had missed them over the years. Safe in the knowledge that his brothers were there and had his back, Jake let his head rest back on the chair and let their voices and laughter wash over him.

Thoughts swirled in his head about Charlie, Afghanistan, his wife Jenna, and being home in Windsor Peak. Being back brought so many memories of Jenna, it was all he could do to not look for her everywhere he went. He could almost smell her perfume sitting here, a spot where they had spent so much time together. Looking up at the stars, he wondered if she could see him, and how much he had disappointed her with all he had done since he lost her. Coming home might have been the best or worst thing he had done, and he had no idea which way it would end up.

Chapter 5

Saturday morning dawned too early for anyone who had soaked themselves in whiskey the previous evening, yet Jake couldn't force himself to stay in bed after so many years of getting up and out before the sun. He staggered down the stairs and would kiss Stella for having a fresh pot of coffee out if he could find her. Pouring himself a large mug, he took the black coffee out to the porch to enjoy the early quiet. Most mornings he got up and went straight for a run, or a workout of some kind, but his present physical state forced him to slow down, and he was determined to appreciate it.

The two dogs, Twix and Reese, dropped to the porch next to him after emerging from somewhere behind the house. He dropped a hand to pet Reese, who rested her head on his leg. Not to be outdone, Twix laid across Jake's feet, as if to make sure he wouldn't go anywhere without them again. It was a safe guess that Stella was out collecting eggs from the chickens and had sent the dogs packing, so he was optimistic that a big country breakfast could be in his future. That was about as far into the future as he was willing to look, at least until he was able to have some kind of conversation with Charlie.

Hearing the door behind him, he held his half-full coffee cup into the air. "Thanks for getting this started, I needed it this morning."

"What?"

He whipped around too fast, causing the ache in his shoulder to ramp up. "Oh, hey, bud. Sorry, I thought you were Stella. What are you doing up so early?"

"Hockey practice." He jogged down the steps and towards the freestanding garage across the driveway, coming back out a minute later with a large hockey bag and a couple of sticks.

"Need a ride?"

"Nope." Charlie busied himself by zipping his bag and adjusting the straps, so they were ready to grab.

"Long walk with all your gear." Charlie studiously ignored him as he examined the tape at the end of a stick. "I'd be happy to drive you, and maybe see you on the ice."

"My friend PJ's dad always picks me up. He's the coach." The words were curt.

A pickup truck came up the driveway, windows rolled down and two people were visible through the windshield. He heard Charlie's bag hit the bed of the truck and the sound of his son's voice talking to the passenger as he gathered his sticks to toss in with his bag. A man who looked to be in his early forties, dressed in hockey sweats and a baseball cap, climbed onto the porch with his arm outstretched.

"You must be Jake. I'm Phil, I coach the boys' team. My son mentioned this morning that you had come home, he was with Charlie last night at the driving range."

Jake struggled to his feet, tangled with dogs, and burdened by the sling. "Nice to meet you."

"I hear you used to be a hell of a player yourself, so I see where Charlie gets it from. Once you've healed up, we'd love to get you on the ice with us." Phil grinned, and Jake couldn't help but like him.

"I'll see what PT suggests, it could be a while." Jake paused and looked toward the truck where Charlie was now sitting with

PJ in the backseat, talking with their heads close together. "And see if Charlie would like that."

"Oh, you know how kids are. They think they don't want us to help because how could we possibly know more than them?" Phil let out a barking laugh. "By the time they realize what we could teach them, we'll be too old to do it. Better get these two to the rink, but nice to meet you and look forward to seeing you around."

Jake watched him jump into the truck and head back towards town, enjoying an early morning with his son. His stomach clenched at the knowledge that this stranger knew his kid better than he did, and possibly better than he ever would. Not only did he not know how kids behaved, but he also didn't know how much about the one who mattered the most, and that knowledge tasted sour in his mouth.

***

"Jake, get ready. We're leaving in fifteen minutes." Patrick stuck his head in the living room door where his brother was watching a movie.

"I'm not going anywhere." Jake clicked the volume up on the TV.

"Yes, you are. Brothers' night out." Patrick leaned against the doorframe, not pushed off that easily. He was already dressed for the night out, wearing jeans and a button-down shirt that accentuated the blue eyes that had helped him become famous. His black hair was combed neatly, and his perfect five o'clock shadow showed off his chiseled chin. Jake considered his own sweats and t-shirt, unshaven face, and too long hair, and decided it was unfair to have a movie star for a brother.

"Not going."

Patrick came fully into the room. "You and I both know that Dan is looking for an excuse to see Kendra, so we are going to Windsor Peak Palace to watch the Red Sox game and pretend he's not still obsessed with his high school girlfriend."

"Why can't it just be you two?"

"Because I said so. We came here to be with you and have some brotherly time, and this is part of that. Now get ready." Jake watched Patrick disappear and knew he would have to go along. It was rare that Patrick put his foot down, but when he did, they all needed to fall in line.

As he walked by his son's closed door he paused, wondering if enough time had passed so that he could apologize again for being a sad excuse for a father. He stood there long enough that Dan passed by, giving him a shove towards the door and a nod, but he decided to leave Charlie alone. He quickly changed into clean jeans and a long-sleeved T-shirt, ran a brush through his hair, and headed down the stairs to meet his brothers.

"Looks like a busy night," Dan commented as he pulled into the nearly full parking lot.

The original town hall of the town had been converted into a bar and grill years before the brothers were born, with the first floor containing the restaurant and the second floor turned into an apartment for the owner. The exterior hadn't changed much in the years that followed, the regal looking pillars and white paint shining among the brick buildings that made up the downtown area. A large porch had been added to the front, allowing guests to spill outside while waiting for tables, and a small garden out back provided space for outdoor events.

As they walked into the Windsor Peak Palace, it felt as though all conversations paused. "Well, if it isn't the Burrows boys, it's been a long time!" A former teacher from the boy's high school days was at the bar, having a burger with his wife. "I heard you were home, Jake. Nice to see you safe. Have you met my wife, Megan?"

"Nice to meet you," Jake shook her hand politely. "It's great to see you as well, Mr. Nelson. "

"It's Mark now, we are all adults."

"Mark tells me you have been in the military and overseas?" Megan asked.

"Yes, ma'am."

"I work at the VA clinic in Burlington," Megan stated. "I greatly admire your service."

"Thank you. Not sure how much longer I will be doing it due to this injury, but I appreciate it." Jake looked to where his brothers had secured three bar stools at the far end of the bar, where it was secured to the wall. "I better catch up with them before they cause trouble. Nice to meet you, and nice to see you, Mark."

The couple wished him well and went back to their meal, and Jake made his way through the crowd who all wanted to welcome him home. He hadn't realized how secluded he had been on his visits to see his family until now, as he saw faces from his childhood he hadn't seen in years. Finally getting to his brothers, he dropped into the barstool to Patrick's right that was against the wall. "I hate you for this."

"You love me. And you love the attention." Patrick pointed at a beer placed in front of Jake. "And you love me for that.'

Dan was scanning the room, ignoring his brothers. "Any sign of Kendra?" Jake asked.

"What?" Dan spun around to face the TV. "I was just seeing who was here, not looking for her."

"Sure, you were," Patrick snickered.

"You two are such idiots. Why did I agree to this?" Dan shook his head.

"Look alive," Jake clinked his beer to Dan's. "She just walked in." The brothers all watched as Kendra Knight entered from the swinging kitchen door. Jet black hair was pulled back into a neat ponytail, accentuating her sharp cheekbones and startling green eyes. Tall and slender, she was both striking and approachable in her jeans and t-shirt.

"Jake," Kendra's voice cut through the noise in the bar. "It's so good to see you. Are you okay? I heard you were injured. And Patrick, so nice to see you." She let her gaze cross to Dan for the slightest moment. "Dan."

"Kendra," Dan mimicked her tone, turning back to his beer.

"How are you, Kendra? I heard you bought this place?" Patrick, ever the peacekeeper, tried to cover for his brother's behavior.

"Yes, I worked for the Hughes' for so long, basically running the place for the last couple years when they moved to Florida. They offered me a deal to purchase it over the next few years, and I couldn't turn it down." Her attention was grabbed by a waitress by the kitchen door, and she held up one finger to her. "I should run, it's the busiest time of the night. Nice to see you guys!" She squeezed both Jake and Patrick's arms as she walked away, ignoring Dan's back turned to her.

"Well, that went well." Jake remarked into his beer.

"Shut up, Jake," Dan growled.

"No, really. You schmooze for a career, and you couldn't even try to charm her?" Jake shook his head.

"Seriously, shut up, Jake. Just because you have a sling on doesn't mean I won't hit you."

"No one is hitting anyone," Patrick elbowed Jake in the ribs. "Let's order some food and relax, and maybe when it quiets down in here you can try again."

"I didn't want to try the first time," Dan mumbled as he picked up his menu.

"Then you did phenomenally well," Jake responded.

Patrick nodded at two women sitting at the bar chatting with Kendra, heads huddled together and occasionally shooting death rays from their eyes towards Dan. "I think her friends are ready to attack you."

Dan glanced down the bar before averting his eyes. "They have always been close, so no surprise they would hate me now."

The brothers ordered food and more beer, settling in to watch the baseball game, which the Red Sox were winning for once. They were frequently interrupted by old classmates and friends welcoming Jake home, or the occasional celebrity spotter asking for a selfie with Patrick. Fortunately, most of the leaf peeper tourists only came to town during the day, and those staying at the Inn tended to stay there for dinner rather that visit the Palace, which suited all the locals well. Once the snow started and ski season began, the mix of weekenders from the cities south of Vermont would surge, and Patrick would struggle to be out in public and relax. Although his brothers loved to tease him, they understood how uncomfortable he could get when he just wanted a night out with his brothers.

"You okay?" Jake asked Patrick quietly as he sat back down after a solid ten minutes of taking selfies with fans.

"Sure, yeah." Patrick grabbed the last buffalo finger and added it to his plate.

"We can go if you want," Dan offered.

"No, really. It's fine. Part of the life, you know?"

"We can ask people to leave you alone," Jake said. "Or let Kendra know you don't want to be bothered, and she can shut them down."

"No, that's not a good look. It should settle down for a while, I think people are getting used to be being here now." He looked around the room quickly. "Plus, people are recording me and taking pictures, so if I say no or someone gets stopped coming up to me, it will be all over social media later."

"You should get credit for all the people you do talk to." Jake was mad on his brother's behalf, that he couldn't just relax and enjoy a night out.

"It's no big deal, really. I should have brought a hat or something, but it will be fine."

Kendra paused as she was walking by, listening as Patrick spoke, then disappearing into the kitchen. She returned with a baseball hat with the restaurant logo on the top and slid it to Patrick on the bar.

He smiled at her as he fit it to his head, pulling it low to cover his face as much as possible. "Thanks, Kendra. This is perfect."

"Perfect for me, you mean," she said, grinning at him. "Best promo I could do."

He laughed and tugged it down a little lower. "Happy to help."

"Hey, Jake, we have open mike nights on Thursdays if you want to come in." Kendra leaned over to talk to him.

"Little tough to play guitar with the arm in a sling, but thanks Kendra."

"You can still sing with an arm injury, can't you? Tuesday is karaoke, maybe you and Patrick can come knock our socks off."

Patrick perked up at the news of karaoke. "Oh, that would be fun. What song can we do that Dan can maybe be a background dancer?"

Kendra laughed and snuck a glance at Dan, who was glaring at his brother. "Some of us are talented in other ways."

"Yes, you are." Patrick patted Dan on the head, getting his hand swatted away by his brother.

"Kendra," Dan started. "How have you been?"

"Since you left for college and never contacted me again?" Her eyes shot daggers. "Just fine, thanks." She walked away once again, as they all stared after her in stunned silence.

"Dude, you never even broke up with her?" Jake asked quietly.

"Honestly, you need to shut the fuck up about her," Dan hissed.

"That's cold, man." Patrick pretended to shiver. "It's almost like you invented ghosting! Do you still do that now?"

Dan stormed away, leaving Kendra behind for the dartboard. Jake couldn't help to notice that Kendra's eyes followed him as he walked and noted that information for later. Jake tilted a chin in his direction, and gave Patrick a quick shove, indicating he should follow their brother and soothe things over.

As Patrick walked away, Jake surveyed the room, his eyes settling on a couple at a table in the far corner. The woman was facing him, her brown curls springing around her face as she quickly averted her eyes from him. The man had his back to him, but even from across the room Jake would bet this was a first date going horribly wrong. The man was talking and laughing loudly, while the woman appeared to be looking everywhere but in Jake's direction, but he saw her eyes dart towards him every few seconds.

"Kendra." He waved her over. "Is that Shea Kerrigan over there?"

"Yes, with that loudmouth Bob Conley." She rolled her eyes. "No idea how that happened."

"Are they a couple?"

"No. Bob is a one date kind of guy; most women don't even make it through the whole date." She laughed. "I faked a stomach bug myself."

"Watch our seats for me, okay?" Kendra nodded and went back to pouring drinks.

Jake made his way across the room, feeling nervous and unsettled in a way he hadn't since he was a teenager. He tried to meet her eyes as he walked, wanting to know he was entering friendly territory, but she evaded him until he was right next to their table. He clapped a hand on the man's shoulder, stopping him mid-sentence. "Hey pal, mind changing seats with me for a minute?"

The man looked stunned. "Change seats?"

"Yes, I'd like to have a minute with Shea," Jake stared at her as he said it.

"Well, we are in the middle of something right now…"

Bob was cut off by Shea. "Please, Bob."

He huffed and stood up from the table. "I guess I'll be back in a minute."

Jake sank into the empty seat, feeling tongue tied as he finally sat face to face with her. Her eyes were a soft gray-green color he hadn't remembered from years ago, but the brown curls that bounced around her face reminded him of the young girl she had been in high school. She was much prettier than he remembered, although he doubted that he had paid her much attention when he was a senior and her a freshman. "Hi."

"Hi," she answered quietly. "I heard you were home."

"I should have let you know; I always forget how fast word travels in this town. I probably wasn't even fully parked in the driveway before the rumor mill kicked into gear. I'm sorry," he said sincerely.

"What happened to your arm?" she asked gently.

"Long story. I'm okay," He sighed. "I really am sorry not to reach out. This is weird, right?"

She laughed. "We've been writing letters and emails for so many years, I almost forgot you were a real person who could show up in the middle of the worst first date ever."

"I can't thank you enough for all that," Jake started. "It meant the world to me to have someone to talk to."

"It did for me too, but I hope you aren't ending our pen pal relationship," Shea joked, but looked a little worried he was.

"No! The opposite. I'm hoping maybe we can be real life friends now?" He saw Bob approaching from across the room. "Kendra mentioned karaoke on Tuesdays, would you want to meet us here? I will most likely have both my annoying brothers along, but they can be entertaining."

"Yes, I'd love that." She paused as Bob stood beside Jake. "So nice to see you, Jake."

"You too." He sat and looked at her for a second longer, then stood. "Thanks, Bob."

Jake made his way back to the bar, his head spinning. It hadn't occurred to him that he could run into Shea, he was so used to just thinking of her as someone on the other side of a computer screen. His hand was shaking as he reached for his beer, and quickly grasped the side of the bar instead. *Get a grip,* he told himself. *You aren't a teenager with a crush.* He sat back down, back to the wall, and looked over to where his brothers were playing darts. A sudden crash from behind the bar had him jumping up from his seat, feeling his heartbeat kick into high gear. Just as quickly he felt someone squeeze his bicep and turned to see Kendra behind him.

"Sorry, the busser is new and just dropped a tray. Are you okay?" Her concerned gaze looked him over.

"Sure, yeah. No problem." He slid back onto the chair and tried to slow his breathing down.

"I can get you some water?" She persisted.

"No, really, I'll be okay." His pulse was still racing, his hands clammy and tingling.

"Look at me for a second." He raised his head to look into her calm eyes. "Just breathe. In and out."

He did as she said and felt better after a minute. "Sorry, Kendra, I don't know what happened."

"PTSD can do that to you. You'll be okay." She pointed to the kitchen. "I am right in there if you need me, or if you need a quiet spot, my office is just inside the kitchen door." She looked over and saw his brothers approaching through the crowd, and quickly departed.

"I just kicked your pretty boy brother's ass in darts," Dan declared as they sat back down at the bar. "I would challenge you, but you're injured, so you can have a pass."

Jake stood up, ready for the challenge and the distraction. "Only takes one arm to throw darts, so today is your unlucky day."

They left Patrick at the bar as they made their way to the dart board, with Dan casting a look over his shoulder. "Friend of yours?" he asked Jake.

"She was in high school with us," Jake responded. "Still works there as a teacher."

"And you know this how?" Dan asked.

"Might have exchanged an email or two over the last few years," Jake tried to be nonchalant about it.

"Oh, really? If I win, I get to ask ten more questions about this," Dan dared.

"And if I do, I get ten questions about Kendra," Jake dared back, and saw his brother's brow furrow as he hesitated.

"Deal." They shook on it and set about their game. After soundly beating his brother, his laughter and gloating quieted for a moment when he realized Shea was gone. He looked around for a moment, trying to spot her curls at the bar or by the ladies' room, but gave up as Dan poked him to move. Dan looked glum as they headed back to their barstools.

"Lay it on me," he said, looking around to make sure Kendra wasn't in sight.

"Oh, Danny, it's not going to be that easy!" Jake laughed.

Chapter 6

Somehow, Shea managed to get through the rest of the night, although she had no idea how she had suffered through Bob's incessant stories. Bob had been handsome in his own way, with his blond hair and brown eyes, ruddy complexion, and fit physique. He just wasn't for her, and she had known from the moment they met when he came on too strong.

Jake had proved to be the perfect distraction, watching him as he interacted with his brothers and dwelling over their brief conversation had kept her sane. Still picturing his smile and feeling the butterflies in her stomach, she let herself into her small house and greeted her dog, Muffin. A rescue of indeterminate origin, Muffin was both small and fierce, protecting Shea from any potential threat while also attempting to hide behind her in panic. The dog was jumping anxiously around Shea's legs, as though she had been gone for days and not just a couple of hours. She clipped the leash on and headed back out the door for their nightly walk, still reeling from the turn her night had taken.

As she walked down her front steps, the door across the street opened, shining light briefly on the porch before closing again. She heard quick footsteps coming her way and waited as her best friend crossed the street, a wine glass in each hand.

"I figured you needed this if you were home this early!" Christine Chambers was a perky redhead who had befriended Shea when she and her husband had moved in across the street. "Was it awful?"

"So bad. I never should have allowed that setup to happen. Remind me never again to agree to a bet that could result in me being set up on a blind date." Shea took a healthy sip of the wine. "Something interesting did happen though."

"What? Oh, this sounds juicy!" Christine's voice went up a notch in excitement.

"Do you know Charlie Burrows?" Shea asked.

"The freshman? Please tell me he didn't hit on you." Christine sounded horrified.

"No! His father is back in town."

"Okay…" Christine drew out the word, making a motion with her hand to go on.

"We may have been writing to each other for the last few years," Shea admitted quietly.

Christine stopped walking. "And you are just mentioning this to me now? I need all the details. Did you know him in school? The Burrows all grew up here, but I don't know how old they are compared to you."

"I didn't really know him, he was a senior when I was a freshman. I knew his girlfriend, who then became his wife, but didn't know him well. I passed him some schoolwork once for Patrick when he was in Los Angeles for an audition," Shea responded.

"Now Patrick I wouldn't mind seeing," Christine laughed.

"He's here too."

"WHAT?" She shrieked and Shea hushed her, looking up and down their quiet street to make sure they hadn't disturbed any neighbors. Other than a lone dog bark that had Muffin perking her ears up, the street remained quiet.

"Yes, Jake and both his brothers were at the bar."

"How gorgeous is Patrick in real life?" Christine fanned herself.

"They all are, honestly." Shea reached down to untangle the dog's leash from a bush. "Patrick is the quintessential tall, dark, and handsome, with his dark hair and those blue eyes. But he is so friendly looking, and that doesn't come across in his movies, I don't think. He smiles a lot, I should say. Dan looks a lot like Patrick, with the same dark hair and eyes, but he looks more serious. More buttoned up, I guess. And Jake —"

"Yes?" Christine waved her hand for Shea to continue.

"He's just as handsome as Patrick, but in a different way," Shea considered her words. "His hair isn't as dark, and his eyes are more hazel, I think. He has more lines on his face, just looks more…. weathered. Or like he's lived a tougher life, I guess. And he's just all muscle and hard edges, with this scowl that says to stay away. But if he smiles, it will take your breath away."

"I am so mad that we didn't go down there for dinner tonight. I wanted to, but Ryan said it would seem like we were snooping on your date. Okay, back to Jake. So, you didn't know each other, but you have been writing?" Christine looked perplexed.

"His wife Jenna was on the soccer team with me. I made it as a freshman and no one was happy, but Jenna made a point of being nice to me and offering me rides, so the rest of them fell into line. She was popular like that; everyone followed her lead." Shea stopped to collect Muffin's deposit on the grass before they started walking again.

"I can't imagine anyone not liking you."

"Not so much they didn't like me, but I was younger and took a spot they thought one of their friends should have."

Christine harrumphed, looking upset on Shea's behalf for a slight almost twenty years prior. Shea laughed and gave her a quick side hug.

"Jenna was so nice to me, when she was killed, I sent Jake a card with my condolences. He sent back a thank you note, nothing exciting. But then I heard he had enlisted and was deploying, so I sent another card, this one just saying how much I appreciated her friendship and what she had done for me. He wrote back and included how to contact him overseas, so I wrote to him. Pretty soon we were emailing almost every day."

"This is mind-blowing. I can't believe I didn't know you had a secret boyfriend."

"No! It's not like that." She took a deep breath, trying to prevent her cheeks from turning bright red. Fortunately the dark night hid her blushing, so her friend couldn't see how the idea of Jake as a boyfriend had flustered her. "He would write to me about the war, tell me stories about the people he would meet. I would tell him stories about school and the town. No romance or anything like that."

"Don't tell me you haven't thought about it. You just admitted he was gorgeous and described him like he's a Greek God."

"Oh, and he is. Imagine Patrick but more.... grownup maybe? I don't know how to describe it. And when he smiles—"

"Girl, you are so gone."

"No! I can't think like that. I'm wondering if he will even be able to talk to me face to face, we shared a lot of details in our messages." Shea stopped walking suddenly.

"It's always easier to say things from behind a keyboard."

"I've been so worried the last few weeks because I hadn't heard from him. I kept looking at Charlie in school, trying to figure out if he had gotten any news. Now I know he was injured overseas, but I don't know the extent of it." She finished the wine in a gulp. "He was already a little unsure of whether he should stay in the military, so I wonder if this will factor into his decision."

"Maybe he will stay here? This could become a thing."

"I don't know if he's over losing Jenna. If I'm being honest, I was already half crazy about him before he showed up tonight, and that was without seeing how he looks as an adult. The teenage Jake was good enough, but the adult version? It's almost too much of a good thing. What if I fall for him and he's not able to do the same?"

"That's why they call it falling, Shea. You can't help what happens, just how you handle it when you land."

They said goodnight on the sidewalk and Shea took a quick shower before crawling into bed, Muffin sliding in under the covers with her. Her brain wouldn't turn off, thoughts of Jake and what it would mean that he was in town were swirling. Knowing he was safe was a huge relief, after weeks of worrying about him. His last message to her was seared in her brain from having read it so many times trying to figure out why he had stopped responding to her. As she and Muffin got comfortable in bed, she pulled up the email on her iPhone and read through it again.

Shea,

I hope your first day of school went well. It seems like yesterday that I was right there in the halls of Windsor Peak High, comparing schedules with my friends and hoping to have a fun year. I know Charlie must be in the middle of that, and I hope his year will go well. If you happen to see him during your day, I wouldn't mind hearing a little about his school life…

This tour should be ending in the next few months and I'm spending a lot of time thinking about the future. I have some young men alongside me this tour, and it's making me think about my life a lot. One is only nineteen, he was in the foster care system his entire life, and enlisted as soon as he turned eighteen because he was tossed out of the house he was living in. He looks at the military as his family, it gives him the stability he has been searching for. I've taken him under my wing and can't help but feel fatherly to him. The other is twenty and has a newborn at home. Every time I see him, he's staring at pictures of the baby or trying to get a video call to go through. That was me, fourteen years ago. Trying to figure out how to be a dad but doing it without Jenna, who would have made it so easy for me. It's got me really thinking about my place in Charlie's life, and if I've made a huge mistake in leaving him with my dad.

Maybe it's time to come home again? I don't know if Charlie would want me there, and I'm not even sure that Windsor Peak is home anymore. But maybe it's more important to be with Charlie than to spend the next five years in and out of war zones.

Sorry this is short, we are heading out today. Might be a bit before I can reply again, but I will look forward to reading your messages when I get back online.

Take care,

Jake

Shea had responded to him for the next several days, then once a week, wondering why he wasn't responding. Now she knew he had been injured, and likely in the hospital, for all that time. The questions he had been asking himself had certainly come around to face him head-on, and she couldn't help but wonder what decision he had made.

Chapter 7

Charlie jumped when a knock sounded on his door early Sunday morning, kicking himself for not turning down the volume of the video game he was playing. "Come in," he called out, and gave a sigh of relief when his uncle Patrick appeared.

"Hey, Charlie. What are you doing up so early?"

I'm used to the early wakeups for hockey, but I have the day off today." He leaned back in his chair and stretched.

"Any chance you want to join your old uncle for a run?" Patrick knelt to tie his running sneakers as he asked.

Charlie hesitated, then shrugged. "Sure, why not?" He stood and started walking down the stairs with Patrick, already dressed in shorts and a T-shirt.

"Will you be warm enough?" Patrick questioned.

"Hey, I live in Vermont, you city dwellers have thinner blood!" Charlie teased as they headed out the front door.

They set out at an easy pace, heading towards town in a companionable silence. As they entered the center a of their small town, Patrick remarked how little had changed since he was Charlie's age. The same diner sat on the corner, although a new coffee café had opened across the street. A small market, pharmacy, and hardware store were mixed in with a floral shop, pizza parlor, pub, and some small specialty stores. Everything was clean and inviting, if a little on the older side. Red brick buildings mixed with the older white buildings on the street, with a large park directly in front of the new town hall and church. The streets were clean, and lined with flowerpots filled with colorful mums, and benches provided plenty of spots for residents and tourists to linger.

"I see why you and Dan escaped," Charlie stated.

"That's a strong word," Patrick said, slowing down so he could speak easier. "I never saw myself leaving here, honestly. When I was *discovered* and flown out to audition for my first show, I didn't know what to think. Going from a small town to a big city is a challenge, to say the least, never mind being your age when it happened. Then suddenly living out there, me and your grandfather, like fish out of water. When I signed a contract to be on the show, thankfully Dan agreed to go to law school in California and let me live with him until I turned eighteen. There's no way your grandfather would have made it if he had to stay in Los Angeles any longer."

Charlie laughed, thinking back to his last trip to visit Patrick in Hollywood for a movie premiere. "When we were out there last year, both Grandpa and Stella talked the whole time about how they couldn't wait to get back to Vermont. I can imagine how him living there must have been."

"The studio was going to help me get emancipated, but I could barely do my own laundry, so I didn't want to leave the security of dad and Stella completely." Patrick shrugged, like talking about becoming famous as a teenager was so normal. "Dan would have to speak about his reasons for leaving, but neither of us hated it here. I used to dream about this place when I was in Los Angeles, I couldn't wait to get back. I only tolerate New York because it's a short drive to get back here."

"You visited a lot at least, when you could." Charlie glanced over at him. "And took me on some pretty sweet vacations. Not to mention the movie premieres."

"I always enjoy spending time with you and having you out in California with me makes it feel more like home." Patrick smiled at him. "I wish I was home more, Charlie. I know it was hard to have your dad gone all the time."

"Grandpa and Stella were here," Charlie heard the edge in his voice and knew his uncle did as well.

"You know he loves you, right? And he thinks he was doing it for you. Or for your mom," Patrick sighed. "I don't know what goes on in his head all the time, but I do know that he thought he was doing what was best for you."

"Ditching your kid is never what's best for them." Charlie puffed out a frustrated breath.

"He tried to have you with him. You don't remember because you were a baby, but after he finished boot camp, he had you with him for almost two years. It was brutal for everyone, but he tried so hard to keep you with him. He would get orders to leave in seventy-two hours for some new hotspot, and one of us would have to rush down there to get you. It was brutal on him, and you, to always be back and forth. His entire support system was hours away, and none of us were able to move closer." Patrick paused for a breath and then continued. "You were in this tiny little apartment. He had you in daycare, but if you were sick or it was a weekend, he had to get someone to come watch you. He was barely making ends meet, even with Dan and I giving him money any time he would accept it."

Charlie stopped running, turning to stare into the window of the bookstore. "I really don't want to hear about this."

Patrick stopped and put his arm around his nephew. "I know. But I think it's important that you know how hard he tried. So maybe you can let him try now and be open to it. We haven't brought up what it was like during those years before because you seemed so happy, and we wanted your dad to have a chance to explain the past. This might be the time for that to happen."

"Is that Patrick Burrows?" Charlie winced at the sounds of his high school principal's voice.

"Hello, Mrs. Turner. How nice to see you again!" Patrick turned on the charm while Charlie laughed into his water bottle. "How is everything with you?"

"Well just fine, Patrick. We just love having Charlie at our school, at least when he decides it's worth his time to come." The principal lowered her gaze on Charlie. "How's that stomach bug treating you?"

"Feeling much better now, thank you." Charlie studied the sidewalk as he spoke.

"Now Patrick, I don't know how long you are in town, but we have a few fundraisers coming up that could certainly use your name attached to them. Want to set up a time to come in and talk about it?" She pulled a phone out of the massive bag hanging from her arm. Although not more than five feet tall, Abigail Turner made up for what she lacked in height with her sturdy frame, built from years of attacking the moguls on the ski slopes. Her hair was now cut into a neat bob, mostly brunette but some streaks of grey. She never seemed to age, although she had been at the high school for at least twenty-five years in some capacity. Now tapping on her phone, she looked to Patrick again to see if he was checking his schedule as well. "Would you like to come in on Monday? It looks like I have a few minutes before lunch."

"I don't think me going into the high school is a great idea, Mrs. Turner. Why don't I send you an email and see what I can do?"

"Why wouldn't it be a good idea?" She looked honestly perplexed at the thought.

Charlie let out a low laugh as Patrick removed his hat and sunglasses, turning so he faced the open window of the coffee shop. Within a minute, the front door crashed open, and four girls came rushing across the street. "Oh my god, are you Patrick Burrows? Will you take a selfie with me?" They were all thrusting cell phones at him and trying to get their hands on him.

As Patrick dealt with his fans, Charlie turned to see Mrs. Turner with her eyes nearly bulging from her head. "He is pretty well known," he commented.

"People really did love that show, didn't they?" She mused.

"Not to mention the superhero franchise he is a part of. And the Broadway show that he just starred in."

She nodded. "Yes, perhaps it would be better if he emailed me. Will you let him know?" She turned to walk away. "And I will see you at school on time Monday, Charlie."

"Yes, Mrs. Turner. Enjoy your weekend." Charlie moved toward the bench nearby, willing to wait out his uncle's fan club, but he saw Patrick's hand waving toward him.

"I am in town for a while visiting with my family. I'm sure most of you know my nephew, I am going to finish my workout with him now. I would appreciate it if you could all just treat me like any other person from Windsor Peak, and I'll be happy to visit with people when I'm free." He had fully extracted himself from the grips of the head cheerleader who had never looked

Charlie's way before this very moment. "See you all later!" He called out over his shoulder as he started jogging, dragging Charlie along with him.

"Does that ever feel normal?" Charlie asked as they made their way out of town.

"No. I wish people would just see me as a normal guy who grew up here, but it always takes a few days for that to happen. One hit TV show and suddenly I can't walk down Main Street in our little Vermont town."

"One little TV show?" Charlie teased.

"Oh, shut it." Patrick bumped Charlie's shoulder and laughed.

***

Jake heard Charlie and Patrick enter the house laughing, and he made his way to the kitchen where they were both leaning on the island. "How was your run?"

"Fine." Charlie's smile had vanished when his father entered the room, causing some momentary chest pains for Jake.

"It was not fine. We ran into Mrs. Turner, who is still somehow able to make me behave like a thirteen-year-old who was caught smoking in the bathroom. Not that I ever did that," Patrick quickly said to Charlie. "She wants me to do some appearances for her to raise some money. I'm still scared of her, so I'll allow myself to be paraded all over town rather than say no to her."

"She always did know how to get her way," Jake replied. "How is school going for you, Charlie?"

"Fine."

"Everything is fine, huh?" Jake felt irritation brewing inside him and tried to tamp it down.

"Yup." Charlie shifted away from the island. "I think I'll go shower."

"Anything to avoid me," Jake said to his son's back.

He stopped for a second, then before going up the stairs got in his parting shot. "Learned from the best."

Patrick sighed. "I just spent all morning trying to get him to cut you a break, and now I am going to have to spend my afternoon giving you the same lecture."

"I don't need a lecture," Jake growled. "I need him to actually talk to me. I'm trying to make things better."

"And you think that should happen overnight?" Patrick wasn't afraid of his brother. "You just appear, and everything is fine? He hasn't had a relationship with you for almost fifteen years, other than the occasional phone call or text message, and random times you have spent your leave here. You can't blame him for being hesitant."

Jake sank into a chair. "I wish it was that easy. I don't know what I'm doing here."

"Here in the physical sense or metaphorical?" Patrick asked as he grabbed a banana and started peeling it.

"Both, really," Jake's voice dropped as he acknowledged his true feelings. "I don't know how to be a dad."

"Yes, you do." Patrick sat across from him. "Look, I'm not a father, so maybe I don't know anything. But our dad is one of the best. And we've been watching him our whole lives, so I have to think some of it has sunk in. We grew up like Charlie, without a mom. If anyone can relate to him, it's you. The difference is, he lost his father at the same time, and now has to adjust to the idea of you coming back into his life. So, give him some time and grace, would you? And give yourself the same, because just showing up here and wanting to fix the relationship was brave and a dad-like thing to do."

Chapter 8

Jake pulled himself out of bed early, unwilling to spend any more time pretending to try and sleep. The night had been rough, his shoulder had been throbbing, and when he finally drifted off, he was woken quickly by a nightmare, and spent the next hours struggling to get into a restful sleep. When he finally found himself drifting off, he would swear he could smell Jenna's perfume and hear her laughing, causing him to sit up too fast looking for her. She often came into his thoughts at night as he drifted off to sleep, and every single time he woke up quickly, disappointed that it was only a dream.

Cursing himself for moving so suddenly that he made his shoulder pain worse, he stood under a cold shower long enough to feel halfway human. Following the scent of freshly brewed coffee, he poured himself a mug and sat at the kitchen island, watching as Stella whipped together eggs to pour into a casserole dish.

"You okay, honey?" She asked, looking at him with concern. "You look exhausted."

"Bad night," Jake admitted.

"Want to talk about it?"

"No, thank you. I appreciate your offer, but I'll get through it."

She leveled him with a gaze that would have had him confessing to anything when he was a kid. "You are dealing with a lot of stress in your life, and you were shot. That's a lot to get through, and you shouldn't be doing it alone."

"I'm not, I promise." He sipped his coffee and considered his words. "Being here really makes me think about Jenna, more than usual. Sometimes I dream about her, especially when I'm really tired, but it's easier when I'm not in a place where I spent a lot of time with her. I can see her everywhere around here, so it just brings a lot back to the surface. And then yeah, the injury and stress with work, and things with Charlie, it is a lot."

"Charlie will come around, I have faith." She wiped the corner of her eye with a tissue. "And your dad and I, we miss Jenna too. I see so much of her in Charlie, he has her ability to make friends with anyone and make them feel special. It's a wonderful trait to have passed down."

"That's nice," Jake said quietly.

"I know it hurts to talk about her, but keeping her memory alive is important. And it makes her more present in Charlie's life, and she deserves that."

"You're right, as always." Jake listened as a door closed upstairs, and the shower turned on. "I promise, I will talk to him about her. I just wanted to have things better between us first, if that's possible."

"Like I said, he will come around." She put the casserole in the oven, setting a timer before starting to wash the bowls.

"Do you always make such an elaborate breakfast? I seem to remember bowls of cereal on my school mornings." Jake grinned at her as she splashed some water in his direction.

"Three of you to get up and out the door, not to mention three lunches to make. It's much easier with just one. Charlie likes a little extra protein these days, especially going into the weekends when he has games. Says it makes him feel stronger, but I think he's trying to put on some muscle to impress girls," she said with a wink at Jake.

"Any idea when his games are this weekend?"

"I put them all on the calendar right in the pantry, so have yourself a look. Your dad and I get to all of them, we love watching him play. Reminds us of when you three were playing, it's nice to have a second chance to watch someone grow as a player. When they say time goes too fast, they aren't kidding." She placed the casserole into the oven. "It feels like an hour ago I was watching your dad tie your skates, and then it was over in an instant. It's nice to have this time with Charlie, we really try to soak it in and enjoy it."

"That's nice," Jake mumbled, guilt causing his stomach to roll.

"Not that we didn't enjoy it with you boys. But there were three of you and lord did you know how to cause chaos. We spent more time trying to keep everyone where they should be than actually enjoying it," she laughed. "We were outnumbered, and outpowered, by you boys."

"We were so lucky to have you," Jake corrected himself. "We *are* so lucky to have you."

"I'm the lucky one," She insisted. "When your mom died, it was so tragic. Ben and I had been friends since we were little, we grew up next door to each other. Patrick was an infant; Ben couldn't handle all that and his own grief. We got through it together, and I feel blessed that I got to help raise you all."

"Ben couldn't handle what?" Jake turned as his father entered the kitchen, dressed for a golf outing.

"We were just revisiting history, Benny. Nothing to worry about." Stella passed him a cup of coffee and Jake saw the smile pass between the two of them.

"Are you golfing today, Dad?"

"Yes, your brothers and I are going out. Want to ride along?" Ben asked as he sipped his coffee.

"No, thanks. I have some appointments at the VA this morning." Jake heard the heavy steps of Charlie coming down the stairs and sat up straighter, turning to face the kitchen door. "Morning, bud."

Charlie grunted, then stuck his head in the refrigerator.

"I made that egg, potato, and bacon casserole you like, honey. Just give me a couple minutes to get you a plate and some toast." Charlie smiled at her and dropped a kiss on her head, taking his glass of orange juice to sit at the table.

"How many games do you have this weekend?" Jake asked.

"Just one."

"Tomorrow?" Jake persisted.

"Yeah." Charlie pulled his phone out of his pocket and studied the screen.

Jake looked to his father, who made a motion with his hand to keep the stilted conversation going. "How's the team you're playing against?"

"They're okay. I think we should beat them." He started eating the breakfast placed in front of him, after thanking Stella.

"I'm really trying here," Jake started after a couple minutes of silence. "Do you– "

"Trying? Trying what?" Charlies angry face looked up from his plate. "Trying to feel better about yourself?"

"I'm trying to have a relationship with you," Jake explained, feeling stung.

"Well, that's not possible right now." He slammed his fork onto the now empty plate and stood to walk to the sink. "And here's why. A relationship means both people matter, right? But with us, it's only you that matters. You decide when to come here, when you want to talk. You chose to leave without saying goodbye after we had a fight, and then to take the cowards' way and text me. So now I am deciding that I don't want to talk to you, and I don't want to feel guilty because the guy who dumped me like a bag of laundry when I was a baby suddenly wants to be buddies."

With that, he shouldered his backpack and headed out the front door. Jake heard a second set of footsteps, and the door closed a second time but didn't see who had gone after him. His grief and guilt were so thick it was like a cloud surrounding him. Breathing was difficult, and he felt a crushing in his chest that could only be his heart exploding. He wanted to rage, to throw things and punch someone, but had lost the ability to even move. Feeling his dad's hand on the back of his neck pushing his head down until it was near his knees, he fought back fruitlessly. "Breathe, Jake. Relax and breathe."

"I…. can't….chest…."

"You're okay. Just breathe. I'm here, I've got you."

Jake felt a small hand slide into his, and knowing it was Stella he held on with all his might. Slowly his breathing started to regulate and the pressure in his chest loosened its vice-like grip, allowing him to sit up. Stella was next to him, tears rolling down her cheeks. His dad pulled him into a rough embrace, nearly causing him to fall off the stool.

"We got you, don't worry," Ben's words were muffled into Jake's shoulder.

"He's right," Jake's voice cracked. "I should leave. This is too much for him."

"You aren't going anywhere," Stella asserted. "That's the most he has said to you since you got here, so let's focus on that. Maybe this is the breakthrough you needed."

"How do I fix this?" He searched his dad's and Stella's faces, but neither had an answer for him.

***

Dan was chasing him down the driveway, still dressed in pajama pants and a T-shirt. "Charlie! Slow down."

"Gonna be late for school. I'll see you later."

"I'll walk with you. But give an old man a break, this pace is brutal." Dan pulled on his arm, trying to get him to slow down.

"I don't want company," Charlie nearly yelled.

"Tough shit." Charlie shot a surprised look at his uncle, who nodded. "I'm coming, and we are going to talk."

"I can't even think straight, never mind talk." Charlie kicked a stone on the ground, sending it flying into the trees. "He makes me so mad."

"I heard what you said to your dad," Dan huffed. "Jesus, I'm out of shape."

Charlie half laughed, then sobered up quickly. "Everything I said is true."

"It is true. But it's also just your perspective. Have you thought about hearing him out, even just once?"

"Why should I?" Charlie was infuriated. First his dad acted like he was the victim, and now his uncle was playing along. "I'm the kid, aren't I?"

"Yes, you are. And you're acting it."

"Wha—" Charlie sputtered.

"I realize your age. But you're only a few years away from being the age your dad was when he had you, and when he lost your mom. Can you imagine that?" He looked at Charlie, who remained stubbornly silent. "Right now, can you imagine that in three years you have a baby and you're a widow?"

"No," he said begrudgingly. "But that doesn't make it better."

"Yes, he screwed up. A lot." Dan stopped to check the road before they crossed onto Main Street, "But he also kept you safe, made sure you were in a loving home and were able to have consistency in your life. He has made sure you had everything you needed for school, hockey, and anything else you pick up that you enjoy, even when he is thousands of miles away and can't see you doing it. While you don't like his decision to serve, he is a hero. He has saved a lot of lives with what he does, and a lot of people look up to him. Not saying you have to, but maybe you want to be more open to his perspective."

"I'll think about it," Charlie muttered, turning into the school walkway. "Are you going to walk me all the way to homeroom, or can I go now?"

"Little monster," Dan growled, before pulling him in with an arm across his shoulder. "I know this hasn't been easy on you, and we are all here for you. I don't want you to think I'm just on your dad's side because I'm not. I'm neutral, and here for both of you, and I want to see things get better for everyone. I will always be here if you want to talk or if you need anything."

"What if I need a million dollars?"

"Well, then I guess I'll have to start playing the lottery." Dan gave him a little shove. "Or you should hit up moneybags Patrick, he can hook you up."

Charlie laughed and felt a little lighter as he walked into the school.

Chapter 9

Jake drove back from Burlington happy to be free from the sling, which his therapist had tossed aside minutes after he sat in her treatment room. She was reluctant to commit to him ever regaining full range of motion in his shoulder but was pleased enough with his healing to get permission from the doctor to send him out sling-free. He still wouldn't be golfing anytime soon, but his fingers itched to strum his guitar and he thought he might just be able to pull it off if he was careful.

At the last second, he pulled into an open spot in front of the Windsor Peak Palace, hoping to catch Kendra before the lunch crowd descended. The front door was still locked, but he made his way down the alley next to the building and snuck through the propped open kitchen door, waving to the kitchen staff as he entered.

"Jake! Good to see you!" A former hockey teammate of Jake's was prepping the grill station and called out the greeting.

"Hey, Ernie, good to see you. Is Kendra around?"

"Sure, she's in the bar checking stock. Head on through."

Jake pushed through the swinging doors and saw Kendra behind the bar with a notepad, hard at work. She smiled as he walked in, but he caught her checking behind him to see if he was alone.

"Just me today, I'm afraid."

"Always good to see you, Jake. But we aren't open yet."

"I just needed a quick favor, if you could help me." Jake felt nervous suddenly, which was ridiculous. "Do you happen to have Shea Kerrigan's phone number?"

"Ohhhhh, interesting." Kendra drew the two words out. "Did you find something of hers you needed to return?"

"Kendra," Jake's low voice held a warning. "Don't make me ask you who you were hoping to see behind me."

"Patrick, of course," She replied smoothly. "I do have Shea's number, so I'll save us both the questions and text it to you." She busied herself on her phone and Jake felt his buzz in his pocket.

"Thanks, I appreciate it." He hesitated. "I do think you and Dan should talk but I also want you to know that I'm your friend too, if you need to vent."

"I appreciate that," she said, smiling at him. "But I don't think you need to hear about our problems, you have enough to deal with."

"It's a good distraction for me. Did he really go to college and just never talk to you again?"

"I wish it was that simple." Kendra stopped what she was doing and stared into space for a minute before continuing. "You were young, and so in love with Jenna, so you didn't see that we had our own problems. Dan and I always wanted different things, and being in love as a teenager just wasn't enough."

"What was it that you wanted?" Jake asked, curious because they had always seemed so in sync.

Kendra smiled sadly at him. "It really doesn't matter anymore. Dan looks happy in his life, and I've moved on."

"You seem pretty angry for someone who has moved on," Jake pointed out.

"Not angry. Just not willing to get drawn into the Dan web again." She turned back to her task, dismissing him and any discussion about his brother.

"If you need me, I'm here," Jake told her. "I have to run; I'm going to meet the guys at the golf course for a quick beer when they finish their round. I'll see you later?"

"Sure, have fun!" She ducked her head under the bar as he headed back through the kitchen to leave.

He ducked out the door then pulled the phone from his pocket, saving the phone number Kendra had sent him. He stared at it for a full minute before putting the phone back in his pocket and climbing into the SUV. Pulled the phone out again, making sure the contact had saved, and then dropped it on the passenger seat.

It seemed like a huge step, although it was just a simple text. He had been emailing her for years, but seeing her the other night made him realize he maybe wanted more than a friendship behind a screen. He knew it was ridiculous to think about Jenna before texting Shea, especially since he had been on a lot of dates and slept with many women between Jenna's death and now. So why was he making such a big deal out of Shea?

He groaned as he grabbed the phone once more, opening a text to Shea and then staring at the blank screen debating what he should say.

Shea, it's Jake. Kendra gave me your number, hope you don't mind.

There. Brief, but effective. He thought for another minute before finally hitting send and tossing the phone into the back seat so he could drive home without distraction.

Chapter 10

Shea heard her phone buzz from her desk but continued her lecture on Shakespeare, hoping at least part of what she was saying would sink into the heads of her freshman class. They all groaned when they had learned what they would be reading next, although she knew most of them would end up finding the humor in the play once they started acting it out in class the following week.

Once her class dismissed, she sat at her desk and grabbed her cell phone, shocked to see a text from Jake. Although they had emailed for years, he had never asked for her cell number, and she wasn't sure it had been a line he wanted to cross.

Debating what to respond with, she finally texted back stating she didn't mind at all and was happy to hear from him. She saw three dots appear quickly, then disappear again before a message came through asking if she was still willing to meet him for karaoke on Tuesday. She agreed quickly and put her phone down as her best friend came into the classroom carrying her lunch bag.

"What are you doing?" Christine taught math in the classroom next door, so her best friend was never too far.

"I just got a text from Jake." Shea pulled her lunch bag out of her tote under the desk.

"No! What does it say?" Christine made a move to grab the phone and Shea swatted her hand away.

"He wants me to meet him for karaoke at the Palace on Tuesday night." Shea saw her friend's expression and quickly added, "With his brothers. It's a group thing, not a date."

"It's the closest thing to a date you have had in a while, so I'll take it!" They started walking down the hall to the teacher's break room.

"I had a date this weekend," Shea said indignantly.

"With Bob, that doesn't count. We have tried to fix you up with much better options over the years, and you always say no, so that choice made no sense to me." Christine stopped walking suddenly. "Unless you were waiting for Jake this whole time?"

"Of course not," Shea protested, unsure if she was lying to herself and her best friend. Accepting the blind date with Bob had been out of character for her, and she still didn't have a reason other than she was feeling particularly lonely on the day her friend had offered. Jake, a crush from her freshman year in high school, had become a good friend and confidante over the years of writing. Although she knew at least part of her would love to see what it would be like to be romantic with him, she had never crossed the line in their messages, nor had he.

"If it's a group thing, can Ryan and I come on Tuesday?"

"You sure Ryan is going to want to do that?" Shea asked about her friend's husband.

"Of course," Christine responded. "You know he doesn't mind what I plan, as long as it's not a night football is on."

"As long as you don't embarrass me," Shea replied, giving her friend a knowing look.

Christine shrugged. "Sometimes I can't help myself, but I will do my very best. When you said he will be with his brothers, does that mean Patrick is going?"

"Yes, I assume so."

"I heard some girls in my class talking about him, but I couldn't hear much. This adds some excitement, Ryan loves his movies and I'll enjoy watching girls fall all over themselves in front of him." Christine opened the door to the teachers' lounge, letting Shea pass in first. "Oh boy, I just realized how Ryan is going to react. He's obsessed with those movies, always talks about how crazy it is that a guy who grew up in Windsor Peak plays his favorite character. He's definitely going to be over the top excited to meet him."

"Let's not tell everyone about this, okay?" Shea asked quietly as she passed her friend.

"Your secret is safe with me!" Christine responded. "Other than telling Ryan because I tell him everything. Now let's talk about what you are going to wear on this non-date, because you need to knock his socks off. In a platonic way, of course."

***

As she packed up her classroom at the end of the day, her phone's incessant buzzing became more than just her book club group chat that tended to over-text the week before a meetup. Other than the one time a month when her phone blew up, she never got this many messages in a short time span.

Sudden fear that something had happened to her parents, or her sister, gripped her heart. Her parents had moved to Florida years prior, and her sister had followed them not long after. It was a constant battle to get them all to understand that she loved them, but she also loved where she lived. However, she worried that something would happen to one of her parents when she was so far away.

Grabbing her phone from her bag under the desk, she swiped it open quickly to see she had eighteen new texts and several missed calls. Christine came into the room just as she saw who they were all from and dropped her phone on the desk in exasperation.

"What was that? You can't be fighting with Jake already."

"No, not at all. I just heard my phone going crazy and looked, and it's all these texts and calls from Bob." She held up the phone to show her.

"That's…really creepy, Shea. How did things end with you the other night?" Christine grabbed the phone to scroll through the messages.

"I thanked him for a nice dinner, shook his hand and went home. He made a move like he was going to try and kiss me, but I just ducked and got in my car quickly." Shea threw some essays in her bag, hoping she had time to grade them at home.

"This is a lot." Christine was scrolling through the text messages, which all seemed to get angrier as they went on. She clicked on the most recent voicemail and they both cringed when his loud voice filled the classroom.

"Shea, this is Bob. Your date from last night? I've been trying to reach you, call me back as soon as you get this. We forgot to make plans at the end of the night, and I want to see you again."

"Too bad, Bob, because I don't want to see you again." She looked at her friend. "What should I do?"

"Nothing," Christine decided. "Ignore it. He lives a few towns over, and even though he has some friends in town, the chances of running into him are pretty slim. He'll find someone else and move on quickly, I'm sure."

"Are you saying I'm forgettable?"

"Well, in this case, I sure hope so!" Christine handed her back the phone. "I'm sure he will get the point when you ignore the messages."

As she said the words the phone began to ring again, with his name appearing on the screen. Dropping the phone again to the desk, Shea groaned, knowing she was going to have to deal with him at some point or another.

***

Arriving at home that evening, Shea was shocked to see a huge display of flowers sitting outside her front door. Rushing up to see who they were from, and secretly hoping they were from Jake, she ripped into the card. *Shea, I enjoyed our evening together. Let's do it again soon. Yours, Bob*

Clutching the card, she stepped past the flowers and opened the door, letting Muffin jump all over her as they reunited. "Hi baby," she crooned, dropping to the couch so she could get her bearings while being greeted like a long-lost princess. "Let's get your leash and go for a walk." Muffin jumped off her lap and ran to the front closet, where the dog's gear was stored, and waited patiently for the door to open.

As they stepped out past the bouquet of flowers again, Shea debated kicking them over. Seeing Ryan pull into his driveway across the street, she quickly changed her mind and picked up the vase, running to catch him before he went inside.

"Ryan!"

"Hi, Shea. Pretty flowers." He stopped on the entry as she approached.

She thrust the vase at him. "Here, give these to Christine. Don't tell her they came from me, just a romantic surprise from you."

"I can't do that, Shea. You should keep them; this must have cost a fortune."

She shook her head. "Please, take them. I'll only throw them out."

"Why would you do that?" He looked stunned.

"Remember Bob, who I had that awful date with last weekend? He sent them."

He took the flowers from her and looked at her thoughtfully. "He's trying to get a second date?"

She sighed. "Yes, but he's trying a little too hard. Text messages, phone calls, now the flowers. I don't know what to do."

"Be blunt. Tell him you aren't interested. Most guys are dense, this is the only way to get through to him," Ryan advised her.

"I don't want to be rude."

Ryan gave her a sympathetic look. "It's rude to send someone a barrage of unwanted messages and gifts, yet he doesn't seem concerned. Don't give him the courtesy he isn't giving you."

"You're right." She gave him an impulsive hug. "I'm so glad Christine has you."

"I got the good end of that deal," he winked at her and turned to walk inside as she and Muffin started their walk.

Was Bob more than a nuisance? She was worried if she didn't nip it in the bud, he would be a bigger problem, but confrontation was not her thing at all. It shouldn't be necessary, in her opinion. He asked her out again, she declined. That should be the end of it. Instead, she was left feeling unsettled that Bob had been to her home when she wasn't there, and unsure of how to get the message across to him without being cruel.

She thought back to their date, remembering how Bob had come on a little strong. Trying to hug her when they first met, reaching for her hand at dinner. Talking about future dates and trips they could take together; all things Shea knew even before Jake walked in that she didn't want to do. He didn't seem to be the type of guy who took a hint, so she was going to have to bite the bullet and address him, she decided.

Once she had returned home, she realized she had several missed calls and text messages from Bob. Thankfully her phone had been in do not disturb mode, after all the buzzing that happened in the classroom. Finally feeling fed up, she sent a quick text response to Bob. *Thank you for the flowers, but I am not interested in a second date. You are a nice guy and I wish you well, but please stop trying to contact me.*

She hit send and dropped her phone onto the kitchen table, hoping that would be the end of her interactions with Bob. She wanted to be excited to hear a text message come in, and be able to hope it was from Jake, not dreading every sound her phone made.

Chapter 11

Jake came in from the barn with a basket full of eggs that he handed off to Stella, seeing Charlie sitting at the island with an open book in front of him. "What are you reading?" he asked, trying to get a glimpse of the text.

"It's homework," His son replied.

"Is it any good?"

"No." The one-word answers were torture for Jake.

"Anything you do like to read?" he asked, hoping to start some kind of dialogue.

"My birth certificate is entertaining." Charlie finally looked up, meeting his father's eyes. "Tells the story of two people who I really don't know, but they brought me to life."

Jake could feel the blood rushing to his head, feeling rage as he heard Charlie dismiss his mother in that way. "Do not ever speak about your mother like that again, do you hear me?" His voice was a low growl and he saw Charlie shrink back a little before pulling himself up in his chair.

"How could I speak about her when I know nothing about her? She never existed in my world." Charlie's face was getting redder, and his fists were clenched on his lap.

"Charlie!" Stella was between them suddenly. "Do not speak to your father like that."

"It's true! He ran off to fight all these wars, but they won't bring her back!" Charlie banged on his chest with his closed fist. "I'm sitting right here, right in front of him, proof that she was someone who cared about him once. You would think he would want to be with me, not with a bunch of dudes in some weird country!"

Jake sank into the stool that was fortunately positioned behind him, because suddenly his legs didn't want to work anymore. "That's not how it was," he said so softly he wasn't sure Charlie even heard him.

"That's exactly how it was!" Charlie continued to rage. "You left me here! You haven't given me a thought in the last fourteen years, and now you're injured so I'm supposed to jump and be your best friend? That's such bullshit."

"Language, please," Stella murmured, placing her hand on Charlie's arm, showing her support for him.

"Stella! He deserves it!" Charlie turned to Jake once more. "I don't want to talk to you about my day. I don't want to hear about yours. I just want you to leave me alone. Figure out your problems on your own, or with someone else. I'm not your guy." With that, he gathered his belongings off the island and stormed out of the room. Jake could see the tears in his eyes and was grateful when Stella squeezed his hand and then rushed after Charlie. She would be able to make sure he was alright before he had to go to school.

"Jake," His father's voice came from down the hall, where his office stood by the front door. "Come here please."

Jake rose, feeling like he had gone back in time to when he was twelve and misbehaved with his brothers, as he walked to the office. His father stood behind his desk and indicated that Jake should close the door before he walked over to two chairs in the corner of the office, pointing for Jake to sit in one.

Ben sank into his chair, where the soft leather had formed to his body over the years, so it was only comfortable for him. "That was a lot for this early in the morning."

"I know. I'm just trying to fix things with him, and I don't know how." Jake thrust a hand into his hair, making it stand up straight from his head. "Everything I do is wrong."

"That's not true." Ben said, leaning forward in his chair.

"It is! I have screwed up since the day he was born." Jake let out a ragged sigh.

Ben shook his head. "I was there the day he was born, and you were incredible. You and Jenna beamed that day, and for the next few months. You were a good dad to him, and you still are. You pay for everything that kid wants to do, you make sure he has everything he needs. Hell, you probably even send Stella money for groceries. So don't say you've done everything wrong."

"Okay, I've just done the most important things wrong," Jake said wearily.

"Son, you have to stop beating yourself up. You served your country. You had a reason for going, do you remember what it was?"

"Of course. I did it for Jenna." Saying her name brought her face into his head, her smile warming his heart. She had sat right here in this office with his father, in these very chairs, getting help with her math homework on a regular basis. If he closed his eyes, he could hear her muttering as she worked out the solution.

"Ok, let's talk about Jenna. It's time, Jake."

Jake stood and began pacing around the room. "She didn't want to go to work that day, did you know that? She didn't even want to be in New York! I thought I was helping her by forcing her to go, saying I would stay with Charlie. I promised I would always take care of her, and I sent her to die."

"Did you know the terrorist group was going to target that train station?" Ben asked quietly.

"Of course not!" Jake erupted. "But that doesn't change the fact that she wanted to stay home, and I told her to go."

"There is nothing you can do to change what happened. Yes, it's awful that Jenna was killed. It's horrible that she didn't get to see Charlie grow up. We all loved her, and we all mourned with you." Ben stood to take his son by the arms. "But we didn't have to lose you too. I am so thankful that you are home, and that you have a chance to fix things with Charlie. It's time to face what's left of your life and go forward. Now you have guilt over Jenna, guilt over your friends you lost in the war, guilt over Charlie. You need to forgive yourself and let the guilt go."

"I don't know how to do that," Jake whispered.

"None of us do," Ben gathered his son in his arms. "We will figure it out together. You took the first step, you came home, and you made the appointment to go see the counselor. Now you have to start back at the day Jenna died, and deal with that and everything that has happened since. You've seen some awful things in war, I can see it in your eyes. It's time to allow yourself to live, Jake. To allow yourself to be happy."

Jake pulled back, seeing the emotion on his father's face. "All of the people that died, Dad, they didn't get to live or be happy."

"All the more reason for you to do it," Ben explained. "Jenna and all those soldiers, they didn't lose their lives so that you would suffer for the rest of yours. Jenna's death was a tragedy, and completely unfair. But would she want you to live like this?

If it had been you that day, would you want her to live the rest of her life as a tribute to you? The soldiers you have lost, they signed up for that same war you did, they knew the risks. Do you think they expect you to relive their deaths every day?"

"You make it sound easy," Jake whispered.

"I know, and it's not. The first step might be the hardest, and that's going to the counselor, addressing all of this. Maybe once you share it with someone, it won't be just your burden to carry. I will listen, and you know your brothers would as well. If you need us, that's why we're here. We love you, Jake. Let us help you." Ben paused as the front door closed loudly. "Charlie will come around. He's hurting too, but he has Stella to help him through it, and he and Patrick have always been close. Focus on healing yourself and whatever small steps you can take with him, stop expecting to jump right into his life."

"You're right," Jake felt exhausted. "I have an appointment today at the VA, when I was there for the orthopedic surgeon yesterday, I ran into Mark Nelsons wife Megan. We saw them at the Palace the other night, she had told me she works there. She was able to help me get an appointment for every day this week with a counselor, I can't imagine how long that would have taken if it wasn't for her."

"I'll send her flowers myself," Ben declared. "I always did like Mark Nelson when you boys were in high school, he wasn't much older than you at the time. I'm so glad she was able to help."

Jake checked his watch. "My first appointment is in an hour, so I should head out soon."

"Be open, Jake. Let them help you."

"I'll try, Dad." Jake paused before opening the door. "And thank you. I appreciate you more than you know."

"Oh, I know, Jake. And I love you too." Ben was wiping his eyes as Jake left the room, fighting back his own emotions once again.

Chapter 12

Dan was hunched over a computer at the small desk in his childhood bedroom, staring at the screen as his fingers punched angrily at the keyboard. Jake stood and watched for a minute, unnoticed, before he cleared his throat and watched his brother jump.

"Shit, you scared me." Dan pushed back from the computer and looked at his brother. "What's up?"

"You okay? You looked a little annoyed there." Jake indicated the computer.

"Nothing new. Just trying to keep a colleague from poaching my clients, they start circling as soon as anyone is out of the office longer than six hours."

"I wanted to see if you felt like going to grab some lunch? I'm feeling antsy, I was already to and from the VA for appointments and have nothing to do before we go to the Palace later for karaoke." Jake was surprised at how anxious he was to see Shea again and wasn't ready to admit that to anyone just yet. They had been texting back and forth for the last few days, and he looked forward to hearing his phone chime in the hopes it was a message from her. The hours were dragging before he would see her in person, and he wasn't sure what to expect of the night ahead.

"I can't," Dan replied. "Sorry. If I don't deal with these clients now, I won't be able to relax later. But I am *not* singing, no matter what you two idiots try to say."

"I take that as a dare, and I accept." Jake pushed off the doorframe he had been leaning on. "I'll find Patrick and let him know you have issued a challenge."

"It was not a dare or a challenge, and you know it!" Dan yelled after him, earning a wave from Jake.

Patrick was in the barn, wiping down his mare after a morning ride. "You going for a ride?" he asked, surprise on his face as his brother entered the barn.

"No, not quite ready for that yet. Feel like grabbing some lunch in town with me?"

"I have an appointment at two, so as long as we are done by then that works." Patrick led the horse into her stall.

"Appointment for what?" Jake asked.

"None of your business." Patrick emerged from the barn, and they started walking towards the house. "Ready for your date tonight?"

"Changing the subject so quickly? Now I'm really intrigued."

Patrick laughed. "Really, though, you dating is exciting."

"It's not a date."

"Keep telling yourself that." Patrick looked at his brother. "When was the last relationship you had?"
"Relationship?" Jake stopped to think. "Jenna, I suppose."

"That's what I thought. You've never mentioned a woman to us or brought anyone home. You know you are allowed to get involved with someone, right? Even to fall in love?"
"My brain knows that. But it just hasn't clicked with anyone. I've met plenty of women and gone on dates, but it just never goes too deep."

"I loved Jenna." Patrick held up a hand to stop his brother from interrupting. "And I know she would never want you to spend fifteen years alone and lonely."

Jake felt his chest constricting and tried to remain composed. "I know."

"So cut yourself a break and enjoy your date with Shea. She seems like good people, I always liked her when we were kids." Patrick slapped him on the back. "Let me take a quick shower and then you can take me out to lunch."

"You're paying, movie star. I'm just a humble first sergeant." He watched his brother run into the house, grateful Patrick was willing to help him stay distracted.

Jake sat down heavily in one of the chairs on the porch to wait for his brother. He knew that everything his brother and father had said was true, Jenna would have hated for him to be living alone and miserable. She radiated happiness wherever she went, making people feel good just by smiling at them. He had soaked in her joy for so many years, being away from it was like being thrust into complete darkness and never being allowed to see the sun. Her laughter, so quick and easy to generate, had given him confidence, and her rapture when he played the guitar was the reason he had loved playing. So many things in his life were because of her, and so many of the things he had denied himself since her death she would be disappointed in him for.

Number one on that list, she would have really hated that he lived apart from his son, that he hadn't been able to push his own emotions aside to allow himself to have a loving relationship with their son. As much as he hated not being able to solve everything quickly, he had to tread slowly and repair the damage he had done. While he was at it, he had to give himself permission to open his heart to the possibility of someone other than Jenna, because just the thought of Shea's smile let a little light shine on his dark, battered heart.

***

Seven o'clock finally rolled around, and Jake was wearing the floor out by the front door waiting on his brothers to be ready. He had told Shea they would be there by half past the hour, and he wanted to make sure he arrived before her. "Are you two almost ready?" He yelled up the stairs, earning a glare from Stella.

"Walk up there, Jake. You know all the shouting drives me crazy."

"Sorry, Stella." He heard footsteps in the hallway above him and was relieved to see two sets of legs coming down the stairs. "About time. You two done with your makeup?"

"Hey, we aren't the ones with a first date tonight that we changed outfits three times for." Dan poked back.

"Not a date."

"Keep telling yourself that," Patrick laughed.

"I'll drive," Dan stated, shaking his keys.

"Fine by me, let's just go." Jake hustled them out the door, waving goodbye to Stella as he closed the door.

"Remember how we had to drag him out on Saturday night, Dan?" Patrick remarked as he buckled his seat belt.

"I do, and now he can't get there fast enough. Wonder what changed?"

"I cannot believe I invited you two to come along," Jake grumbled from the backseat.

"Technically Kendra invited us, and then you decided to bring a date. But we don't have to worry about the details, let's just focus on your love life tonight!" Patrick turned the radio up and sang along, leaving Jake to start out the window and admit that the feeling in his stomach was nervousness at seeing Shea again.

When they entered Windsor Peak Palace a few minutes later, Jake and Patrick headed straight for an open table, where Jake chose a seat against the wall, watching as Dan stood by the bar clearly searching for Kendra. "It's so sad," Patrick commented.

"That they broke up?"

"No, just how pathetic our brother is." They laughed, and then Jake's attention was diverted as the door opened and Shea came in. She was with a man and woman that he didn't recognize, and his stomach dropped as he wondered if she had brought a date.

"Am I on a blind date with the redhead?" Patrick whispered, nodding toward the three heading to their table.

"Knock it off."

"Hi," Shea was in front of him now, and Jake jumped to his feet.

"Hi." He smiled, feeling clumsy suddenly. "This is my brother Patrick. Please ignore him as much as humanly possible."

"Nice to meet you." Shea indicated the couple behind her. "This is my friend Christine, and her husband Ryan."

Ryan shook hands with Jake. "Great to meet you both." He glanced back at his wife as he reached for Patrick's hand. "I am definitely not saying that I am a huge fan."

Patrick laughed. "Come sit by me, my brothers never praise me." Dan arrived back at the table, allowing for introductions all over again, before Jake finally sat with Shea to his right.

"I'm glad you could make it."

She smiled back at him. "Thanks for not thinking it's weird that I brought friends along."

"Weird? When I brought my two brothers? They are the very definition of weird."

"Heard that," called Dan from the other end of the table.

They all paused in conversation to order drinks, hearing the waitress out about the daily specials and when the karaoke would begin. "The sign-up list is over there." She pointed to the side of the stage, and Patrick immediately jumped up to add their names to the list. Christine followed, with Ryan begging her not to choose a duet.

"How do you and Christine know each other?" Jake asked.

"They moved in across the street from me a few years ago. We both teach together at high school, so we spend a lot of time together," she laughed. "We share in the quest of trying to convert all our students to love our subject the most. I'm convinced I can make everyone love English class if they just have an open mind."

"Some must?" Jake questioned.

"Oh, sure," Shea nodded. "I get a few every year who are avid readers, and who love reading and writing. They are in the minority, but most of them come around by the end of the year. I try to keep it fun, picking books I think they'll enjoy. And I give them options other than just writing essays, which they appreciate. Things like acting out a scene or writing a poem rather than writing something for me. They don't realize they work just as hard, and most of the time learn twice as much, then if they just wrote a three-page essay."

"It sounds like you are a great teacher."

She waved a hand. "I try, but enough about work! How are you? How have things been since you came home?"

"I'm doing okay. Got cleared by the doctor to start PT and stop wearing the sling, so that helps."

"Do you mind if I ask what happened?" She looked worried. "I had a message from you and then nothing, and suddenly you are here."

"I know, I'm sorry. I had a concussion and really couldn't tolerate looking at any kind of screen, so I couldn't email you to let you know I was in the hospital. And I only got your phone number this week from Kendra, I don't know why I had never asked you for it." He looked over at his brothers and their new friends, laughing and enjoying the night. "I won't go into a lot of detail and ruin this night, but I was caught in an ambush. Explosions, bullets, all the things you don't want in a day at work. I was one of the lucky ones."

"I'm glad." Shea reached over and put her hand on his arm, causing him to meet her eyes. "And I'm sorry about those you lost. I know how hard that is for you."

He swallowed past the lump in his throat, feeling the light pressure of her hand on his arm and the warmth it provided, and not wanting to ruin the moment. Dan started them all as he lunged to his feet, bumping the table in the process, reaching for the tray of drinks Kendra was carrying.

"Dan, leave it. You'll make me drop it," Kendra warned.

He sat back down, looking wounded. "I just wanted to help." Accepting his beer from her outstretched hand, he took a sip before asking, "Any chance you could sit with us for a few minutes?

"No, sorry. I'm way too busy." She turned to head back to the bar, and Patrick howled with laughter.

"You don't get shot down often, brother, but when you do it's epic."

"I thought it was nice of you to ask her," Shea said softly, receiving a small smile from Dan in return.

"They'll go at each other all night if we let them. Luckily Patrick will be on stage half the night performing, and the other half will end up swarmed with fans once they get comfortable. They shouldn't ruin our night too much." Jake tapped his finger on his beer in time with the song being badly sung by the first performer. "Are you planning to sing?"

"Me?" Shea asked. "Absolutely not. No one should have to suffer through that!"

"Come on, it can't be that bad."

"It's worse than you could possibly imagine. And go on a stage where someone who just finished a Broadway musical is performing? I'll pass."

"Patrick is good, I'll give him that."

Shea studied his face. "Are you a better singer than him?"

"Guess you'll have to find out. I just heard them call my name, which means Patrick signed me up to go first."

Chapter 13

Watching Jake climb the stage, Shea felt a nervous anticipation she hadn't expected. Her every nerve ending had been on fire since she first came into the bar, and watching Jake get set to sing had her on edge. Would he be singing to her? She shut the idea down immediately, seeing it was ridiculous. She wasn't even sure if they were on a date or just out as friends, and he wasn't giving her many clues. Despite the years of confiding to each other in messages, they weren't used to being around each other or having a normal conversation. She had to relax and see what would come, as unsettling as that might be.

As he started singing, his whiskey-and-smoke voice washed over here and silenced out all the noise in the bar. He had pulled a barstool on the stage and was sitting, commanding the entire room. She smiled when the notes of a Hootie and the Blowfish song started, one she hadn't heard in years. His brothers reacted with catcalls and grins, singing along from the table along with everyone else in the bar.

Christine slid over closer to Shea, whispering in her ear. "This is so hot."

"Go back over with your husband!" Laughing she pushed her lightly, then returned her focus to the small stage.

As the song trailed off, he looked up and caught her eye, winking quickly before sliding off the barstool and heading back to the table. Then he was off the stage to thunderous applause, and the crowd demanding he sing more, which had Patrick jumping to his feet.

"Thanks to my brother Jake for opening for me! If you all don't mind, I'd like to give him a quick round of applause to thank him for his service to our beautiful country." The crowd rose to their feet, cheering for Jake, before turning their attention back to Patrick. "Now I'll show him how it's done!" The opening notes for a pop song from one of the young blond singers from the nineties started playing, causing the crowd to laugh and cheer for him.

"He always knows how to shift the spotlight," Jake murmured as he sat back down next to her.

"You were amazing. I can't believe you can sing like that." She was fangirling and she didn't care.

He shrugged. "I was always the one hanging out with Patrick when we were little, and he wanted to sing and play instruments, so I went along for the ride. My dad has always said that our mom was the musical one, so we must have gotten it from her."

"When did your mom pass away? You don't mention her much."

"When Patrick was born. Something went wrong with the delivery; we just suddenly had a baby brother and mom was gone. Dan and I were little, I was 2, he was 4. He has some vague memories of her, or he says he does at least. Stella moved in right away, and she kept us all clean, alive, and out of jail."

"That's so sad."

Jake reached over and squeezed her hand. "Don't get me started on sad, especially when my brother is doing his best Britney right now."

She laughed, glad he had both lightened the mood and was still holding her hand under the table. His hand felt rough but warm, and she felt their contact in every cell of her body. "Are you singing again?"

"I will do one with him, but we will wait a bit before then." He leaned a little closer to be heard over the sound of the cheers Patrick had earned and was egging on by taking multiple bows on stage. "Can I ask a strange question?"

"Yes, it's true that I like pineapple on my pizza." She smiled at him. "I'm kidding, go ahead."

"We are definitely revisiting that statement." He took a sip of his beer. "Do you consider this a date?"

The wine must have gone straight to her head, because without hesitation she replied. "I'd like very much if it was one."

He smiled at her. "Me too."

"And then you can take me out again soon, without all the riffraff."

"You have a deal." They both laughed and she felt herself relax into him as he let go of her hand to drape an arm around the back of her chair. She met Christine's gaze across the table and saw her friend's excitement at seeing what was happening between her and Jake, but luckily Patrick rejoined the table and Christine was distracted before she could say anything embarrassing.

"Are you two done attention seeking?" Dan asked his brothers.

"Never," Patrick assured him, turning to take a selfie with a couple passing by the table. "I don't know how you go through life being as boring as you are."

"Boring? I don't seem boring when I'm taking care of your contracts for you, do I?"

"Is that a serious question? Because that is when you are the boringest of all the boring."

"Boys," Jake commanded. "We're in public, so let's at least try to be civilized."

"Yes, sir." They both responded with snappy salutes. Shea couldn't help but laugh with them, earning her a side eye from Jake.

"Encouraging them only leads to more."

"As long as it's not directed at me, that's okay."

"They wouldn't dare."

When Dan's name was called to sing, he groaned and threw a nasty look at his brothers before trying to decline. The crowd chanted his name until he took the stage, glaring at Patrick when the song "Sorry" by Justin Bieber came on the screen. To his credit, he tried to make the best of it, looking in Kendra's direction as he sang. She stopped working to watch, and a small smile emerged before she ducked her head and went back behind the bar again.

"I know they dated, but I assume it ended badly?" She inquired quietly.

"When he went to college, he ghosted her. Years of a relationship, a serious one, and then he was just gone. She won't even look at him if she can avoid it."

"But she was married, right? Her daughter is from that marriage?" Shea didn't know Kendra very well, they had been too many years apart in high school to overlap. Kendra's daughter was young, still in elementary school, so Shea didn't know her well yet. However, she had met the little girl in the restaurant a few times and she was both adorable and sweet. Kendra had been nice enough to accommodate Shea when she wanted to host a book club meeting in the bar on Sunday afternoons, setting aside a small area away from the football fans. When they met to discuss the possibility, Kendra had been so kind, and had remained so during all of the meetings the book club had held.

"Yes, she married another local guy, and he was much worse than Dan could ever dream of being. Big drinker, gambler, you name it." Jake looked towards where Kendra was standing. "I don't know the entire story, but from the few emails I've gotten from her over the years, life without him is a lot easier than life with him. I think when he left and didn't look back it was the best thing to happen to her."

"That's awful. I'm glad she is away from him."

"Me too. Now enough about her, tell me why you won't sing."

She laughed and they settled into an easy conversation, feeling more relaxed than she had in a long time. They didn't lack for things to talk about, alternating between their own private conversation and bantering with the rest of the table. Shea couldn't believe it when the lights dimmed, indicating the last call for the bar.

"I'll have to leave you once more, to do this with Patrick, then I can get you home if you'd like?"

"Go sing, and then we can figure it out."

The brothers took to the stage, singing a Lynyrd Skynyrd song, bringing the crowd to its feet with calls for more. Waving off their new fans, Jake left the stage while Patrick thanked everyone on Kendra's behalf for coming out before stepping down.

"Did you drive here?" Jake asked her as he sat down.

"I rode with Christine and Ryan."

"I was going to offer to take you home myself, but I drove with Dan. I can steal his car and take you home if you want?"

"Probably makes more sense if I go home with them, I don't want to make Dan's night worse than it's already been."

"You're probably right. I can touch base with you tomorrow to make plans if that works?"

"Perfect." They both stood, along with the rest of the table, and Shea felt nervous again suddenly, unsure of where to put her hands or how to say goodbye.

Jake leaned down and kissed her on the cheek, letting his lips linger slightly as her skin tingled from his touch. "Have a good night sleep."

She smiled at him and waved to his brothers before walking to the car with her friends, anxious to get home so she could relive every moment in her dreams.

Chapter 14

"Do you have practice this morning?" Jake asked Charlie as he sat hunched over a bowl of cereal.

Charlie responded before putting a spoonful in his mouth. "No."

"This afternoon?"

"Yup." Another bite and crunch.

"Need a ride?" Jake threw out, sipping his coffee.

"Nope."

"How's school going?" This was almost a conversation, so Jake was going to keep trying.

"Fine." An eye roll accompanied the word.

"Kids at school must have heard Patrick was in town."

That earned a snort of laughter that was quickly subdued. "You could say that."

A whole sentence! Jake couldn't believe the happiness those four words gave him. "Lots of kids trying to earn an invite over?"

"Yeah," Charlie stopped as Patrick entered the kitchen.

"Good morning! What are we having for breakfast? Frosted Flakes? Been a long time since I had this." He grabbed a bowl and started pouring, then glanced at his brother and nephew. "Did I interrupt something?"

"Ye—" Jake started, getting cut off by Charlie's louder "no."

"I thought I heard my name as I came down the stairs." Patrick stated.

"Just talking about how the kids at school act when you visit." Charlie dropped his dishes in the sink and headed out of the kitchen. "See you later."

"Sure you don't want a ride to school?" Jake called out, hearing the door close as his answer once again.

***

Jake picked up his phone and put it back down ten times in five minutes, causing Dan to glare at him over his laptop screen. "Either text her or don't but stop slamming your phone on the table."

"Hardly a slam." He drummed his fingers on the phone. "Is it ridiculous to text her? I'm a grown up. Texting her seems wrong."

"Then call her," Dan suggested.

Jake consulted his watch. "She's at school."

"Wait until later."

"I don't want to wait too long. What are the rules with that?" Jake picked up his phone again. "Maybe I should google it, you don't seem to have much of a love life going."

Dan sighed. "You can text her. It's not like it was when you were dating Jenna, most people text now instead of calling."

Jake considered it for a minute, then picked the phone up again, talking as he typed. "Hi Shea, it's Jake. I had fun last night. Was wondering if you were free on Friday?"

Dan cut in. "Why are you introducing yourself?"

"What if she didn't save my number?"

"She saved your number. Don't introduce yourself. And make it clear you are asking her on a date, because bringing her to karaoke with your brothers was probably a little confusing." Dan grinned. "Even if we are way more charming than you."

"Fine." Jake typed, debated, and then hit send.

"You didn't want to check it with me first?" Dan asked.

"I've used up my quota of relationship advice for the day. I'll roll the dice with this." His phone chimed, and he grabbed it quickly. "Must have worked, she said she had fun and would love to have dinner on Friday."

"Congratulations. Now can I work?" Dan went back to typing, leaving Jake to stare at the text message from Shea.

***

"Have you seen Grandpa?" Charlie's voice broke through Jake's focus on the book open in his hand.

"I think he went with Stella to the nursery to pick out some new plants for out front. Can I help you with something?" Jake closed the book on his finger, looking towards his son.

"Is Dan here? Or Patrick?" Charlie was looking up the stairs as he asked.

"No, they went golfing."

"Oh." He stared down at his feet for a long minute. "I need a ride to hockey. Coach can't get me today."

"I can take you!" Jake jumped to his feet, feeling in his pockets for his keys. "Let me just run upstairs and grab my keys, I think they must be up there."

"I'll be out front."

Jake took the stairs two at a time, grabbed his keys off the bureau and raced back down. "Want me to grab anything for you?"

"No, I got it." Charlie slid the bag and sticks into the back of the SUV then went to the passenger side.

"Another year and you could be driving," Jake remarked as they set out down the driveway.

"Yup." Charlie was focused on the view out the window.

"How's your team doing this year?"

"Pretty good."

Jake struggled to keep the short conversation rolling. "What's the record?"

"Thirteen and one."

"Wow. That's better than pretty good. I don't think I have ever been on a team that started out that strong."

"Even when you won the state championship?" Charlie glanced at him before quickly averting his eyes back to the road.

"Well, that was the high school team, this is your club team, right?"

"Yeah, high school won't start until after Thanksgiving."

"Our high school record that year wasn't great, I think we started out seven and three. Then we went on a streak in the playoffs. Dan was hurt the first few games, so he likes to take credit for the season turning around, but I think it was just team chemistry."

"That helps," Charlie nodded.

"I think we still have the video around somewhere, if you ever want to watch it."

"That might be fun."

They pulled into the rink parking lot far too fast for Jake, despite how slow he had driven. "Want me to stick around?"

Charlie hesitated, looking around the parking lot. "I guess that's fine."

Jake walked with him into the rink, nodding to the other fathers who were standing around in the lobby as he watched Charlie disappear into the locker room. He made his way into the rink, choosing a spot in the corner where he thought he would be the least disruptive to his son as he practiced, and settled in for the hour. Pulling his phone from his pocket, he sent a quick text to Shea.

At the rink to watch Charlie's practice. He let me drive him and we had a full conversation on the way here.

She responded quickly, sending a smiling emoji and words of encouragement that he read quickly before putting his phone back in his pocket. As the team took to the ice, he got so caught up in watching them skate, the hour flew by.

He waited in the lobby, catching up with a few familiar faces from his hockey days, until Charlie emerged still sweaty from the practice. Waving to his old friends he followed his son back to the car.

"Want to grab a pizza?" He dared to ask, fully expecting Charlie to say no.

"Ummm —" Charlie glanced at his phone, then at Jake. "Yeah, I guess so. Think Stella will be mad?"

"I'll send her a quick text. I know she wasn't sure who would be around for dinner anyway. I bet she and your grandpa will stop for dinner in Burlington, so this way she won't have to worry about us. Your uncles can fend for themselves."

They drove in a somewhat comfortable silence to the local pizza spot, where they parked and made their way to a table by the window. Jake saw several kids around Charlie's age around a few video games in the front of the restaurant and pointed them out. "If you want to go play, I can order for us."

"You sure?" Charlie looked surprised.

"Sure. What do you want to drink?"

"Just water is fine, I'm thirsty. Thanks!" He darted off to meet his friends, and Jake ordered his water and a beer for himself from the young waitress. When she delivered the drinks a minute later, he decided to order the food as well. "We will take the Caesar salad, an order of breadsticks, and a large half cheese, half pepperoni pizza."

He pulled his phone out again, sending a group text to his brothers, dad and Stella letting them know he and Charlie were grabbing pizza.

None for us? Came the response from Patrick.

You and Dan can grab dinner at the course. Your Dad and I are having dinner in the city. Stella responded, followed by a second text. *Enjoy your evening, Jake.*

He enjoyed watching Charlie play the game with his friends, seeing how he lit up when he laughed, and how the other kids clearly enjoyed his company. When the food was delivered, Charlie pointed at the table and headed over, sliding into the booth across from him.

"This okay?" He gestured at the food.

"Might be enough for me, not sure what you'll eat."

Jake laughed. "We can always order more, I was thinking we could save room for ice cream next door."

"If you were thinking sundaes, you have a deal," Charlie busied himself eating, but Jake was able to sneak in a few bits that almost made it feel as though they were having a full conversation. He now knew that his son preferred math to English, that he enjoyed the movies his uncle starred in, and that he was still in an age where girls were mild distractions but not worth the energy to pursue.

"I was already dating your mom at your age," He shared, and Charlie's eyes widened slightly. "Things were different then; we didn't have all the social media and texting nonsense you guys deal with now. It was probably a little less pressure to have a girlfriend. All we had to do was go for horseback rides, go skating or skiing."

"Did you do all that together?"

"Oh, yeah. She could outski me though," He laughed to himself. "But I drove her crazy on skates. She couldn't skate backwards no matter how hard I tried to teach her, and she hated that I was better than her."

"Well, you played hockey, she didn't."

"That's true."

"Do you miss her?" Charlie looked down at the fork he was playing with, asking the question softly.

"Every damn day. Every minute. She loved you so much, I don't think I've really told you that since you were little, but she did. You can see it in the pictures you have in your room."

"I wish I had known her." He traced a pattern on the table with his finger in the drops from his soda glass.

"I know that our situations are different because I had a great dad and Stella, and you got stuck with me. But I do know what it's like to miss someone I never had a chance to know."

"You aren't so bad. And I had Grandpa and Stella," Charlie mumbled. "I'm going to run to the bathroom."

The rest of the night was lighter, as though a small hurdle had been jumped. They got ice cream sundaes for the whole family and brought them home before Charlie disappeared upstairs to do his homework.

"How did that go?" Dan asked quietly after they heard the bedroom door close.

"Really good. I feel like I'm finally getting a chance to fix things with him."

"I'm glad," Patrick chimed in from the couch before turning the volume up on SportsCenter.

Chapter 15

Shea and Muffin returned from their evening walk to find Christine settled on the front porch, looking at something on her phone. "Hey," Shea called out as they came up the driveway, not wanting to startle her.

"Hey yourself. Sorry to take over your porch, Ryan is driving me crazy with yelling at his fantasy football team, so I escaped here for some girl chat. Do they really need to start the games on Thursdays now?" She slid the phone into her pocket and stood to follow Shea into the house.

"I don't mind, you should have let yourself in."

"The weather is still nice enough that I didn't mind being out there for a bit. In a month that will all change." Christine fake shivered as she dropped her coat on a hook by the door.

"Want a drink? I'm going to make myself some tea."

"Whatever you're having works."

Shea puttered in the kitchen for a few minutes, putting tea bags into two mugs and getting out a bag of cookies from the pantry. They both settled into their favorite spots in the living room, Christine lounging on the couch while Shea curled into a club chair under the front window. "What else is new?" Shea asked her friend.

"Oh, no, we are not here to talk about me," Christine shook her head. "We haven't had five minutes alone to discuss the fireworks that were going off the other night between you and Jake. Where do things stand between you now?"

"He asked me to go to dinner tomorrow night," Shea felt her cheeks growing pink as she said it.

"Oh, that is so exciting! I wish I could be here to help you get ready, but Ryan and I are going up to Montreal for the weekend." Christine looked thoughtful. "Maybe I can change it, I wonder what the cancellation policy is."

"Absolutely not. You go away and enjoy the time with your husband!" Shea was adamant.

Christine looked down at her tea mug. "I'm supposed to ovulate this weekend. We have been trying so hard, so we thought maybe a change of scenery would help."

"I'll have my fingers crossed for you," Shea promised. "And then I'm not going to think for one more second about your weekend activities."

Christine laughed. "Better we focus on yours. Where are you going for dinner?"

"I don't know, he didn't say. Somewhere local, I'm sure."

"He is smoking hot. I hope you don't mind me saying that, but the eyes and the muscles, and the singing. Whew." She fanned herself.

"Down girl! Don't make me more nervous for tomorrow!"

"You'll be fine. You two looked pretty cozy, no one else at the table was even in your conversation most of the night. And you have years of talking already, so this should be a piece of cake." Christine sipped her tea as she dismissed her friend's concerns.

"It's very different from emails," Shea started. "I can't quite explain it, but it's both like having my best friend home again and a total stranger. If that makes sense."

"I think it does," Christine nodded. "You've only known each other through those messages."

"And through his wife."

"Hmmm. I see what you mean." Christine waved her hand after a minute of thinking. "No, you can't bring her into this. If I died tomorrow, I would want Ryan to find someone new after a significant amount of grieving. And Jake has done that twice over."

"You don't think this is weird?"

"Weird? I think it's awesome. You haven't dated – other than Bob, that disaster doesn't count – since you broke up with Luke." She made a face. "That dirtbag. If I ever see him again…"

"I appreciate it, but best just to ignore him if you do."

"Ignore him? He cheated on you and stole from you. I thought you would marry him, and instead he almost destroyed you."

Shea sighed, thinking of the pain she had endured at the end of the five-year relationship. She had no idea they were having any kind of issues, until one day another woman had turned up on her doorstep, pregnant and screaming that he was the father of her baby. Shea had been stunned. Luke had been talking about moving in with her, and claimed to be saving for an engagement ring which was why he never had money to take her out. Instead, he was using all his money to support this other woman a few towns over. He managed to clean out Shea's savings account while clearing his belongings from her house, along with taking several of her more expensive items. Although it had been three years since she had last seen him, the pain still stung when she thought of Luke. Especially knowing he was now married and had a second child with the woman he had cheated on her with.

"He was a jerk," Shea agreed. "And yes, he turned me off from dating for a long time."

"Jerk is putting it mildly. He deserves to be thrown in a pit of snakes and have the lid put on top. Or into a shark tank with some hungry great whites." Christine plucked a cookie from the open bag on the table in front of them. "I wonder if a part of you was maybe holding out for Jake. Did you ever have a little crush on him in school?"

"Oh, I think everyone had a crush on one of the Burrows boys at some time or another. Jake was older, had a little bad boy edge to him that Jenna smoothed out." Shea thought back to her teenage years. "I can't say I didn't notice him a little."

Christine hooted with laughter. "I'd notice him if I were blind. But please don't tell my husband that I'm here gushing over your boyfriend."

"He's not my boyfriend. Let's get through a date first, okay?"

"Deal. But I want all the juicy details. Pretend we are teenagers, not mature adults who should know better. I want to feel like I am on this date with you."

"That's a little much. But I'll give you enough details to make you happy." Shea nibbled on a cookie, trying to settle the nerves in her stomach.

"How much do you know about his relationship with Charlie?" Christine inquired. "And his family, they seem very close."

"He has talked about all of them in his emails. He's always been close to his brothers; he describes them as his best friends. Same with his dad, and Stella, she's lived with them almost his whole life," Shea explained. "Charlie he struggles with, they have a complicated relationship, but he's trying."

"Don't give him too much of a pass. That's how we miss the warning signs in life, being so dazzled by the good that we overlook the bad," Christine warned her.

"You're right. It's a tough situation, from the outside I don't know how I would leave my child the way he did. On the other hand, I've never lost a spouse in a terrorist attack, so I guess I wouldn't know how I would react?" Shea ran her finger around the edge of the mug she held. "I feel like he's finally coming back to himself in a way and realizing how much time he's lost with Charlie. He's been saying that for a while now and thinking about whether it's time to come home. This might be the kick he needed to decide."

"Do you think he's ready for a relationship?"

Shea rolled her eyes. "Your guess is as good as mine. The one thing we have never talked about is love lives, so for all I know, he could have been dating this entire time."

"Maybe make sure he doesn't have a girlfriend back in Virginia," Christine warned.

"Oh, I never thought of that," Shea admitted. The thought of him dating someone else, or having a girlfriend, made her feel a little sick to her stomach. "Good idea, I'll have to ask him."

"Has he said anything about when he's supposed to leave?" Christine looked worried. Shea knew her friend was probably dreading the idea even more than she was, because it would be on her to pick up the pieces if Jake left.

"Not really. Should be a few weeks before he really knows what's happening."

"Have you given any thought to what will happen if he does have to leave?" Christine asked the question gently, and Shea knew her intentions were good. "I can't imagine being here and having someone I cared about in a war zone."

"I haven't let myself think that far ahead," Shea confessed. She really didn't want to think about Jake leaving, or anything that could happen beyond their first official date. "I don't know what will happen this weekend, or during the time he is home, so I have to just wait and see. I've always worried about him anyway, so I guess it wouldn't be much different?"

"I think you're wrong.," Christine challenged her. "Worrying about a friend is very different than worrying about someone you could be falling in love with."

"Christine, we are nowhere near there," Shea rolled her eyes. "Don't get ahead of yourself."

"I'll try not to, but you don't let yourself be blindsided by burying your head in the sand. Deal?"

Shea agreed, although her mind was already spinning. Spending just a few hours with Jake had already consumed her thoughts more than any man she had ever dated before. What would happen after they went on a date? Or spent a night together? She pushed the thoughts out of her head and focused on her friend, who had moved on to gossip about some fellow teachers and talk about the upcoming Harvest Festival.

After an hour, Christine stood and stretched. "I should head home, any minute now Ryan will realize the house is empty and panic."

Shea gave her a hug. "I really hope things work out for you this weekend."

"Right back at you," Christine said, hugging tight before heading out to cross the street.

Shea grabbed her phone as she carried the mugs to the kitchen and went to let Muffin out into the fenced yard one last time before bed. A text from Jake popped up and she clicked on it eagerly. *Hope your night is going well. Had dinner with Charlie and think I finally made some progress. Looking forward to tomorrow night.*

She leaned against the counter and considered her response, before typing *Glad to hear things went well! I had some girl time with Christine, heading to bed shortly. Also looking forward to tomorrow!* She tucked the phone in her pocket to keep herself from waiting for a response from him. Having a second thought, she pulled the phone back out and typed quickly before she could stop herself. *Do you have anyone waiting for you back in Virginia?* Biting on her lip as she saw the bubbles quickly appear, she let out a sigh when she saw his response. *Like a girlfriend? No, I would never have asked you out if I did.* She smiled and sent one last text, telling him to have a good night's sleep, before sticking the phone in her pocket. She could easily spend all night texting with him, asking questions about his time with Charlie or his day, but she had to hold herself back. Better to see where they were after some alone time before becoming even more invested in his life.

Chapter 16

Hearing his phone ring, Jake pulled it out of his pocket and saw his commanding officer's cell number on the screen. "Major Taylor, how are you, sir?"

"Jake, wanted to check on you." His voice came through in the same manner the Major always presented himself, crisp and efficient. "Any update on the injury?"

"I had some appointments here at the VA," Jake started. "It's going to be a little bit before I know much more. I need to see the doctor who will decide if I can return to duty or not."

"Sure hope so," his boss said. "We miss you around here. I get word from Afghanistan that your troops are all asking about you every five minutes. I know you still have time left on your convalescent leave, but always good to know which way this is going."

"I'll touch base with Sergeant Banner, ask him to smooth things over." Jake replied. "Maybe try to call a few of the higher-ranking men, ask them to spread the word that I'm fine and hope to return."

Silence met his statement, followed by a cough on the other end of the line. "Don't rush back for anyone else, Jake. Make sure you are ready before you try. The last thing I want is a soldier who's only half in, that could end very badly for more than just you."

"Yes, sir."

"I spoke with Chris Hartings' parents earlier this week. Do you remember him?"

Bullets were whizzing by his head as he grabbed the fallen soldier, dragging him to behind a half wall that would protect them. Shouting orders to his troops, telling them to circle and figure out where fire was coming from, take out the enemy. Holding the wound, trying to stop the blood. Heat, dirt, blood, shouting, tears.

"Jake, are you there?" His boss's voice brought him back to the present.

"Sorry, sir. Just lost service for a minute."

"Anyway, they would like to speak to you. If you are up to it." The Major's voice was softer than usual, expressing a sensitivity that he was not known for.

"I'd be happy to, if you have their contact information." Jake wrote down the phone number recited, double checking to make sure he had it right and he could read it, since his hand was shaking so badly.

"I told them you were home recovering, so you may not be able to call. No pressure."

"I appreciate that, sir. I will try and call them today." Jake swallowed past the lump in his throat.

"Jake." He paused so long Jake checked to make sure the connection was still there. "I know your history. I also know you are one of the best we have. Those two things cause me some conflict, because I do consider you a friend and I want what's best for you. If you find yourself struggling with anything, you have my number."

"Thank you, sir."

"This isn't from your commanding officer. This is from your friend, Steve." He cleared his throat. "Keep me in the loop on your progress as well."

"Will do. Thank you for everything."

The phone beeped, indicating the call had been disconnected. Jake sat where he was, staring at the numbers on the paper in front of him for so long they became a blur. Then he stared at it some more.

***

Dan walked by, leaning over to see what he was looking at. "Whose number is that?"

Jake couldn't find the words he needed suddenly.

"Hello? You awake?" Dan prodded him.

Jake shook his head. "Yeah, I'm awake. Just don't know what to do."

"About what?" Dan sat next to him at the island, trying to pull the number closer to him but Jake clamped a hand down on top of it. "Wow. Whose number is it? Can't be Shea, you already have her in your phone. Another woman?"

"No, it's not another woman," Jake growled. "It's personal."

"Ok, and I'm here because I'm your brother. We don't keep secrets from each other. Spill."

Jake took a deep breath. "About three months ago, I lost a soldier in Afghanistan. His name was Chris Harting. This number belongs to his parents."

"Want to tell me what happened?" Dan asked, gentler now.

Jake examined his hand, still covering the phone number, for lack of anything else to do.

"I'll take that as a no," Dan stated. "How about if I sit here silently while you call them?"

"I don't know if I can."

"Yes, you do." Dan's voice expressed a confidence in him that Jake wasn't feeling. "You would have already thrown it away if you didn't care enough to call. Or you never would have written it down. I know you, and you always talk to the parents. Why is this one different?"

"This kid," Jake said, picturing him as he spoke. "There are some that I just connect with in a different way. Some that I see myself in, and others that I can't help but wonder why the fuck they are there. They want to see the world, or get out of a small town, but they have so much life in them. It's a dark world, military life, lots of difficult personalities and people who are a little rough around the edges. This kid was the opposite. He—"

"Reminded you of Jenna," Dan guessed quietly.

"Yeah."

"And he died with you, I'm guessing."

"In my arms."

"Well, I can't speak on this from any experience," Dan started. "But I can tell you with absolute certainty that if my back was against the wall, there is no one I would rather have at my side than you. And if I were a kid, or even right now, I know that even in my last moment if you were next to me, I would feel okay."

Jake leaned forward, placing his forehead on the cool granite of the island. He felt his brother's hand on his back and knew that Dan would sit next to him for as long as it took for him to be able to move again. The desire to pick his head up and smash it back down onto the solid surface slowly dissipated, the pressure on his back the only thing connecting him to the present moment and the knowledge that he was safe.

***

When Jake was finally able to sit up, he had no idea how much time had passed. But the fact that Patrick now sat calmly and quietly at his other side indicated that a significant portion of time had lapsed, while he was trying to force his dark memories away from the brightness of the day.

"I'm going to make this call," he managed to rasp out, before having to stop for a moment and collect himself. "I'm going to do this, and then I want to get blackout drunk. You guys got me?"

"We got you," Dan's voice was calm and solid.

Picking up the phone with shaky hands, he tried to dial twice before putting it back down again. Looking to him for approval, Patrick pulled the phone and slip of paper away and entered the number. He put it back on the counter in front of Jake, just needing the green button to be pushed.

"I don't know if I can do this," he whispered, staring at the phone.

"It can wait," Dan suggested.

"I can call them for you," Patrick chimed in. "Introduce myself, say I'm your brother and we wanted to send our condolences."

Jake shook his head. "They want to know about his death. I appreciate your offer, but they need to talk to me."

"We can do it tomorrow if you would rather," Patrick replied, looking at Dan. "Dan's right, it can wait."

"No, I need to get this over with." Jake groaned at the sound of his words. "That sounds awful. I don't dread talking to them, just the subject matter."

"We know," Dan said softly, before holding his finger over the call button. "Ready?" He looked for Jake's nod before hitting call.

The phone rang three times before a woman picked up, sounding breathless over the phone's speaker. "Hello?"

"Hello, yes. Ma'am, this is First Sergeant Jake Burrows calling."

"Oh my. Sergeant, can I get my husband? He will want to talk to you as well. Just one second." They heard some muffled sounds and then the sound of her yelling, and seconds later she was back. "He's here now. Thank you so much for calling."

"Of course. I wanted to express my condolences and apologize for being so delayed in reaching out to you." Jake sounded as robotic as he felt, trying to go through the motions that he had done many times over in his career.

"We can't tell you how much it means to hear from you," Chris's father stated. "When our son called or wrote home, ninety percent of what he said was about his hero, Sergeant Burrows. He told us that you had kept him safe in many situations, and that he had learned so much from you."

They heard a sniffle, and then the woman spoke again. "He admired you so much, Sergeant."

"Please, call me Jake." He cleared his throat. "I'm honored to have known and led your son. He was truly remarkable, and I learned way more from him than I could have possibly taught him."

"Is there anything —" The dad's voice cut off, followed by a choked-out sob. "At all you could tell us about when we lost him?"

"You know a lot of it is confidential," Jake started, feeling his brothers close in around him. "But I was with him. He wanted to be home with you both. His last moments he spent talking about home, and how he longed to see you again. I did everything I could, I promise you that."

"Jake, we do not hold you responsible, don't you think that for one second." Her voice was soft, but the tears could be heard with the words. "Our son wanted this adventure, and he knew what the cost could be. He has blessed us a million times over in his lifetime, and he continues to give us signs every day that he is with us. Our faith is strong, and we know we will see him again."

"We wanted to thank you," his dad cut in. "We heard from one of his best friends that you carried him out, made sure he came home to us. Having him home to be laid to rest near us gives us immense peace."

"I ummm—", Jake cleared his throat again. "I wish it had ended differently."

"So do we," the dad's voice came through the line. "Jake, if you are ever able to visit us here in Indiana, we would love to meet you in person. You and your family will always be welcome here."

They ended the call, promising to keep in touch, and Jake sat for a moment staring at the light dimming outside the window. Feeling Dan stand up, he watched as he crossed the kitchen, grabbed a bottle and three glasses, and pointed to the porch.

Chapter 17

The parent teacher conferences ran late, so Shea decided to stop at Windsor Peak Palace on her way home and pick up some takeout food. Ryan had offered to walk Muffin for her, knowing how these days dragged on for teachers, so she had gladly accepted. He had texted her a picture of Muffin secure on their sofa, so rushing home wasn't necessary. She hadn't heard from Jake since early in the morning, and it was shocking to her how quickly she had gotten used to texting back and forth with him all day.

The crowd was light when she entered, and she quickly spotted Kendra behind the bar. Hopping onto a bar stool, she pulled a menu toward her and considered the options.

"Hi." Kendra slid a coaster in front of her. "Want a drink?"

"I'm just going to grab some takeout," Shea explained. "Long day of parent teacher conferences."

"Then you definitely need something," Kendra laughed. "Wine or coffee?"

Shea considered her options. "Maybe one glass of white wine, while I wait for the food."

"Perfect." Kendra turned to grab a bottle and poured expertly into the glass. "Here you go."

"Thanks," Shea said before taking a sip.

"You and Jake looked like you were having a good time at karaoke," Kendra said, leaning closer over the bar.

"Yes, it was a lot of fun."

"I hope you don't mind that I gave him your number?"

"No, thank you." Shea ducked her head to hide her blushing cheeks.

"None of my business, but Jake is one of the good guys in the world."

Shea sipped her wine, considering her words. "I think so too. They all seem to be, the brothers I mean."

"Yes, most would say that." Kendra grabbed a glass and started rubbing it with a dishtowel. "How are things with your book club?"

"Great! We can't tell you how amazing it is that you let us do it here, it's been so nice." Shea noted the change in topic but didn't know Kendra well enough to push her on the tension that was evident between her and Dan.

"Happy to help," Kendra replied. "I heard you were doing a table at the Harvest Festival?"

"Well, the school librarian is, and asked me to help," Shea explained. "The elementary school does a book fair each fall as a fundraiser, so she wanted to extend it to sell books at the festival. We hope to draw in more readers that way, when they do the fair in the school the kids tend to be drawn more to the little gadgets that the company insists on sending along."

"Oh, I am very familiar with those. My daughter brought home a bag full of pencils, posters, and fidget toys last year, but not one book." Kendra rolled her eyes but was clearly pleased to be talking about her daughter.

"Exactly! We thought if we got some of the high school kids to help at the table, read with the younger kids, and focused on the books it would help. The festival is the perfect time to do it."

Shea toyed with her wine glass. "As a matter of fact, we have so many volunteers now, I only need to do one shift, early Sunday morning."

"That's great! You'll have a chance to enjoy it that way." Kendra turned to take an order from two men who had just sat at the bar and passed them beers quickly before coming back to stand in front of Shea. "I got pulled into the organizing committee this year, so I'm nervous about how it will go."

"From what I have heard, it seems like this year is going to be amazing," Shea enthused. "The manager at the Inn told me that they were booked solid all weekend, and I know all the Airbnb's have been booked for months. It's amazing to get that many tourists into town so early in the season."

Kendra nodded. "It should help the local businesses, which is the goal. As great as the local community is, having the tourists in gets us through the slower parts of the year."

Shea saw the bag with her food coming out from the kitchen and polished off her glass of wine, digging in her purse for a credit card. Kendra ran in through the computer quickly and handed her the slip along with the bag. They said their goodbyes and Shea headed to her car; happy she had the foresight that morning to drive rather than walk to school.

She pulled her cell phone out quickly before starting her car and was happy to see a text from Jake had come in while she was talking to Kendra. He apologized for being quiet all day, said he had a lot going on but was looking forward to their date and wished her a good night. Feeling relieved, she texted him back quickly, telling him to enjoy what was left of his day and that she would see him soon. Feeling more settled, she drove home, analyzing how she should feel about Jake so easily becoming a part of her regular daily routine.

Chapter 18

Charlie was dropped off by his friend PJ's dad after their hockey practice and saw his dad and two uncles in their usual spots on the porch. He took his time when putting his equipment in the garage, laying out the gear so it could dry thoroughly and collecting laundry to put in the washing machine, but they were still there when he came out. He briefly debated pretending he was heading to the barn and sneaking in the kitchen door, but finally decided to just get it over with.

Climbing the stairs, he could hear Dan's low voice, but wasn't able to make out what he was saying. His dad held a glass loosely in one hand, head hanging down but clearly listening to Dan's words. Charlie hesitated on the top step, not used to the three of them ignoring him.

Patrick stood and walked toward him, then ushered him in through the front door. "Your dad has had a rough night. I don't want you to think alcohol is the solution to a bad day, but in this case, it kind of is."

"What happened?" Charlie couldn't prevent the words from spilling out.

Patrick sighed and leaned against the wall. "I wish I could share that, but it's your dads' story to tell."

Charlie rolled his eyes. "Typical."

"Hey, I've been open with you, Charlie."

"Sure, you have, when you want to." He pointed outside. "He hasn't."

"First of all, let's not forget that I'm the adult here," Patrick warned him. "Secondly, maybe if you showed him that you cared occasionally, he would share things. Dan and I are doing our best to make sure he's safe and it would go a long way to have you be nice to him. Now go up to your room and try not to sulk."

Charlie stormed up the stairs, furious at his uncle. Patrick was usually the one he could depend on, the one who was able to make things better. Now he was out getting drunk with his father and taking his side on everything. This was great.

He hesitated at the top of the stairs, looking at his own closed door and then across at his dad's room. The idea that his dad wouldn't be safe here made no sense to him. His dad survived war so many times, what could possibly hurt him in Vermont?

Ice ran through his veins as he realized what they were afraid of. His dad always seemed so solid and confident, the idea of him hurting himself would never have entered his mind, and now he couldn't shake it. That's what they were scared of, and why they weren't leaving. Some kind of suicide watch, apparently. There was no way his dad would do that. Right?

His uncles' voices grew louder for a moment, then the front door closed, and all was quiet again. Before he had time to debate the decision, he darted across the hall to his father's room and looked around, nervous at invading his space but needing some answers.

If he were going to hide a gun somewhere, where would he put it? Knowing his father, it would be locked up somewhere safe, but it didn't seem like anyone thought he was thinking all that clearly. He opened the drawers quickly, running his hands through the clothes and coming up empty. A quick look in the closet showed his shirts hanging neatly and shoes lined up on the floor. The nightstand contained a book and a phone charger, and under the bed only the empty duffle bag. He was just lifting the guitar out of its case to check underneath when he heard the door creak behind him and turned to find Stella behind him.

"What are you doing?" She asked from behind a pile of clean laundry stacked in her arms.

"Nothing!" He almost yelled, then dropped the guitar back in the case and winced at the sound.

"Doesn't look like nothing." Stella studied him. "Are you snooping or wanting to learn the guitar?"

He kicked at the desk chair, having trouble meeting her eyes. "Snooping."

"What are you looking for?"

"A gun." She gasped and would have dropped the laundry if he hadn't lunged forward and grabbed the pile. Placing them on the desk, he sat heavily in the chair in front of it. "Not for anything bad, Stella, I would never."

"Then what, Charlie? Why would you be looking for a gun?" She sat on the bed and watched him as he struggled to come up with the words.

"I heard Dan and Patrick talking. They are worried about my dad, and I just thought – "

"They are worried about him, sweetheart. He's been through a lot, and we can all see how he is struggling. But I don't think your dad would ever hurt himself if that's what you're worried about."

"I didn't think so either! But they seemed so worried, and I thought maybe he wasn't himself? I just freaked out and came in here looking."

"It would mean a lot to him if he knew you cared enough to look."

"Please don't tell him."

"No, I won't. But you could ask him yourself, tell him you are worried."

"I don't think that's a good idea. He really doesn't seem like he wants to talk about where he's been and what he's done. We just started talking about hockey, it's kind of a big jump to ask someone if they are going to hurt themselves."

"I agree, it's a hard conversation to have. And I can tell you honestly that it's not a fear that I share with the other men in this house. Your dad is very proud, and very strong, and he's doing what he can to get the help he needs. As a matter of fact, he is the first one to help someone else get help when he sees they need it, and I don't doubt he would look out for himself the say way."

"What should I do?"

She rose from the bed and gathered the laundry, stopping to squeeze his shoulder before she left. "Just be open to him. Don't be so quick to say no when he offers help, or to ignore him when he asks about school. You've been acting a little rudely towards him, and I have let it slide because you have been through so much in your life, but there are limits. If you are worried about your dad's mental health, then help him by making life a little easier around here."

"And what if he ups and leaves again?"

"Only he can make that decision, and if he does go back, we will figure it out together. Okay?"

He hugged her tightly, accepting the comfort she offered. "Okay."

"Now get your butt out of here and stop the snooping!"

Chapter 19

"Morning," Jake greeted Charlie as he entered the kitchen, backpack over his shoulder. "Would you like some breakfast? I was about to make myself an egg sandwich."

"No time," Charlie responded, grabbing a banana, a granola bar, and a bottle of water before turning to leave.

"Have a good day at school!" Jake yelled to his back, the closing door the only response.

"I'll take some breakfast," his father's voice called from his office.

"Me too," Patrick's voice resounded from upstairs.

"Me three," Dan chimed in as he came down the stairs, laptop in hand.

Jake set about making breakfast for all of them, adding one in at the last minute for Stella who would be coming in from her small cabin any minute. Although she had a full kitchen and all the luxuries of a full house, the cabin provided her with some much needed quiet and privacy from the main house. Jake had often envied her the solace she found in that one-bedroom cabin, and often debated sneaking into it as a teenager with Jenna for some alone time – but they had always chickened out and spent time in the hayloft of the barn instead. Thinking about Jenna with a piece of hay sticking out of her golden hair brought a smile to his face and an ache to his heart, but at least the smile had come first.

"What are you doing today?" Ben asked as he came into the room.

"I need to head up to Burlington for a PT session and some appointments," Jake responded. "Then a whole lot of nothing."

"Not nothing," Patrick responded. "We're golfing this afternoon."

"What part of the bullet to the shoulder is confusing for you, Patty?"

"You know I hate that nickname," his brother responded. "And the sling doesn't prevent you from driving my beautiful self around the course while we enjoy each other's company."

"I'll pass."

"Your loss." Patrick poured himself a cup of coffee and pulled out a second mug as Dan came into the kitchen.

Patrick turned to see what Jake was cooking. "That looks delicious and fattening. I'm going to gain twenty pounds this week at this rate."

"Why are you worried? You don't have anything coming up, do you?"

"It's much easier to gain than it is to lose. I have about six months before I head to Georgia to film the next movie in the series, so I need to stay on top of it. That spandex doesn't hide much."

"Spandex…" Dan and Jake erupted into fits of laughter only brothers could have at a sibling's expense.

"Yeah, yeah, very funny." Patrick rolled his eyes. "I'll make sure you see the checks, see how amusing it is then."

"I guess moneybags is paying for golf, so I'll be there." Dan took his breakfast from Jake and sat at the table just as Stella came in.

"Who is daring to make a mess in my kitchen?" Her outrage came with a smile.

Jake dropped a kiss on her cheek and handed her a plate. "Just some sandwiches, but Dan and Patty will be on cleanup duty, so I made sure the bacon splattered a lot."

"As soon as that sling comes off, I'm hitting him," Dan said to Patrick.

"Not if I get to him first!"

***

Jake pulled on his shirt in the exam room, having just finished being poked and prodded by a new doctor at the VA hospital. He had seen the orthopedic surgeon earlier in the day and was finishing his medical appointments with the primary before going to physical therapy and then to see the psychologist. It was a long day, but it was easier to get it all done at once than to make the drive multiple times a day. The primary doctor had made a lot of humming noises as he did his exam, and asked Jake to dress and meet him in his office down the hall once ready.

Knocking on the office door the nurse had directed him to, he heard the doctor call out for him to enter. The doctor was behind his desk, which was covered in paperwork and folders ready for him to review. He raised a weary glance at Jake and gestured for the chair across from him. "Thanks for taking the time to chat."

"No problem," Jake responded. "I appreciate you seeing me today."

"I'm reviewing your chart and your existing disability rating. You were pretty high on the rating to begin with, as you know."

He flipped open a folder in front of him, reading from the pages within. "PTSD, insomnia, concussions, knee injury, back injury, hearing loss. That was all before this incident, and you were already creeping close to one hundred percent. I wanted to see what your thoughts were. The orthopedic doctor who saw you earlier reported you will never regain full range of motion and may have nerve damage permanently affecting the use of your arm. Did he tell you that?"

"He did." Jake had been devastated when the doctor broke the news to him but tried to hold his emotions back. After all, he still had both arms and both legs, and he knew plenty of people who weren't so lucky. Some residual pain and the inability to move in certain directions wasn't the end of the world, and he had to keep telling himself that so he wouldn't focus on the negative. Like whether he would ever be able to play hockey with his son, or ski without risking further injury. Or even go back to the Army, if that's what he ultimately decided he wanted to do.

"My duty is to make sure soldiers are fit to serve. I don't like telling anyone they are not when they want to be, but I also don't want someone hurt because I let them go back to a job they weren't ready for. Or worse, have other people die because of a decision I made." He pushed the glasses up on his nose. "I hope my bluntness doesn't come across as not caring. I do care. I won't clear you for duty if I don't think it's the right decision, but if you tell me that you aren't ready to retire, I can at least give you more time to heal."

"I appreciate your direct approach." Jake met the doctor's eyes. "To be honest, I have been pushing the thought out of my head entirely."

"Not surprising, if I'm being honest." The doctor looked at him kindly. "The PTSD can make facing difficult decisions even more difficult."

"Can I follow up with you in a week?"

"Please do. Let's make another appointment for a week from now, I can look you over again and we can talk." The doctor opened the laptop in front of him and clicked around for a minute before shooting a rueful grin at Jake. "I should know how to make an appointment, but I don't. Do you mind having the nurse do it for you?"

Jake shook the doctor's hand and left his office, his mind whirling. He quickly made an appointment with the nurse for a week later, agreeing to the time and day without really hearing what she said. The brief conversation with the doctor had rattled him more than he expected. Suddenly he was a week away from a decision that would impact his entire future, and he didn't know which way he wanted it to go. Resolving to focus on his physical therapy, he pushed the thoughts of his future aside. Focus on the tasks at hand, get the job done, and then take the next item on the list.

Chapter 20

The exertion of his physical therapy was a welcome relief, and one he wouldn't have minded extending. Counting repetitions, pushing his body beyond what it wanted to do, these were things he understood. His last appointment of the day, with his counselor, was far less comfortable. Pushing his mind and emotions beyond where he wanted to go was uncomfortable and difficult, but he had vowed to be fully honest and confront his past and future.

His counselor welcomed him into her room with a smile. She was in her early sixties, if he had to guess, and had a grandmotherly vibe that he found extremely peaceful. Even when she pushed him, it was with a gentle hand, and he felt entirely safe in her presence.

"How have your appointments gone today?" Dr. Katz asked as she settled into her chair across from where Jake sat.

"Good. PT was rough but that's to be expected." Jake fiddled with the zipper on the sweatshirt he wore. "Had my physical."

"Oh?" Somehow the one syllable held a whole wealth of meaning and questions.

"The doctor thinks it might be time for me to retire."

"What do you think about that?"

He choked out a laugh. "I knew you were going to ask me that. I honestly don't know."

"How are things with your son?" She changed directions so quickly his head felt like it was spinning.

"Getting a little better," Jake admitted. "We went to dinner the other night, had some time together where he wasn't looking for an excuse to get away."

"It's understandable that he would struggle with you being home. He has a routine, and you disrupt it. You can't take that personally." She crossed her legs.

"Well, I do. But I also know that it's ninety percent my fault," He sighed. "I should have tried harder when I was away. The last time I was home, he was really pushing me to talk about his mom, and I couldn't do it. Every time I tried to find the words; I would just freeze up. When he freaked out the final night I was home, saying he had read about Jenna's death online and didn't see why it was so hard for me to talk about, I said some things I regret. I told him it was easy for him because he didn't know her, and now he's reminding me in little ways that I said that."

"Do you talk about what she was like when she was alive?"

"I did the other night. Seeing how he lit up and soaked in every word, I realize this is what he has wanted." Jake thought about his words. "Or at least, part of what he wants."

"What's the other part?"

"Me, I think." He met her gaze. "A dad who's here, who coaches the hockey team with his buddy's dad. Who can help him get ready for his first date or help him with his homework."

"Do you think you could be that person?"

Jake sat, letting the question hang in the air while he considered his response. "I think so. But I also think I'm that person in a different way to hundreds of young men on their way to war. The difference is, Charlie has been safe here with my dad and Stella. These soldiers that I train, that I serve alongside, they don't have that safety."

"You can't keep everyone safe." Her voice was gentle, but persistent.

"I know."

"Do you, though?" Her questioning gaze had him second guessing himself. "Because we have talked a lot about how you are carrying the guilt of not keeping Jenna safe, and that was completely out of your control. What happens to troops in a war zone is out of your control. You getting shot was out of your control." Dr. Katz stared at him, waiting patiently for his response.

"My brain knows that, the rest of me is struggling to keep up," he finally admitted.

"Let's talk about what would happen if you weren't in the military. Have you thought about civilian life at all?"

Jake thrust a hand into his hair, distracting himself with the thought that he needed a haircut. "No. I can't say that I have."

"What do you think it would look like?"

He shrugged. "I'd live here, I wouldn't want to move Charlie. Probably find some kind of job, or maybe go back to college."

"What were your plans before Jenna died?"

"I was taking classes at Windsor Peak College and was about to start working with a construction company. They were paying good money, so I didn't mind doing the hard work so that Jenna and I could afford to eat." He thought back to those days, getting up at dawn and hauling lumber, or perched on a roof nailing tiles. "It wasn't my dream job, but I came to like it."

"Could you see yourself doing that now?"

"Not really, if my shoulder is as fu-," he swallowed. "I mean, as screwed up as the doctor thinks."

"You're allowed to curse here, Jake. This space is whatever you need it to be, and I can promise you, I won't be shocked."

He chuckled. "I would imagine, I know how foul mouthed so many of us can be."

"There are other options other than doing the labor," Dr. Katz pointed out. "You could be a contractor, or an architect."

"True," Jake admitted. "I really haven't thought about it as much as I should have."

"Even if you wait to retire, in five years you will need to have a plan," she pointed out. "So, let's think about what being a civilian means to you, outside of the work and the family. What do you think of when you hear the term?"

He sat and thought, trying to put his thoughts into words. "When Jenna died, I spiraled. I could barely remember to take a shower, and it was a struggle to get out of bed every day. Some days I didn't," he remembered. "When I went to boot camp and I suddenly had this structure, all the rules to follow. You get up at a certain time, you dress a certain way, you eat what you are given. It's all regulated."

Dr. Katz nodded. "Yes, that's all true."

"What if," his voice trailed off for a second. "What if I fall apart again? What if without that structure, all the rules, I don't know what to do with myself again?"

"Let me ask you this, Jake. Have you struggled in this time you've been home? Have there been days you didn't know what to do, or didn't want to get out of bed?" Her gaze was even and non-judgmental.

"No," he admitted. "Not at all."

"So do you think that fear is enough to keep you in the military?"
"Probably not."

"I'll ask you again - are you ready to retire?"

Jake shook his head, hating his answer before it left his lips. "I don't know."

Chapter 21

Shea held the phone up, trying to show Christine her outfit over FaceTime. "Can you see?"

"Maybe go in front of the mirror and flip the camera? That would work better," Christine suggested. Christine had left for her romantic weekend in Montreal with Ryan immediately after school, kicking herself the whole way to the car for not being available to help Shea get ready.

Shea rushed to the full-length mirror in her bedroom, showing her friend the jeans and sweater she was wearing for her date with Jake. "Too casual?"

"No, it's perfect. I would have gone for a little more cleavage, but that's just me." Christine laughed when Ryan agreed loudly. Her voice quieted as she asked Shea if she had heard from Bob again.

"Unfortunately, he keeps calling and texting. I don't know what to do."

"Did you tell him to leave you alone?" Called Ryan from the driver's seat.

"I texted him that I wasn't interested in seeing him again and asked him to please stop. He seems to have taken that as encouragement," Shea answered. "He keeps promising more and more elaborate dates, as though I would be bribed into dating him."

"It might be time to block him," suggested Christine. "Back to the good date, what time will Jake be there?"

"He said seven, so just a few more minutes." Hearing a knock on the door, Shea saw her panicked face looking back at her from the phone screen. "He's here."

"Good, go have fun. Text or call me when you get home to give me all the details. Or tomorrow morning if things go really well!" Christine and Ryan yelled their goodbyes as she disconnected the video call.

Shea took a deep breath and then rushed to open the door, caught off guard once again at having Jake be right in front of her. She smiled nervously and waved into her living room. "Hi. Do you want to come in?"

"Hi," He answered, and stepped inside, looking around. "This is nice." He reached down to pet Muffin, who was declaring her undivided love to him by trying to climb into his hands. "Who's this?"

"That is Muffin, who I somehow rescued three years ago." She introduced Jake to her dog, laughing as he was licked across the cheek.

"Somehow?"

"I was tricked," She confessed as she grabbed her jacket from the closet. "A friend works with the rescue and begged me to foster a puppy for a week. Swore they would find her a home quickly, but they had no one to take her that night. I agreed, and we didn't even make it home before I had called my friend and said I was keeping her."

He laughed, the sound warming the living room. "Puppies have a way of doing that to you." Clearing his throat, he straightened up and met her eyes. "You look nice."

"Thank you. So do you." She smiled. "I'm a little nervous. And I can't believe I told you that."

"I feel the same. I had a thought about how to fix that." Before she knew what was happening, he had taken the three steps to close the distance between them, and placed both hands alongside her cheeks, pulling her lips to his. The lightest brush of his lips had her breath catch in her throat, and then he was pulling back and smiling at her. "Maybe now we can relax a little. Should we go? I made a reservation at Marriano's."

She let him help her slide the jacket on, and shivered as he ran his hands down her arms. The kiss may have been meant to break the tension, but suddenly she felt like every nerve ending in her body was on alert. He slid her hand into his and followed her out of the house, waiting while she made sure the door locked behind them before leading her over to his SUV and opening the passenger door.

As they drove the short distance to a neighboring town where the Italian restaurant was located, she shared stories with him about her week at school. The students gave her an endless supply of small talk, and even though she knew she was rattling on, he seemed entertained. As they entered Marrianos, the smells of garlic and the warmth of the candlelight settled what was left of her nerves. She followed the hostess to the table in the corner and felt Jake's hand on the small of her back directing her into the chair opposite the one she had been heading towards.

"Do you mind if I sit there?" He asked, indicating the seat against the wall.

"No, not at all." She shrugged off her coat and he helped her hang it on the back of the chair. He seemed flustered suddenly, and she wasn't sure what had caused it.

"I feel like there is something off with you," Shea stated after the waiter had delivered their drinks.

"Really?" Jake sipped from his water glass and then sighed. "Yes, you're right. I had an incident with Charlie this morning and I can't shake it."

"Want to talk about it?" she asked gently.

"It's a lot of what we have talked about for years in our messages. I struggle with how to be a dad to him when I miss so much, and he is resentful of me being away." Jake looked pained as he explained.

"Is it you being away that's the problem? Because I would think a lot of soldiers go through similar deployments and are away from their families for long periods of time."

"You're right." He seemed to be considering her words and how he would respond. "Admittedly I have been gone more than the average soldier, by my choice. He says he is angry because of how I left last year. We had a fight; I don't even know what it was about when it started. But it turned into the usual, with him yelling about his mom and me being gone all the time. I honestly can't remember most of it, but I was seeing red. My therapist now says it's my trauma response, to block things out and move on. Don't I sound fancy?"

She reached over for his hand. "I'm sorry you've had so much trauma you have a built-in response to it."

"I should be able to face it. Instead, I stormed around for a few hours, then packed up my stuff and left around two in the morning. I left a note, and texted him later the next day, but the damage was done." Jake cleared his throat. "I had walked out again when he needed me. But in my defense, I didn't know at the time he needed me, I can only see that now."

"Hindsight is a powerful tool."

"Now I don't know what to do. He is so angry; I don't know how to get through to him." Jake looked tortured.

"I have a lot of experience with angsty teens," Shea said. "Most of the time they just want to feel like they are heard. They are at this age where they act grown up so much of the time, but they're still little kids inside who are just looking for security and comfort. I see it a lot with the kids whose parents struggle to keep a roof over their heads, or with kids in the foster system. They act out in a million different ways, but all they want is to know they are safe."

"How can I make him feel safe if he won't talk to me?"

"Just keep trying. If he asks you about anything, be honest with him. If you keep showing up, even after hard conversations, he will realize you aren't so bad." She squeezed his hand, and they both paused to order their food from the hovering waiter.

"You give good advice." He smiled at her, and she felt warm inside. "Let's talk about something else, I want to learn more about you."

"I've been writing to you as though you were my diary for years, so I think you know more than most people!" she declared. "I should probably be embarrassed over some of the things I told you."

"Like winning the pie eating contest at the Harvest Festival?" Jake grinned at her.

"Hey, that's not embarrassing, I'm proud of that!"

"The picture of you with blueberry covering every part of your head was one of my favorites. Will you be entering again this year?"

"I should, to defend my title. But I think I'll let someone else have a turn this year. I volunteered to work at the book tent for part of the day, so I don't know that I'll have time. You, on the other hand, would be an ideal contestant." She considered him thoughtfully. "I could see you face first in a pie."

He laughed, "I think maybe I'll suggest it to Patrick instead. He would raise more money for the town fund if he were entered, people would come from all over to see that."

They settled into an easy conversation, and Shea found herself relaxing more with each laugh they shared. With each laugh they shared, the nervousness she had felt about going on a date with Jake Burrows had faded.

***

Jake helped Shea back into the SUV and was surprised when he realized they had been in the restaurant for over three hours. Even with planning out every detail of the date, including calling ahead to request a table where he would feel comfortable, he hadn't expected it to go as well as it had. Normally when he took a date to dinner, he checked his watch after an hour, wondering if enough time had passed so that he could try to take her home for the night. His relationships tended to end within a week or two, so he tried to move as quickly as possible.

Pulling into the parking space outside her house, he went to open his door and was stopped by her hand on his arm. "As much as I appreciate the gesture, if you walk me to my door, I'm going to invite you in. And I really don't want to ruin this by moving too fast."

"I could walk you to the door and then refuse to come in?"

"But would you?" Her fingers tangled with his on the center console, and he felt his resolve weakening with just that light touch.

Pulling her over so she was close enough, he kissed her with what he intended to be a gentleness proving his restraint. What resulted was steaming up the windows of his SUV so quickly he felt like he was a teenager again, and when he tried to pull her across the center console to his lap he finally came to his senses. "Wow. I guess I would not. You are hard to resist." He was glad to see a glazed expression in her eyes that told him she felt the same way he did at that moment.

"I should go before we combust." She reached across and kissed him once more, before opening the door and half running from the car to her door. "Thank you for dinner and an amazing night."

"When can I see you again?" He yelled from the car window, watching as she unlocked her door.

"Is tomorrow too soon?"

"Not at all. I'll call you in the morning, sleep well!" He drove home, humming along to the radio, feeling lighter than he had in years.

Chapter 22

Charlie crept in through the kitchen door, trying to avoid waking anyone in the house since it was well past his curfew. He couldn't help it if suddenly kids were inviting him to things, and girls were paying attention to him. He had cheerleaders practically fighting over sitting next to him at the party, so he lost track of time. Having his uncle in town was an attention grabber, with all the girls wanting an invitation to come hang out at his house, so he would take it. As soon as Patrick left the girls would move on, so might as well enjoy it while it lasted. Besides, his grandpa and Stella had set his curfew, but they were usually long asleep by the time Charlie got home.

Grabbing a bottle of water and a granola bar, he made his way up the stairs to his room, stopping at the door when he heard a noise coming from behind his father's closed door. It sounded as though something had fallen, and then he heard his father's voice shouting. Glancing down the hall at his uncle's rooms and realizing no one else was awake, he opened the door slowly, scared he would see his dad being attacked.

The room was dark, with just the faint glow of the moon coming in through the window. His dad was in the bed, thrashing around among the one sheet that remained on the bed. The pillow and blankets were strewn around on the floor, and the book that had been on the nightstand was across the room. Charlie couldn't see anyone else in the room, so he crept forward, jumping when his dad started to yell again.

"Get down! Get down! Stop! Don't go that way!" The panic in his voice was causing Charlie's chest to feel tight, he didn't know what to do.

"Dad?" He approached the bed, where his father was thrashing against the covers. Reaching out to shake his dad's good arm, he fell backwards to the ground when his wrist was grabbed in an ironclad grip. "Dad! Wake up! It's me! Charlie!"

"Get down!!" His father screamed again as he pulled on Charlie's arm so hard tears came to his eyes.

"DAD!"

"What's going on?" The light flipped on in the room as Dan rushed in, looking ready to fight. "Charlie, are you okay? What's happening?"

"He is having some kind of nightmare and I can't wake him up."

"Jake," Dan's voice boomed, and he shook his brother's shoulder.

Jake startled and tried to sit up quickly, wincing as he moved his shoulder wrong. "Shit. I'm sorry. I was having a..." He realized he was holding Charlie's wrist in his hand and saw his son on the floor next to the bed. "Charlie, did I hurt you? Fuck. I'm sorry. I don't know what happened."

"I'm okay." Charlie edged backwards on the floor until his back was against the wall. He could see the hurt on his dad's face when he realized he was putting that much physical space between them. "You were yelling so I came to make sure you were alright."

Jake's head hung as he sat on the edge of his bed. He was sweating, his shirt was clinging to him in wet patches where the sweat had soaked through. His breathing was uneven, and Charlie could see his pulse jumping from a vein in his neck. Jake looked toward Charlie, then hung his head. "I wish I could explain. I'm sorry that I scared you. I would never do that intentionally."

"Where were you in that dream?" Charlie's voice was barely a whisper.

Jake looked to his brother for help, but Dan just shrugged. "Afghanistan."

"Was that when you got hurt?" Charlie asked as he saw Dan slip out the door to the hallway.

"No. Other people did, but not me." Jake stood and moved to sit next to Charlie on the floor. "We were in a village. It wasn't supposed to be dangerous. We were just passing through; we had been there several times before without an incident. This time was different, they were ready for us to come, and we walked into an ambush."

Charlie' stomach started hurting, and he had to stop himself from running out of the room.

Jake took a deep breath. "I could see my friends ahead and they were falling so fast, I couldn't even get to them. I grabbed one kid, he was barely older than you, and I dragged him to safety and started calling for help. He died right there in my arms."

Charlie really felt sick now, like he could throw up. He knew people died in war, but he hadn't ever thought of it happening right in front of his dad. Or that people were shooting at his dad, for that matter.

"I really don't want to tell you more, if that's okay." Jake leaned back against the wall, looking at Charlie for the first time since he started talking.

"That's okay," Charlie offered him the bottle of water, which Jake took gratefully. "Can I ask a different question?"

"Sure."

"Have you ever thought of hurting yourself?" His voice was no more than a whisper.

Jake's sharp breath hissed out again in a long exhale before he spoke. "Oh, Charlie. I'm sorry you even have to worry about that." He took another deep breath. "There is one thing I'd like you to know."

Charlie looked at him, waiting patiently for him to continue.

"Through all of it, every incident, especially this time when I got hurt. But even on the good days, when things went right, and on the bad days where there was chaos or pain. Days like that one I just dreamt about. Through it all, the only thought in my mind was you." Jake squeezed his son's leg, and Charlie surprised himself by grabbing the hand and holding on. "You were my entire focus. I had to survive for you. And that stays the case now. I know I'm hard to live with sometimes, and it can get dark, but I'm doing everything in my power to heal my body and mind, for you. I promise you; I won't leave this world without fighting like hell to stay in it with you."

"But if that's the case—" Charlie stopped the words from coming out, unsure of how far to push his dad.

"You can say it, ask it, whatever."

"Why did you keep doing it?" Again, the words were barely audible.

"I wish you had known your mom," Jake stared off, as though he could see her. "She was so beautiful. So kind and good. She was light to my every dark thought, every dark emotion. And every time I think about what happened to her, I get so angry. I kept going back because every time I felt like I was getting a little bit of vengeance for her, and for you. They stole her from you. She would have been the best mom to you, Charlie. She loved you so much."

"What if what I wanted was a dad here, instead of revenge for a mom I never was able to know?" Charlie could hear his voice shaking and couldn't believe that the words had made their way out.

Jake felt the tears behind his eyes. "Well, then I'm more of a screw up than I even thought possible. But I think you need to understand the man that I was when your mom was killed. I was broken. I wasn't even half a man; I was just a broken shell who couldn't think of anything other than what happened to her. I blamed myself for it, and in the days that followed that blame got stronger and stronger."

"Why would you blame yourself?"

Jake paused so long that Charlie was sure he wouldn't answer. "That's something I think I should tell you about a different day, if that's alright? Not that I want to put it off, but a middle of the night conversation when I'm half in Afghanistan, half in Vermont, maybe isn't the time."

"Okay." Charlie was disappointed, it was the closest he had come to knowing more about what happened the day his mom died. Yes, he knew the general story from news clips, but never from his dad.

"Back to when I enlisted. I could barely take care of myself, and every day I felt like a failure to you. You would cry and I would cry right with you, because I didn't know how to fix either of us. The only thing I could think was that if I avenged her, that would fix me. And I can honestly say I didn't realize it would be this many years before I could try to be a dad. I felt like I was leaving you in the best possible hands, way better than you being stuck with me. I knew your grandpa and Stella would be what you needed; I just wish I had felt strong enough to give that to you myself. I can't go back to change things, Charlie. All I can do is ask that you give me a chance now."

"Will you leave again?" Charlie shifted on the floor, trying to find a comfortable position.

"I can't promise that I won't because my orders aren't over. But if you ask me not to re-up, I will do that for you." Jake could see the emotion on his son's face and felt the need to lighten the moment. "Of course, that would mean that I am around to ask why you are getting home at two in the morning, so that could be interesting."

"Oh, I've been home for hours!" Charlie got to his feet and reached down to help his dad up. "I was just getting a snack when I heard you."

"You got dressed in the same clothes you left in to get a snack?" Jake grabbed his son before he could leave the room, embracing him with the one good arm he had. "I love you, Charlie. Even when you miss curfew. And I hope you love me when I'm not perfect."

Charlie clung to him. "Will you tell me more about my mom one day? I hate that I don't know much about her."

"Yes," Jake managed to choke out. "I will do that."

"I do love you, Dad." Charlie let go and was out the door before Jake could see clearly through the tears.

Chapter 23

Jake never went back to sleep, instead spending the rest of the night and the dawn hours reflecting on his conversation with Charlie. There were so many things he would do differently if he could go back in time. Allowing Jenna to stay home with their baby instead of rushing her to work would be the first on the list, or at least taking the time to drive her to work that day. How different would their lives be right now if that morning had never happened? Knowing looking backwards wasn't going to do much more than cause him pain, he had decided to fix what he could in the present rather than reflect on the many years he had disappointed his son.

He sat at the kitchen table sipping on a cup of black coffee for hours before anyone else woke up. Stella had been in and out of the house already, offering breakfast which he had declined before running to the grocery store. "All these boys at home and we run out of food before I even get it out of the bags!" She had declared, stopping to drop a kiss on Jakes cheek before leaving. "But I just love having you all around!"

After debating what to say, he sent a quick text to Shea saying he was going to be busy with Charlie all morning but hoped to still see her later. Her quick response gave him something to look forward to, and he allowed himself a few minutes to reflect on how amazing the date had been the night before.

Dan and Patrick had come in together early, heading to the gym for a workout. Dan had squeezed Jakes' shoulder as he came into the room. "How are you doing, Jake?"

"I'm okay, thanks."

"Get any sleep?" Patrick was grabbing bottled waters for them from the refrigerator.

"Not much, but it's alright. I had a lot of thinking to do and was able to work out some things in my head." Jake took a sip of his coffee, realizing a second too late that it was still burning hot. Wincing, he blew on the cup and then tried again, desperate for the caffeine to kick in. "I really screwed up."

"What do you mean? You can't help what happens in your sleep," Dan responded.

"Thanks," Jake said. "But I mean with Charlie. I should have done so many things differently."

"You did the best you could," Patrick said as Dan nodded along. "You can't change the past."

"No, but I hope I can make some changes now for the future." Jake looked at his brothers. "I can't tell you how much I appreciate your support, especially last night."

"That's why we're here," Patrick stated. "Do you want us to stick around? We can skip the gym if you want company."

"No, you go ahead, I'm just waiting for Charlie to wake up."

"That could be a while," Dan stated as they headed towards the door. "Want to come with us?"

"No, thanks. Have fun." Jake went back to staring at his coffee cup, waiting for his son. He didn't mind if it would be hours; his son had waited years, he could handle a few hours.

***

When Charlie came down the stairs, still looking half asleep, he looked surprised to see his father at the table. "Good morning," he said, looking unsure of himself.

"Morning, Charlie. I hope you were able to sleep after all that last night."

"Yes, I did. I hope you're okay."

"I'm much better today, thank you." Jake cleared his throat, realizing he was nervous. "Any interest in going to town and grabbing some food? I thought maybe we could take a walk and talk a little."

"Sure, that sounds good," Charlie agreed. "I have a hockey game at two, so I just need to be back to get ready for that."

"Would you mind if I came to watch you play?" Jake asked.

"Yeah, I'd like that a lot."

"Let's get going then, so we can be back in time." Jake stood from the table. "You good with grabbing something at the bakery and walking around the park a bit?"

"Sure," Charlie agreed, grabbing a hoodie out of the hall closet and heading to the door ahead of Jake.

Once they had their bakery orders and were walking across the street to the park, Jake started what he had been working on all morning. "I wanted to thank you for last night. I know that wasn't easy for you to see. I'm a little embarrassed that you witnessed that if I'm being honest."

"I think it was probably easier to see than it was to live through," Charlie responded quietly. "But yeah, it was hard to see you like that."

Jake forced himself to keep talking, despite wanting to shut down and retreat. "I can't imagine seeing my dad like that. I wish it had been anyone else but you, or that no one heard me at all."

"I don't think that." Charlie looked around, anywhere but at him. "But don't you kind of wish that they didn't happen at all? Wouldn't that be better than being alone with them?"

"You're right," Jake responded. "Guess you are smarter than me."

"No, I wasn't saying that," Charlie objected. "I just feel bad that you think it's normal to have things like that happen. Does it happen all the time?"

"I was only making a joke, but a bad one." Jake had hoped this would be easier, being side by side with Charlie, but he still struggled with the words. "I do have nightmares more nights than I don't, so I have gotten used to them. If you don't mind, I'd like to shelve the nightmares for today. That's a lot to get into, and I'm worried it might be too heavy for you."

Charlie started to object, and Jake held a hand up. "Not that I don't want you to know what it's been like for me, but it's not something I'm used to talking about, and I don't want to burden you with things that are too much. I'm seeing a counselor at the VA hospital, and I think it would be best if I worked through some of it and discussed with her what might be a good amount of information to share with you. If you are okay with that."

"That makes sense. I'm glad you have someone to talk to and who can help."

"Me too." Jake paused. "What I really wanted to talk to you about today is your mom. But only if you want to hear about her, and what happened. And how it has impacted just about every decision I have made since she died."

"Yes." Charlie glanced toward him. "Very much."

"Okay, so I'm going to start back at the beginning. We met as kids, here in school. She was everyone's best friend, from kindergarten right on. She always knew who needed a friend to sit with at lunch, or who would be upset if they were picked last for a game. As we got older, our friendship turned into more. I was head over heels for her from about twelve on, but she didn't pay any attention to me until we were fourteen." Jake paused, able to picture Jenna's young face just before their first kiss. "She was my first everything, and I was hers. We were inseparable, much to your uncle's dismay, although they loved her too. They got resentful sometimes because there used to be the three of us everywhere, and now there were four. But they started treating her like a sister even before we got married.

We talked about graduating from high school and staying right here to go to Windsor Peak College. She lived with her grandmother, and they didn't have the money to send her away to school. And I wasn't going anywhere without Jenna. Her grandmother passed away when we were seventeen, and she was so alone. When she found out she was pregnant with you, it was the first thing that brought her true happiness. Even though we were so young, we were almost done with high school, and all she wanted was to be a part of a family.

I asked her to marry me, and we got married a week later in Burlington at City Hall. I was sure your grandfather would be furious, but Stella made sure he and your uncles came to the ceremony and were happy for us. I know he and Stella thought we were too young, but I was positive we would be together forever."

Charlie was hanging on every word, and Jake felt awful that he hadn't even known the basic facts on his parent's relationship. "Can I ask one question before you go on?"

"Of course."

"What happened to her parents? Why did she live with her grandmother?" Charlie asked.

"Her parents were the ultimate hippies. Lived out of a van, moving from place to place every month," Jake explained. "Her grandmother had always lived here, as a matter of fact, Jenna's dad went to school with Stella and Grandpa. But her parents, they couldn't stay put in one place for very long. When your mom was four, they got arrested and your mom was going to be sent into foster care. Her grandmother stepped up and took her in and raised her from them on. Her mom and dad would float in occasionally, but never stay for long. I haven't seen or heard from them in years, but I can try and track them down if you would like to meet them?"

"Yeah," Charlie responded quietly. "That might be nice, if they are still around."

"When you were born, you were our late Christmas present. We had secretly hoped you would come early and arrive before the holiday, but you dragged it out and waited until January. Your mom was so uncomfortable those last few weeks, but she loved being pregnant and having that bond with you. The day you were born was the happiest day of my life." Jake gestured toward a bench facing the creek and both settled on it.

Charlie sat, pulling a bagel from the bakery bag, offering Jake his breakfast sandwich. He placed it on the bench next to him, not sure if he could eat it or not. Waiting while Charlie busied himself spreading cream cheese, he allowed the calmness of the day to fuel him with the energy to go on.

"Three and a half months later, I had the worst day of my life. Your mom had been offered a job in Burlington, but the main office was in New York. They wanted her to go there for some training, but she was reluctant to leave you. I finally convinced her to go, said we would stay with Dan in his tiny apartment, and I would take care of you during the day while she did the training." Jake leaned forward slightly, as though protecting himself from the words that were to come. "Even that morning, as she was getting ready, she told me she wasn't ready to leave you. But we were so broke, and my job was starting the following week, so I had the time to be with you while she got comfortable with the idea. She joked that she might have been more comfortable if she was leaving you with Stella," Jake remembered.

"I can't believe Stella let you go to New York without her." Charlie pulled out a bottle of water from his pocket and took a sip.

"True, Stella wasn't happy about all of us going, but we were so sure it would be fine." He cleared his throat. "I should say, I was so sure it would be fine, your mom was a nervous wreck. I convinced her to go that morning, and when I turned on the news a half hour later, I just knew. Terrorists had bombed the subway, the station where she would have been getting off the train. The timing was too perfect, we had ridden the subway the day before to make sure she would be comfortable, so I knew exactly how long it would have taken her."

Charlie's breath caught, and Jake noticed his son had grown paler, but was staring at him waiting for the rest of the story.

Jake took a shuddering breath, forcing himself to continue. "I called her cell phone and there was no answer. I called Dan in a panic, but he was already in the city at class, and everything was shut down. I finally bundled you up into the stroller, and I ran all the way there. I called her until my phone was almost dead, and then had to stop in case she was trying to call me.

When I got to the subway station there were police and fire crews everywhere, but no sign of her. I ran to the office where she should be working, and they were horrified to tell me she wasn't there. I collapsed right in the lobby; my legs just wouldn't work. Dan and I searched for her for days, going to every hospital, every business near where she would have been walking. Even Patrick flew in to help and went on the news asking people to call if they had seen her anywhere. Grandpa flew in with Patrick and drove you back here, to be with Stella. We were all praying she was wandering the city with a head injury, like you would see in a movie.

The police finally told me I had to stop, that they had found her DNA in the wreckage. Dan drove me straight back here, and I was a zombie for days. Ten days after that, I went to a recruitment office, because I was so full of rage that I had to get revenge. Before that I had no desire to be in the military, no interest in war. But they blew her up, and they bragged about it when they made a video taking credit for the bombs. I needed to make them pay."

Jake bowed his head, exhausted from the emotion churning through him. He waited for his son to say anything, and finally heard him clear his throat and surreptitiously wipe his face with his hands. "I have never had a girlfriend, never mind be in love," He started. "But if someone did that to Stella or Grandpa, or you, I would feel the same."

He couldn't believe that a fourteen-year-old kid had this wisdom and ability to forgive. A huge weight was lifted off his shoulders as his son put an arm around him and hugged him. Jake grabbed him and held on as though his life depended on it,

and they cried together for the first time since Charlie had been
an infant.

165

Chapter 24

Shea seemed to be checking her phone every five minutes, despite telling herself to be patient. She had already talked to Christine and gone over almost all the details of the night before, keeping some private for just her to revel in the memory of. When the phone finally rang just after one, she was so relieved she answered on the first ring.

"Hi, Jake."

"Hey yourself. What are you doing?"

"Cleaning out a closet and trying to stay busy. How was your morning?"

"Emotional. I'll tell you about it later. I was wondering if you felt up to a hockey game this afternoon? Charlie has a game at two, I could swing by and grab you on the way? He needs to be there a half hour early, so I'm sorry for the short notice."

She looked at the time and considered her options quickly. "Why don't I meet you there? I don't want to spring myself on Charlie out of the blue, and if he's riding with you to the rink things must have improved, so let's not push that."

"Good plan. I'll meet you there." He disconnected and she rushed into the bathroom, giving herself fifteen minutes to get ready wasn't ideal but she would make it work. She rushed through her makeup and changed into a clean sweater before grabbing her jacket and running out the door.

Realizing she probably was going to beat Jake and Charlie to the rink, she stopped at the local coffee shop and got two hot coffees to bring to the game. She wasn't sure if Jake drank coffee but was willing to take the chance that he would appreciate the warmth in the rink. She parked a few spots down from where she saw his car and hurried inside to find him standing just inside the door.

"Hi," she was breathless, either from the quick walk inside or just seeing him again.

'Hi," he answered back, smiling slowly at her. "I really want to kiss you right now, but there is quite an audience."

She glanced around and saw several parents from her school, as well as some former classmates of theirs. "Yes, might get some people talking. I brought you a coffee, I rolled the dice and assumed you would take it black."

"You are amazing. I need this more than you know." He took a healthy sip. "Let me guess, you take yours with a healthy dose of cream and sugar?"

"Just a little cream, but I will drink it black in a pinch. Anything to stay awake some days!"

"Let's go grab some seats if you don't mind. I want to make sure I can see all the action." He led her into the rink and indicated the bleachers across from the home bench.

"What position does Charlie play?"

"Defense. Patrick always played there as well, Dan and I were forwards."

"I remember all three of you playing in high school, the Burrows boys were always known for their hockey skills. Among other things." She smiled at him. "The crushes all the girls had on you three…"

"Oh, stop." He laughed. "That seems like a lifetime ago, doesn't it?"

"And yet no time has passed at all." They shared a smile. "Here comes the team now."

They watched the team file onto the ice and start their warmups, and Jake was immediately enraptured watching his son. Growing up in Vermont, Shea understood and appreciated the sport, but seeing Jake glow at his son on the ice gave it a new layer. As the game started, she could feel the tension and excitement rolling off Jake as Charlie made play after play on the ice.

"He's really good, isn't he?" He marveled to her.

"He is! When was the last time you saw him play?"

"It's probably been two years, and he's grown about eight inches in that time. He really developed as a player, and this level of competition is really showing what he is made of." He waved over her head, and she turned to see his family making their way up to them. "Dad, Stella, this is Shea Kerrigan. Shea this is my dad, Ben Burrows, and Stella, who basically raised us after our mom passed away."

"We know each other from town, of course," Stella said, giving her a warm smile. Ben patted her on the shoulder as he passed, saying a quick hello. "Not to mention all the events at school. It seems like every week there is something happening there!"

"They do like to keep the community active." She smiled at Patrick and Dan as they moved to stand behind them, as Stella slid into the open spot right next to her.

"I've heard a little about you, it's nice to get to know you outside of the school and town events," Stella said as she got settled. "It's so nice of you to come see Charlie play."

"I'm happy to be here."

"We can take Charlie home after the game if you and Jake had other plans."

"Oh, I don't —" She looked to Jake for help, but he was watching the game so intensely he didn't see her.

"It's okay," Stella patted her arm. "No rush. I'm just happy to see Jake smiling again."

They all cheered their way through the game, yelling until they were hoarse when Charlie scored a goal in the third period to break the tie. As his team celebrated their win on the ice and they all started moving their way down the bleachers, Shea pulled Jake back to whisper in his ear. "I can head out now if you want?"

"What? No. Why?"

"I don't want to upset Charlie by being here with all of you."

"He won't be upset. Besides, he already saw all of us. Don't stress." They emerged into the lobby, watching as Patrick smiled for pictures and signed some hats for young fans, while they all waited for Charlie to come out of the locker room.

"I wonder if that's exhausting for him," she murmured to Stella, who was watching Patrick like a mother hen.

"It can be, but he's usually fine meeting fans. When he doesn't want to be noticed he does a pretty good job of blending into a crowd." They watched as Patrick waved to a fan and then made his way over to stand between Dan and his dad, back to the crowd. "See? Now he won't be disturbed, he's hiding in plain sight."

"I should learn that trick for parent teacher conferences!"

"Might be worth a try, but I think they would find you. What subject is it that you teach?"

"English," Shea replied.

"Always my favorite class. There is something so romantic about poetry." Stella glanced at Ben, who was deep in conversation with his sons.

"The kids don't appreciate it much yet, but if I can foster a love of reading, I'll be happy."

"Would it be too invasive to ask about you and Jake? How long have you known each other?" Stella tucked her gloves into her jacket pockets while studying Shea carefully.

"We knew each other slightly in school and reconnected after Jenna passed." She hesitated, unsure how much he had shared with his family. "We all went to karaoke the other night. It was a lot of fun."

"And you went to dinner last night I believe?" Stella clearly missed nothing. "I'm happy. This is what he needs. Just be careful, he's hurting in ways we don't always understand, because he never wants to talk about what he has seen. He's taking the right steps to get better, I just want you to know that sometimes his reaction is more extreme, but it has nothing to do with what you think it does. I know that doesn't make sense right now, but as someone who loves him very much, I want him to find happiness. And that means not seeing him blow it because he can't control his emotions. I realize I'm saying way too much, but I am especially protective of Jake after all he's been through. I hope you understand and don't mind me overstepping."

Shea wasn't sure how to respond and was thankfully saved by Charlie emerging with a teammate from the locker room. He high fived his uncles and accepted congratulations from everyone on a game well played.

"Charlie, you know Ms. Kerrigan from school, right?" Jake asked.

"I do. Hello, Ms. Kerrigan."

"Outside of school you can call me Shea, Charlie. Great game!"

"Umm, yeah. Thanks." He turned back to Jake. "The guys are all going to grab something to eat and then head to PJ's house for video games. Okay if I go with them?"

"Of course. Do you need a ride?"

"No, but if you could take my gear that would be great." He held out the bag and everyone took a step back at the stench emerging from it.

"Not it." Dan and Patrick turned and headed for the door. "Have fun, Charlie!"

Jake accepted the bag and sticks, holding it as far from him as possible. "Keep me posted if you need a ride later and be safe."

"Will do." With one last look in her direction, he mumbled a goodbye to the group and ran off to meet his friends. Stella and Ben followed suit, leaving Jake, Shea, and a bag of hockey equipment in the lobby.

"I need to get rid of this stuff before it destroys my car. Want to leave your car here and ride with me, and we can make a plan as we drive? Or want me to drop this off and then come get you?" Jake led the way out of the rink and towards their parked cars.

"I think I'll meet you at my place if that's okay. I'd hate to have to come back here later to get my car."

Jake glanced around the mostly empty parking lot after dropping Charlie's bag inside his car, then grabbed her around the waist and pulled her close to him. "Hi."

She grinned at him. "I think we covered that a few hours ago."

"You're right. What I meant to say was…" He lowered his mouth to hers, and the heat warmed her from her lips straight to her toes. "I'm about to really embarrass us in this parking lot, so we should probably get out of here."

"Good thing you have some self-control, because I am not sure I do anymore." She adjusted her coat and tried to get her brain working again. "I'll see you at my place when you can get there."

Chapter 25

Shea made herself a cup of tea to warm up, then busied herself emptying the dishwasher. Hearing a car pull into the driveway, she hurried to the door to welcome Jake inside. Muffin, confused by the new guest in the house, hid behind her until deciding he wasn't a threat and threw herself on his feet.

"I was thinking we could take her for a walk. Maybe grab some takeout and bring it back here?" Shea suggested.

"Perfect, I could eat." He held the door for her after she clipped on the dog's leash, and they headed down the sidewalk toward town. "You have a great spot here, close to the school and still walking distance to the town."

"I got very lucky. My aunt and uncle wanted to move to Florida, and I had just gotten the teaching job. I couldn't afford to buy the house yet, but they let me rent it for a few years, putting the rent money towards the cost of the house, until I could buy it outright. I imagine I would still be renting an apartment somewhere if it weren't for them."

"That's amazing."

"Yes, they are special. As I'm sure you know, us teachers aren't exactly rolling in dough! They understood that and didn't want to see me working three jobs to make ends meet."

"Three would be a lot. Do you still waitress over the summers at the Inn?" She had mentioned the job in her emails over the summer, sharing stories of the weddings that took place each weekend.

"Not this past summer, I was able to do some tutoring instead, which was nice. And next summer is so far away now, I won't worry about it for a while!"

"Eight more months of school, seems crazy. I wonder where I'll be in eight months."

"Have you given any more thought to your plans? Do you want to go back to the Army? Or to Virginia?"

"Virginia isn't home, it's just where I am stationed. Once I'm retired, I wouldn't want to live there." He sighed. "This week at physical therapy has me questioning if that retirement is coming sooner than I had planned. At some point in my career, it became crazy not to stay in for the full twenty and get my retirement, right? Even though this was never what I expected to be, it turns out I'm somewhat good at it. Now I'm in my thirties and have no idea what I want to be when I grow up."

"If you have to retire now, do you not get the full benefit since you wouldn't have been in the service long enough? Or do they let you retire early because you are hurt?"

"It would be a medical retirement, so I would still get all the benefits. It's not a bad option at all, it's better than sitting in a recruitment office for five years because I'm not fit to serve anywhere else." He held up his hand. "Not that I'm taking a shot at recruitment, they have a tough job and I respect them. But I couldn't do it. I don't think I'm cut out to be in an office all day, so figuring out what I would do as a civilian is a big part of this."

"We can make a list," she decided. "Put all the things you like and dislike on it and start brainstorming some ideas. Of course, you could just be a hot thirty-something retiree! That could work too."

"Well, when you put it like that…" He laughed and grabbed her hand, giving it a squeeze before tucking their held hands into his jacket pocket.

They walked through town, stopping to talk to people Jake hadn't seen in years. The whole population of the town seemed to be out and about on this Saturday afternoon, running errands or going for an early dinner. Shea waved to students playing in the park, and greeted parents they passed on the sidewalk.

"It really is crazy living in a small town, isn't it?" Jake mused as they walked.

"What do you mean?"

"Everyone knows everyone. You can't walk three steps here without someone calling over to say hello or stopping to talk to you." Jake proved the point by waving at an old teammate across the street. "I can't imagine how long grocery shopping would take."

"You've been away for a while," Shea pointed out. "People want to say hello and catch up, because you could be gone again tomorrow."

"You know I'm not leaving tomorrow, right?"

"I sure hope not, but the reality remains that you could be leaving before most people have a chance to see you." Shea stopped to calm down Muffin, who was in panic mode over a golden retriever on the other side of the street.

"True," Jake agreed. "I guess the more time I spent away from here, the more I thought most people would have moved somewhere else. I wasn't expecting it to be the same faces."

"This town is weird like that," Shea remarked. "Some people move here, like Christine and Ryan. But so many more just grow up here and never leave. Or go off to college and come back, I guess. The draw of Windsor Peak is too strong for most to resist. Other than you, of course."

"It wasn't the town I was avoiding," Jake said carefully. "I take back the word avoiding. I don't know what I would call it. I was in a fog, and the military gave me a routine and a purpose. It had less to do with running away from here as it did needing someone to tell me what to do, especially in the first few years after I lost Jenna."

"Did you plan to have a career in the military? When you left, did you think it would be for the rest of your life?" Shea looked at him, waiting for his answer.

"No." He stared ahead, and she wished she could read his thoughts. "I signed up for four years. I never imagined it would turn into fourteen plus years. I think the idea of coming home was scarier than war, if that makes any sense at all."

She squeezed his hand. "I think it does. I hope it's less scary now?"

"Much. Charlie and I had a huge breakthrough last night and this morning, and I feel like we are on the right path."

As they continued walking, Jake shared the details of what had happened with Charlie, and she could see that he was tempted to stay in Windsor Peak to be with his son. While she wished that he was thinking of staying for her, she would take him sticking around under any circumstances. The idea of him leaving when they were just starting what seemed like something incredible was too awful to even think about.

Chapter 26

"Hey," Dan started as he came into the living room, where Jake and Patrick were watching football. "I need to talk to you two."

"Can you talk while not blocking the TV?" Patrick asked, and Dan crossed to sit on the chair next to where his brothers were reclined on the couch.

"I have to head back to the city."

Jake turned to look at his brother before going back to the game. "Ok. Are you leaving today?"

"That's it?"

"Well, you know I appreciate you coming up here. I figured you would have to go back at some point, and you've been stressed as hell working on your laptop." Jake shrugged. "Should I cry?"

"No, but I wanted to make sure you were really okay before I took off."

"I'm really okay." He saw Dan's look. "Alright, I'm mostly okay. But I'm doing the work and will get there. I don't need you to stay if that's what you're asking."

"That's what I'm asking. Because if there is any chance of—"

"I'm not going to do anything stupid."

"Well, that's pushing it," Patrick intervened. "You are an idiot."

Jake rolled his eyes. "I won't do anything that would hurt me or anyone else,"

"Better," Patrick nodded.

"You two are a hoot, you know that?" Dan groused. "You coming back with me?" He directed at Patrick.

"Nah, I'm going to stay here for a while. If you want to leave me your sweet car, I'll take care of it and bring it back with me in a few weeks." Patrick threw out.

"How would I get back?"

"They have planes."

"No, I'm taking my car. I'll head out in a few hours," Dan stated.

"You should grab a beer and watch football with us, and then leave in the morning," Jake suggested.

"Not a bad idea. Is Stella making snacks?"

"Is she making snacks? Is the Pope Catholic?" Patrick snorted.

"Alright, twist my arm. I'll stick around. Hopefully, the Patriots can turn this game around." He gestured at the TV.

"Since you're sticking around, it's your turn to grab beers." Jake held up his empty bottle and clinked Patrick's.

"Oh, I get it. I'll do this one, but you two are taking your turns." Dan went to the kitchen as Jake and Patrick erupted at the offensive line on the TV.

***

Five hours and two football games later, the brothers lounged in the same spots, stomachs full of the food that Stella had brought out all afternoon. Charlie had wandered through with a couple of friends, grabbing snacks before heading out again, declining their invitation to watch the game.

"Are you coming back next weekend?" Patrick asked Dan.

"No," he replied. "Why?"

"It's the Harvest Festival. You have to come back," Patrick stated.

"I don't think anyone will miss me at the Harvest Festival."

"Stella might," Jake said, Patrick nodding his agreement.

"And maybe Kendra, since she is a major sponsor." Jake saw the look on Dan's face as Patrick dropped that piece of information.

Dan leaned forward, resting his elbows on his knees. "Probably make it easier on her and not be there. Clearly, she doesn't want me around."

"Up to you," Patrick assured him. "We won't miss you one bit. But if you want some more time to try and fix what you so beautifully messed up, it might be a good weekend to do it."

"What am I going to do? Follow you around to take pictures of you with fans? Be a third wheel with Jake and his new girlfriend?"

"Ummm, that's a stretch," Jake interrupted.

"Yeah, I never ask you guys to take the pictures." Patrick laughed.

"You mean to tell me you won't be at the festival with Shea? I heard you sneak in late last night, so things must be going well."

"Are you asking me to kiss and tell?" Jake demanded.

"Did you or did you not spend twelve hours with her yesterday?"

"Yes, Judge Dan. I did."

"And do you plan to do the same next Saturday?" Dan continued his interrogation.

"We haven't gotten that far- "

"Jake, give it a break." Dan sighed. "I'll think about it."

"We accept that answer!" Patrick stated, holding his hand up for Jake to high five.

"You two are insufferable. And it's someone else's turn to get beer."

Chapter 27

Entering Dr. Katz's office, Jake greeted his therapist before sitting and placing his coffee on the small table next to him.

"How are you today, Jake?" The doctor asked with a welcoming smile.

"Pretty good," Jake said. "I had an eventful weekend."

"Ok, tell me about it."

"It started when I took an old friend out for a date on Friday night. She and I have been writing to each other all the years I've been gone, but this trip is the first time I've seen her since Jenna died."

"And there is a romantic connection?"

Jake considered his answer. "Yes. Absolutely."

"Is there a but in there?"

He sighed. "I can't stop thinking about Jenna. Feeling unfaithful, I guess."

Dr. Katz leveled him with her gaze. "You know Jenna is not coming back."

"I know. And my family has been telling me that over and over. It's just a weird feeling, I need to get through it." He thought back to Friday night, the first kiss he had shared with Shea. "I think she is worth it, she's the first woman that I've wanted more than a physical connection with. I already feel like I know her so well, from all our messages. But being able to touch her and see her smile, it's even better."

"This is great news. I'm happy you are opening yourself up to the possibility of a new partner." Dr. Katz looked pleased. "What else happened?

"Friday night I had a nightmare." Jake took a sip of his coffee. "Charlie came in to wake me up."

"Let's start with the nightmare. What was it?"

"When we came under fire and Chris died."

"We have spent a lot of time talking about that day." Dr. Katz pulled a pad of paper off the table next to her, poising a pen over the blank page.

"It was the worst in my professional career."

"Why is that particular day so bad? You've lost other soldiers before."

"This one was my fault. I was distracted."

"You train your soldiers, correct?" She waited for him to nod. "Which means they should be able to spot the same things you do. Many of those men with you have been in war before. Is there a chance this enemy was just a step ahead?"

He shook his head. "It was too quiet. The kids weren't running around. I should have seen it."

"But you didn't. And neither did they." Dr. Katz let it sink in for a moment. "What happened with Charlie."

"I had grabbed him in my sleep, pulled him down on the floor next to my bed. I think I hurt his wrist." Jake rubbed his own risk absently. "I finally woke up and saw how much I had scared him."

Dr. Katz held a hand up. "Did he say he was scared of you, or for you?"

"What do you mean?"

"Was Charlie afraid you were going to hurt him?" Dr. Katz asked.

"No, not like that."

"And you would never intentionally hurt him?"

Jake felt stunned by the question. "Of course not."

"Okay, so what happened next."

"I sat next to him. Told him a little about my nightmare. He asked me some questions and asked me why I keep going back." Jake ran a hand through his hair. "I told him I wouldn't if he asked me not to."

"It's not fair of you to put that decision on him."

"I wasn't!" Jake objected, while feeling the truth of her words seep in.

She stared at him. "Are you sure about that?"

He sighed. "No."

"Tell me more."

"Saturday morning, I waited for him to wake up. We took a walk, and I told him about the day Jenna died. And what it was like for me after she was gone," Jake said. "I think that was a conversation that was long overdue."

"How did he take it?"

"Better than I would have." Jake smiled ruefully. "He's such a brave kid. I feel like it opened the wall between us, like I have a chance to fix things now."

"Now you have a new relationship possibility, and a chance to be a dad to your son. It sounds like you have some positive things happening in your life."

"I do."

"We have two good reasons to continue working to overcome your PTSD. Allowing yourself to love again, and to have a relationship with Charlie, that's a big motivation to continue healing." Dr. Katz made some notes on her pad of paper. "Let's dive back into your nightmares and see if we can make some progress there."

"I was kind of hoping you would say I'm cured," Jake said.

Dr. Katz looked at him for a minute before responding. "I think we have a way to go before we can even move to weekly appointments, Jake. I don't want you to think this is going to be easy, or quick. Or that when you finally do graduate to fewer appointments that you should look forward to a time when you never come. You have seen some horrible things, and that doesn't even include losing your wife the way you did. I would prefer you think of therapy as a forever thing."

Jake hung his head, then nodded slowly. "Whatever it takes."

***

Driving home hours later, Jake turned the music up loud to silence his brain. After a session with Dr. Katz digging around in there for his deepest, darkest thoughts, the need to shut it off was strong. Singing along with the songs that played, he forced every thought from his brain, but one was too persistent to get rid of.

Would he ever be able to live a normal, peaceful life?

Chapter 28

"How are things with your future husband?" Christine asked as they walked home from school on Monday afternoon.

"I think you might be moving a little faster than we are." Shea couldn't contain the smile on her face. "But it's going really well. I like him a lot, he is so easy to be around, and we have so much to talk about."

"Good! You deserve this!" Christine waved to a neighbor walking on the other side of the street.

"Let's not get too excited yet," Shea warned. Despite her excitement over Jake being in Windsor Peak, and how much she was enjoying her time with him, she felt strangely unsure of their future together. Sometimes he felt like he had disappeared for a moment, even when he was right next to her, and she couldn't reach him. Not knowing if he was thinking of Jenna, or if he was dealing with his PTSD, or something else entirely was disconcerting. Before she could fully commit her heart, she needed to know what was happening in his head.

"I know you don't want to hear this, but Ryan was home sick today and saw a guy lurking around your house. He went out to ask what was happening, and it turns out it was Bob." Christine cast a nervous glance at Shea. "Ryan asked him to leave and not come back. He was a little unsettled by it."

"Why would he go by in the middle of the day? He knows I'm a teacher." Shea shook her head. "Not to mention it still freaks me out that he must have researched where I lived, because I didn't tell him."

"All the more reason to worry, if you ask me. He's there when he knows you aren't, that's creepy." Christine pointed out. "I'm glad Ryan was there. Ryan said he was flustered when confronted, and said he was hoping to catch you to go for a coffee. Do you want him to report it to the sheriff?"

Shea thought about it as they walked. "No, I don't think so. I don't want to bring any more attention to him. I'll send him another text asking him to leave me alone, hopefully that will do the trick."

"Back to Jake," Christine started. "Does Charlie know you guys are dating? I wonder what he thinks, since you could have him in class next year."

"He does know," Shea shared. "We went to his hockey game together on Saturday, so he saw us together. Jake told me they talked the next morning, and Charlie has no problem with us dating."

"That's good. He probably would have found out at the Harvest Festival anyway, that's when most of the town will see you guys together." Christine looped her arm through Shea's as they walked. "Are you ready for your big debut as a couple?"

"Don't be silly," Shea laughed. "No one will be paying any attention to us. It will be so busy with all the tourists, no one will have my dating life as the top point of gossip after the festival."

"This is true," Christine mused. "There's always someone who gets drunk and makes a complete fool of themselves. Or remember the year the couple tried to get it on in the Port-A-Potty and knocked the whole thing over? Maybe something like that will happen again."

They both laughed, thinking about the poor couple in question. "That was awful, I felt so badly for them."

"I have to ask, though – are you nervous that he might have to go back?"

"I think it will be a little while, so I'm trying not to think about it." Shea laughed. "You are just a beacon of light today, with bad news and now this."

"I hate to be this friend, but you have to think about it. You can't keep your life on hold forever while he's in other countries."

"People do it every day!" Shea objected.

"Yes, married people. Or the ones in serious relationships. If he were to leave next week, would you stay here waiting for him?"

Shea sighed. "I think so. It would be hard not to, now that I have spent this time with him and know how great we could be."

Christine pushed on. "You know you want to have kids, and him being gone for years is going to put that on hold if you are waiting for him."

"We haven't talked about anything like that. I don't even know if he wants more kids." Shea admitted, alarmed that she was falling fast for him and there were so many unanswered questions.

"I liked seeing you with him. I love you being happy, and I don't want to dim that at all. I just want to protect my best friend, and make sure you ask the questions that need answers. I'm rooting for you guys, no question about that, so I'm hopeful you'll be on the same page." They both stopped walking in front of Christine's porch. "Want to come in?"

"No, thanks. I need to go get Muffin and walk her. Go get those tests graded, all I heard today was the grumbling of students worried they failed!"

"Oh, they all know I'll give them bonus points if they seem pitiful enough!" Christine waved to her as she closed the door behind her.

Every day when she got home from school, Muffin acted as though they had been separated for days upon days. Today she felt a little uneasy, looking around the house carefully making sure that there was no way Bob could have gotten into the house. Muffin always acted as though there had been a nuclear emergency when she was left home alone, so her behavior shouldn't have made Shea more nervous, and yet it did. The little dog ran between her legs, jumping up and yelping until Shea picked her up and carried her around the house. After spending a few minutes petting her and reassuring the dog that everything was fine, she clipped the leash on so they could go for their afternoon walk.

***

Shortly after seven that evening, a knock on the door startled her as she sat grading papers at her kitchen table. Feeling nervous, she walked over and peeked out the window before approaching the door and was relieved to see Jake's car in front of her house. Opening the door, she saw him standing on the porch with a bottle of wine in one hand and a bottle of her favorite flavor of sparkling water in the other.

"Hi," He smiled at her. "I was going to call but decided to take a chance and stop by. I wasn't sure if you would want wine on a school night, so I came prepared for anything."

"Come in," she gestured inside, thrilled to see him, and touched that he remembered how much she loved anything that was lemon-flavored. "Mondays are usually exhausting, so I tend to avoid wine as tempting as it is."

"Flavored water it is." He slid the bottle of wine into the wine rack to the left of her refrigerator and put the water on the counter. "How was your day?"

"Much better now." She wrapped her arms around him, soaking in the warmth and strength of him. It was amazing how comfortable and at peace she felt when in his embrace, and she realized she had been missing him all day. In less than a week she had come to look forward to seeing him, and even more sure that she belonged in his arms.

He kissed her before pulling back slightly to look in her eyes. "Am I disrupting your night?"

"Not at all. I was just grading papers, nothing exciting."

"I don't want to interrupt. I can sit and quietly watch some football while you finish, if you want. I just wanted to get out of the house and steal a little of your time, but don't want to make your day tomorrow harder."

She was touched by his thoughtfulness. "If you don't mind, I am almost done. Let me get through these last few, and then I can watch the game with you."

"Yeah? Not going to make me change it to Bravo?"

"I wouldn't dare. Besides, that's recording on the DVR, so I won't miss it anyway." He laughed as she went back to the table to finish her work.

Stealing glances at him on her couch made the task take twice as long as usual, but it was worth it when she finished and settled onto the couch next to him, his arm automatically reaching out to go around her. "How are things with Charlie?"

"Better." He looked thoughtful. "He's not ready to start telling me his deepest secrets or coming to me for advice, but he's not throwing things at me or just angry at my presence. I take that as a win."

"Did he say anything about me being with you on Saturday at the hockey game?"

"No, I'm surprised he didn't ask. Then again, why would a fourteen-year-old be thinking about his dad's love life? That's probably the last thing he wants to be thinking of."

"Especially if it's a teacher from his school that you're dating. That doubles the cringe factor for sure."

"Take that back, I can't have you calling my girl cringy!"

She laughed and reveled in the idea of being Jake's girl. Debating whether to bring up some of Christine's concerns, or the fact that Bob had been hanging around, she decided to just enjoy the moment. No point in ruining a perfectly good football game with relationship questions, especially when they had barely moved past the kissing stage. And bringing up the situation with Bob felt weird as well, especially since nothing had really happened.

What could have been minutes or hours later, Shea felt a blanket being tucked around her. "Oh, did I fall asleep?"

After being thoroughly tucked in, she felt Jake's lips brush her forehead. "Goodnight, sweet Shea," he whispered before leaving her room quickly. She sighed and settled back into sleep, dreaming of the man who had just left her.

***

"Dinner tomorrow? I promise to have you home early." Jake had called as Shea stepped out of the shower on Tuesday morning.

"That sounds nice! And thank you for tucking me in last night, I can't believe I fell asleep on you."

He cleared his throat on the other end of the line. "You're welcome. I wish I could have gotten you up to your bed, but I couldn't risk my shoulder."

She laughed and couldn't resist teasing him. "You wanted to say something about getting me into bed, didn't you?"

He let out a short laugh, then his voice dropped quieter as though trying to avoid having anyone else hear him. "You won't be laughing when that happens."

"Promises, promises," she teased, before telling him to have a nice day and hanging up. The quick conversation had woken all her senses, and now she couldn't wait until the following night when she would see him again.

Chapter 29

Charlie was shooting pucks in the driveway when Patrick pulled in, driving his grandfather's old truck.

"That's a far cry from Hollywood," he called over, hearing Patrick laugh in return.

"You could say that again. I might need to rent a car; this is not fun to park anywhere." Patrick patted the rear bumper of the truck. "Can I shoot around with you?"

"Sure, there are some sticks in the garage." Charlie waited until he grabbed a stick and came back to the piece of synthetic ice he was shooting off. "Want to make it a game?"

"If you tell me the rules," Patrick agreed.

"Call your shot first, and if you hit it, you get a point." The net across from them was covered with a tarp that had a picture of a goalie on it, only leaving a few small spots for pucks to get through. "I'll go first. Five hole." He shot it perfectly into the hole between the goalie's legs.

"Top right," Patrick called before shooting the puck through the hole he had called.

"Nice," Charlie offered, before calling and making his next shot.

"How are things with your dad?" Patrick asked as he stepped up to shoot.

"Is that your shot?"

"Funny guy," Patrick called back to him. "Five hole. Now tell me, how are things with your dad?"

"Better," Charlie told him. "I feel like I get it now, why he felt like he had to join the military."

"Still mad he left you here?"

"Nah," Charlie shrugged. "I get it now, I think. I'm sure this is way better than some Army post. Grandpa and Stella take good care of me."

"Good. I'm glad." Patrick leaned on the stick he was holding.

"Does this mean you're going to leave?" Charlie asked, surprised at how much he didn't want that to happen.

"Not planning on it. I have time, and I can't think of anywhere else I'd rather spend it."

"Bora Bora looks nice," Charlie offered.

"You want to go to Bora Bora?" Patrick laughed. "That's a long flight, I'll let you have it. Plus, I'll spend months on location soon, it's nice to feel like I'm at home before that."

"I'm just saying, if you need someone to hang on a beach with, I wouldn't say no." Charlie shot a puck that bounced off the goalie's face.

"You'll be the first person I ask, very generous of you to offer," Patrick teased him.

"What do you think of my dad and Ms. Kerrigan?" Charlie blurted out suddenly, then clamped his mouth shut. What was wrong with him?

"She's a real nice person," Patrick responded slowly. "I think she and your dad enjoy each other's company."

"That's great," Charlie mumbled.

"Does it bother you that he's dating?" Patrick looked at him, and Charlie squirmed, trying to avoid his gaze.

"No, of course not. He can do whatever he wants."

"I know there must be a butt in there."

"What if he decides to stay here, and they move in together? Would I have to move? What if they got married? Or had kids?" Charlie's mouth was running away from him now, and he had no way of stopping it. "She's a teacher at my school, so that's a little weird too. Not bad weird, just that I have to get used to it. The hockey team keeps calling her my stepmom."

"Oh, I can imagine how your teammates are handling this," Patrick commiserated. "But let's take this piece by piece, okay? If they did move in together, do you think you would want to move with them? Or stay here?"

"This is home," Charlie stated, looking up at the farmhouse. "I can't imagine living anywhere else."

"In a few years you'll go to college, and you'll have to live in the dorm," Patrick pointed out.

"That's different. When I have breaks, I want to come back to this house, have Stella cook my favorite foods."

"Okay, so you stay with Grandpa and Stella," Patrick suggested. "You don't have to move if you don't want to, it doesn't mean you wouldn't have a relationship with your dad."

"You don't think it would hurt his feelings?"

"Is that a real concern of yours? That's quite a change from a week ago."

"A week ago, I didn't know why he went into the military. Now I do." Charlie squinted to look at the sun setting over the mountain.

"So maybe you have a room at both houses, sleep there sometimes and here sometimes. People do stuff like that all the time." Patrick sat on the step to the porch. "Now if they were to get married or have kids, would it bother you?"

Charlie thought about it before responding. "I don't think so. I'm still getting used to the idea of having a dad, you know?"

Patrick nodded. "I get that."

"It would be nice to have siblings, you guys are all so close. It might be nice to have that in the future."

"Alright," Patrick slapped his legs. "I'll tell him to get on it and start making babies."

"Patrick," Charlie warned. "Don't tell him any of this. Promise?"

"You're killing me, kid. But of course, I promise." Patrick started to stand then sat back down. "Oh, and if your friends at school or teammates make fun of you, remind them who you got to sit next to at the last premiere. They'll shut up real quick hoping to get an invite."

Charlie laughed, thinking of the three hours he had spent sitting next to one of Patrick's co-stars, who most of his friends drooled over. She had been nice, and the selfie they took together had kept him popular for weeks. "About that, maybe she could come visit…"

"Keep dreaming, bud." Patrick laughed as he stood and walked into the house.

Chapter 30

The next few days seemed to drag on as Jake attended his appointments at the VA and continued to try and forge a relationship with Charlie. Things had improved dramatically at home, the door-slamming days finally appeared to be behind them. Before school they had made breakfast together, and then Charlie had asked for a ride to school when he realized he was running late.

Jake had driven him and taken advantage of the early morning to bring up a common thread in their lives. "I know you've heard this before, but my mom died when I was two."

"Yeah, she died when Patrick was born." Charlie nodded. "That's when Stella moved in."

"She did. And she's really the only mom I ever knew, I don't have any memories of my mom." He shot a glance over to see Charlie's face, but he was looking out the window.

"We're a little bit like a Disney movie," Charlie finally said.

"How do you mean?"

"All these dead mothers everywhere." He unbuckled as they pulled up at the school but hesitated before climbing out. "Guess we were all really lucky to have Stella. It probably was easier to have her and Grandpa around then to deal with you every day." He shot a smile at Jake to take the edge off the words.

"Plus, they go to bed earlier, so you sneaking in wasn't as obvious!" Jake yelled out the window, making Charlie laugh and wave as he disappeared into the crowd of students.

Driving to the VA hospital, he couldn't help but think of how comfortable he had gotten at home. The last few days he had barely thought of going back to his Post in Virginia, or overseas. It felt like a distant memory, even though he knew he had a clock ticking on his leave time. The further he got from his life in the Army, the harder it was to imagine leaving all this to go back. Things with Charlie were finally going well, and he was about to start his high school hockey season, which would be an exciting time to be around. Shea was an amazing surprise, and every day he became more aware of the possibilities there were if he could open his heart. A stark apartment or a bunk in a warzone were a far cry from where he was at this moment.

***

Finishing the stretches prescribed by his physical therapist, he wandered down to the barn to see the horses, not surprised to find Patrick already there.

"Ready to ride yet?"

"I wish," he responded, rubbing the nose of the horse Patrick was brushing.

"Soon enough. Seems like you're improving every day." Patrick glanced at him over the horse's back. "Any thoughts on what happens after you get cleared?"

"I'm not sure I will." Jake moved to the next stall to give his father's horse some love. "They don't think I'll ever have full range of motion again. My disability ranking was already creeping up, this could put me at a full one hundred percent."

"What does that mean?"

"I won't be able to go back to my job, that's the big thing. Honestly not even sure a desk job would work, because that would require both arms to work well." He sighed. "The doctor suggested I consider medical retirement."

"Lots to unpack here," Patrick gestured towards the table on the porch. "Let's go sit."

They settled in at the table, looking out at the mountains just past their open fields. "I honestly don't know what to do," Jake admitted.

"What part are we talking about?"
"All of it. Work. Jenna. Charlie. Windsor Peak. Shea. It's all tied up together in a big knot, I'm afraid if I pull one string the whole thing will fall apart."

"Things with Shea seem to be moving along nicely," Patrick commented.

"She's amazing. I took her for granted the last few years, not really thinking of her as a person so much as a distraction, which sounds awful but it's true. I needed someone to talk to who wouldn't judge me – I know you and Dan wouldn't have, but I could open up to her pretty easily. Now I've realized that all those emails are tied to someone who's warm and caring and beautiful. A real person, not an email address." He glanced at his brother, seeing the understanding on his face. "I'm starting to feel things I haven't felt since Jenna."

"And that's freaking you out."

"Hell yeah, it's freaking me out."

"Why, though? You're a grown-up, so is she. And as much as it hurts, Jenna isn't coming back," Patrick softened his voice as he spoke about Jenna.

"I know all that in my mind. My heart still feels like it belongs to Jenna, and it feels unfaithful, crazy as that may seem." Jake sighed. "Plus, what if I do go back? Do I have her waiting here for me, so now I have two people who are annoyed that I'm doing my job?"

"You're about twenty steps too far forward. You've gone on, what, a couple official dates?" Patrick held up a hand. "Slow down, you seem like you are trying to create problems when there aren't any."

"My entire career is foreseeing problems and knowing how to deal with them."

"She's not a terrorist, Jake. You can't predict if she meets some other guy tomorrow who sweeps her off her feet, or if a huge job opportunity comes up and she has to move to North Dakota." Patrick punched him lightly in the arm. "Just give yourself a break, see what happens. The first thing you should be figuring out is work and go from there."

"I really can't make any decisions until the doctor tells me whether I'm fit to serve or not."

Patrick gasped dramatically. "Does he know that you need to control everything, and this is unacceptable?"

"Shut up."

"Seriously, though," Patrick sobered. "Would it be the worst thing to retire now?"

"No. It would be sudden, I thought I had five more years. And the thought of sending these young kids into battle without me…"

"There are other you's, Jake. You don't make up the entire Army."

"I know that, but they trust me."

"And yet they are over there and you're here, so clearly they have learned enough from you to do their jobs," Patrick pointed out.

"This is true." Jake looked across to the mountains. "I just thought I had a few years to figure this out."

"Life is tricky, it doesn't want to follow your map." Patrick pointed across the paddock where a grove of trees hid an open field. "I always thought that would be a great spot for a house. Close enough to here to run over, far enough for some privacy."

"You thinking of building one there?"

"Nah, not me. But thought it might be a good piece of information for you to have in that head of yours, as you think about where to land. I don't see you living anywhere but Windsor Peak, nowhere you have been over the last fifteen years has fit you like it does here."

Jake stared out at where his brother had pointed, visualizing a cabin with smoke coming from the chimney and lights warming the windows. It wasn't a bad idea at all.

"Speaking of you," Jake said to his brother. "You don't have to stick around for my sake. I'm sure you have places to be."

"Not really. I leave to film the next movie in a few months, but nothing between then and now. I have a trainer who sends me workouts and checks in with me on FaceTime, but no need for me to be in person with him." Patrick flexed his arm jokingly. "Plenty of people around here I could work out with, and I'm really loving being able to ride and just being me here. Know what I mean?"

"I do." Jake nodded. "After you film this movie, will you head back to New York or L.A.?"

"L.A." He shuddered. "No, thank you. Not my speed at all. I am only there when I have to be, and only keep a house there because it's more comfortable when I have to shoot. I thought New York could be home, but the longer I'm here, the more I question why I can't stay forever."

"You and me both, brother." They sat in companionable silence until Patrick stood and stretched. "You going somewhere?"

"I should head to the gym and have a few messages to return. I'll leave you to the peace and quiet." Patrick slapped him on the back as he crossed to enter the house.

***

A few hours later, Jake yelled goodbye to everyone and set out for Shea's house. This was technically their third date, but it struck him that they had been together a total of four nights out of the last seven. Most of his dates during his military career had been one-offs, or maybe a second date, but never beyond that. There were always plenty of girls hanging around the bars near his Posts, wanting to spend the night with a man in uniform, and he hadn't been willing to go much further than a shallow night together. Shea was the opposite, he felt like he could sit and talk to her all night, as well as listen to her stories. He didn't want to cheapen their friendship by rushing into bed with her, and he had to think about what that meant.

At the same time, the thought of a relationship made him break out into a cold sweat. His rational brain told him that of course Jenna would be okay with him dating, even remarrying. The heart, though, had its own concerns about being given to anyone else. He could still feel Jenna in his arms when their wedding song played on the radio and hear her laughter in his dreams. Fifteen years had passed, and yet he still felt the weight of the wedding band on his finger as if it was just placed there.

205

Chapter 31

Shea was ready when Jake arrived to pick her up and could tell instantly that something was just a little off with him. His smile was a little slower, and he seemed distracted in a way that he had never been before.

"Is everything okay?" She studied him, concerned about what she was seeing.

"Yeah, fine." He frowned. "Why?"

"You just seem like maybe something is wrong. Or are you in pain?"

"No. No pain." He stuck his hand in his hair in a way that she had already become accustomed to, which left hair sticking up straight like a mohawk. "I'm just in my head, I'll snap out of it."

"Anything you want to talk about?"

He stared at her for a beat, then shook his head. "No, I'm good."

"Okay. Guess we should go then?" She had planned a dinner out for them, followed by a play at the community theater in the center of town. The theater pulled students from the local colleges for performances and was usually well done and popular with the locals. After each play they had a small reception in the lobby, raising funds for future productions or to improve the theater, and she enjoyed supporting them.

The local pub was packed when they arrived, but fortunately she had called ahead and reserved a table. As they walked to the table in the center of the room with the hostess, Jake pointed to a small booth in the corner. "Could we have that instead?"

"You can, but we usually leave that open because it's a little dark in the corner." The hostess explained, shrugging when Jake walked in front of them to slide into the booth, facing the crowd. Handing them their menus, she turned and disappeared quickly.

"Are you sure you're okay?"

"I'm fine, Shea." He busied himself with the menu.

"What was wrong with that table?"

He sighed, looking over at the table and then at her. "I'm sorry. I can't sit in the middle of a crowd like that. I need to have my back against a wall."

"Because of your shoulder?"

"No, because I need to keep an eye out."

"For what, Jake? This is not making much sense."

He lowered his menu, looking her straight in the eye. "I need to be on the lookout for bombers. Or anyone with a gun."

Her mouth dropped open. "In Windsor Peak?"

"I know it's not rational." He shook his head. "But I can't relax if there is a possibility that something could happen behind me."

She nodded slowly. "That makes sense after all you've been through. I'm sorry I pushed you."

He grabbed her hand across the table. "I'm sorry I've been bad company so far. I'll snap out of it."

"Will you be okay in the theater? We can skip that if you would rather?"

"Can we see how I feel when we go over there?"

"Of course." She squeezed his hand. "If you're uncomfortable, we can leave."

"You don't have to leave, but I can always wait in the lobby for you. I'll try, though."

"What do you do at Patrick's shows?"

"I've only been to a couple of his premieres, and he can usually arrange so that I'm in the last row on the end." He gave a short laugh. "I don't make things easy for anyone, I'm afraid."

"Is this…"

"You can ask."

"Are you working on this with a therapist? Is this something that might get better?"

"PTSD is a weird thing." Jake leaned back in the booth. "My therapist talks about it like it's normal, and that I'll be able to deal with it when it flares up. I could be totally fine one minute and on edge the next, and not even know what set me off. I can control some of the things that would be an issue, like this seating arrangement, and that helps. You don't want to be around me if a firework goes off unexpectedly, and really any loud noise could cause a reaction. But yes, it's something I'm working on. I don't know that it will ever get better, but I am trying."

"I'm glad. And for the record, I'd be just as happy sitting on my porch sharing a bottle of wine with you as I am going out to dinner. If there are days that you need something quieter, I'm happy to go along with that." She squeezed his hand, happy to see him relax a bit and be more like himself as they ordered their meals and chatted about their day.

***

When they arrived at the theater, Shea managed to grab the floor manager and swap their two fourth row tickets for two in the back of the balcony, on the aisle. She had made an excuse to use the restroom, so Jake had no idea that she was asking, but she saw the relief on his face when they went to their seats and knew that it was the right choice. The show for the month was *Mamma Mia*, and they enjoyed every second of the show and the singalong at the end.

"You have a fine voice," he leaned over and told her as she belted out the title song.

"It's loud in here, you can't hear me!"

"I think we will have to do an Abba duet at the next karaoke night!" He smiled at her, and she knew she would follow him anywhere, even onto a stage with a microphone.

As they exited the theater into the makeshift bar in the lobby, Jake excused himself to go to the bathroom and she got in line to get them drinks. Feeling hot breath on her neck, she turned to find her bad blind date Bob standing so close behind her that she could feel his body heat and smell the liquor on his breath. His face was red, eyes bloodshot, and he looked unsteady on his feet.

"Where have you been, Shea? I've been calling you." He stepped even closer, and she collided with the person behind her as she tried to get some space.

"Hello, Bob. Nice to see you."

"Not so nice on my end, I took you out for the night and the thanks I got was a handshake and unanswered phone calls." He

210

wavered slightly on his feet before grabbing her with both hands. "I think you owe me a good night kiss."

She was struggling with him one second, and in the next standing alone looking at Jake holding the drunk man against the wall, arm across his throat. "What the fuck is happening here?" Jake growled in his face, as Shea leaped forward to try and intervene before the rest of the lobby noticed what was happening.

"Jake, let him go. He can't breathe." She pulled at his arm, which was locked in place. "Jake! Let go!"

"Go outside and wait for me," His voice was so low she could barely hear him.

Glancing over her shoulder, she noticed they were starting to be noticed by the crowd in the lobby. "Jake, we need to go. Let him go."

He stepped back suddenly, so fast that Bob slid to the ground grasping at his neck. "Did you want him to touch you?"

"No! Of course not! But you can't kill him because he's a drunk idiot!"

Bob's voice slurred up at them from where he was prone on the floor. "She sure moved fast with you; she's going to regret picking a neanderthal over me."

"Are you threatening her?" Jake growled.

"Stating facts. You will regret messing with me. And you – "His gaze ran up and down her body in a way that made her want to shower suddenly. "You missed out, but I'll give you a second chance."

Jake stepped forward and she had to hold him back, terrified by the anger on his face. Her hands were shaking, and she could feel tears pricking at the back of her eyes. "Jake, please stop."

"I need to get out of here before I kill him." He stormed toward the door, and she raced after him.

"Jake! Stop. Talk to me." She grabbed his arm, and he shook her off, then stopped and turned to look at her, rage still showing on his face.

"What just happened?"

"I don't know! I was in line to get us drinks and he came up babbling about how I owed him a kiss." Jake started walking again, and she trotted along beside him. "Why are you so angry?"

"I don't know. I just saw him touching you and I snapped." His fists were clenched tightly at his sides.

"Are you angry at me?"

"Did you want that?"

"No! Not at all!"

"I can't be with you and be worried about some other guy, Shea. That's not how I work."

"There is no other guy." She grabbed his arm, trying to stop him from walking. "It's only you, Jake. I don't want anyone else."

He shook his head, then suddenly sank onto a bench facing the open park. "Shit. What did I just do?"

"What do you mean?"

"I scared you. I'm sorry," His voice dropped even lower, so she had to strain to hear him. "I can't help how I react sometimes; this is what I was trying to explain to you."

Seeing him stare out into the darkness, she realized she had felt closer to him when he was overseas than she did at that moment. He felt unreachable. She longed to hold him, but everything about him told her to keep her distance. They sat in silence for what felt like hours but was probably only minutes before he stood up.

"I should take you home."

"Could you tell me what is really happening? I can't believe that Bob is causing you to shut down on me like this." She rose and started walking slowly beside him in the direction of her house, where he had left his car.

She thought he was going to ignore the question, they walked for several minutes without a word exchanged before he cleared his throat. "Driving to your house tonight I was thinking about Jenna. Part of me feels like I'm cheating on my wife. And I know that's crazy and ridiculous, but the more I try to convince myself of how crazy it is, the more time I spend thinking about it. But no matter what, the idea just couldn't shake from my head. Then I saw that guy pawing you, and I just saw red. I can't explain it."

"I didn't want him to touch me," She responded. "More importantly, I don't want you to feel unfaithful to Jenna. I have similar guilt, although I'm sure it's on a different level. She was my friend, and I'm crushing on her husband? If she hadn't died, we wouldn't be together right now, so it makes me feel crappy when I realize my happiness is coming at her expense."

"You didn't do anything to her."

"And neither did you." She stopped walking suddenly. "Would you have been faithful to her? Were you faithful?"

"I was and would have been. I still love her. I'm sorry if that hurts you, and it messes with my head to feel that way, but I do."

"I wouldn't want to replace her in your heart or your head, Jake. But maybe there could be room for both of us? Your past and your future?" She gazed at him, seeing the emotion on his face. "We can both consider that maybe, just maybe, Jenna brought us together?"

He lowered his forehead to hers before wrapping his arms around and holding on tight. "I want to try. So much. Please be patient with me."

"I have nothing but patience. And time." She stepped back from him. "And a bottle of red with our name on it, let's go relax and enjoy the rest of the night without anyone else around."

She was able to lead him to her porch before ducking into the kitchen to get the wine and glasses. Her hands were shaking when she took the glasses out, and she had to put them on the counter and catch her breath. The rush of adrenaline that had driven her home left her in a flood, and she was left feeling legless and unsure of herself. Taking a few steadying breaths before going back to the porch helped, but she still felt unsettled, and saw the same in his eyes.

"I think we should take a raincheck on this," he said quietly, the words tearing through her heart.

"On the wine, or the dating?"

"I don't know. My head…" He shook it sharply, startling her. "I need to get it right. I'm sorry." He gathered her in his arms for a hug that was too brief, before walking across her lawn to his car.

Watching him walk away from her finished her weak legs off, and she sank back onto the porch steps, watching his taillights disappear into the night. Letting the tears fall was the first thing that felt normal in the last hour.

Chapter 32

"Stella," His grandfather's voice resonated across the downstairs hallway to where Charlie was lounging on the couch and checking his social media on his cell phone. Stella hurried down the hall and into his office, leaving the door open, so yet again Charlie was left feeling like a spy. "I just called Mike down at the Vet's office about that medicine for the mare. You won't believe what he told me."

"What?" Stella responded.

"Jake got into some kind of scuffle with a guy at the community theater last night," Ben's voice was quiet.

"What?" Stella's shocked voice rang out.

"Mike said it was quick, but the guy was shaken up and Jake was gone before anyone really could react."

Charlie crossed to stand in the doorway of the office, done with listening in from hiding spots. "He got into a fight?"

"Charlie, hi. Sorry pal, I didn't know you were around." Ben sat back in his chair, looking concerned at being overheard.

"I got in from school a little while ago," Charlie explained. "What happened last night?"

His grandfather looked at Stella, who shrugged, then responded. "I'm not too sure. I haven't seen your dad today, so I guess we'll have to wait and ask him."

"Where is he?" Charlie demanded.

"That I don't know. Stella, any idea?"

"He left early this morning, didn't say much. I just assumed he was going to an appointment." Stella took a step toward Charlie. "He seemed fine this morning, so let's not jump to conclusions."

Charlie pushed back from the door frame as he heard a car approaching. "Here he is now. You want to talk to him alone, Grandpa?"

"You know what, Charlie? I think you should talk to him." Stella's hand was guiding him toward the door, and before he knew it, he was on the porch with his dad walking towards him.

"Hey, how was school?" His dad asked.

"Did you get into a fight last night?" Charlie blurted before he could decide what to say.

"Did I – "Jake stopped walking and stared at him.

"Grandpa just heard from someone that saw you."

"Well —" Jake looked down at the car keys he was jiggling in his hand.

"What happened?"

"Can we sit?" Jake gestured toward the chairs on the porch.

Charlie nodded and sat on the edge of a chair, ready to bounce back to his feet. His father sat slowly, pulling off his sunglasses and revealing the dark smudges under his eyes.

"I don't think I would call it a fight," he started.

Charlie interrupted. "Would you if it were me involved?"

"That's a valid question. I think the answer is still no." He leaned forward so he was closer to Charlie. "I would want you to stand up for anyone who was in the situation Shea was in. She

218

was being touched by a man who had too much to drink, and he was trying to kiss her. I removed him from the situation. I did not hit him."

Charlie bit his lip, unsure of himself suddenly. "You and Shea, you're, like, a couple now?"

"I don't know how to answer that today." Jake looked down and Charlie noticed his cheeks had turned a little pink.

"What does that mean?" Charlie couldn't stop himself from asking.

"It means I like her. A lot. But I know that complicates your life, and it could make hers a lot harder if I had to leave again." Jake looked up at him. "Plus, there's your mom."

"Mom is gone." The flash of pain across his dads' face made him feel guilty for the bluntness, but it was true.

"I know that. It's complicated."

"Doesn't sound complicated to me. You like her, she likes you." Charlie shrugged. "You stood up for her last night, and publicly at that. She must have a lot of people asking her questions today."

"God, when did you get to be so smart?" Jake shot a small smile at him.

"This isn't rocket science," Charlie tried to brush off the praise. "If I told you that I got into a fight because a guy was coming on to a girl, or that I liked a girl and she liked me, you would say the same thing."

"What should I do now?"

"How would I know? I'm just a kid! Go ask Stella." Charlie gestured toward the house, starting to stand before sitting back quickly. "One thing I should say, I guess. I'm good with you dating. Especially someone like Shea. Not that my opinion matters, but I wanted – "

"Of course, your opinion matters. Thank you."

"Alright, so let's go ask Stella how you can fix this. You're probably screwed." Charlie tossed over his shoulder as he started toward the house. "But if there is a way to fix it, she would know."

"Wow. That's cold." Jake caught the door before it closed on him.

"Hey, I tell it like it is."

***

Jake had been walking around all day feeling as though he had woken up from a bad dream, and the talk with Charlie had snapped him out of it. Following his son into the kitchen, where the rest of the family were waiting anxiously, he thought back to the thousands of problems that had been solved around the kitchen table. Bad grades, fights with friends, girlfriend problems, issues between him and his brothers – you name it, they had been discussed in this room. Looking around at the support that surrounded him, he couldn't help but feel lucky to have them all in his life.

"I didn't get into a fight," he started. "A guy was overserved and had his hands on Shea, and I removed them. It wasn't a big deal at all."

"I'm glad you were there for Shea," Stella responded.

"And I'm glad I didn't have to post bail this morning," his father grumbled.

"He screwed things up with Shea," Charlie announced.

"How did you manage that?" Patrick asked.

"I don't know. I was off all night. Just couldn't get out of my head, and then this guy had his hands on her. I reacted without thinking and that may have scared her," Jake admitted, hanging his head as he did so.

"Did she say she was scared?" Stella asked gently.

"No, but I could see it on her face."

"What happened when you left the theater?" Patrick passed him a bottle of water, which he accepted gratefully.

"It's all a blur." He took a long drink from the bottle. "I told her I needed some time."

Patrick laughed, then sobered up quickly. "She's been your pen pal for how many years? How much more time do you need?"

"There's a big difference between writing emails with someone and being in a relationship with them," he snapped back.

"All signs point to you being into her. What's the problem?" Patrick continued to push, met with silence.

"He's thinking about my mom," Charlie's quiet voice inserted.

Stella laid a comforting hand on his arm. "You know she would want you to be happy. I think we have all told you that at some point or another."

"It's a little weird because Shea knew her too. And we only connected because of Jenna." He sounded like an idiot, and he knew it. "Shea said last night that maybe Jenna had brought us together."

"She's right," His father, gruff with his arms crossed and sitting across the room, finally joined the conversation. "Just like how I know your mom sent Stella here. These women of ours, always trying to make our lives better even from the beyond."

"I guess I need to go talk to Shea." Jake glanced at his family, seeing them all nod in agreement.

"Got that right." Patrick pushed back from the table. "I'm going to take these three out for dinner while you go fix your mess."

Chapter 33

Shea had called in sick that morning, the first time in her career that she had ever done so without being ill. She hadn't been able to fall into a restful sleep the night before and woke up with a headache and bags under her eyes. Thoughts of what she could have or should have said and done floated through her mind all night, as well as the haunted look in Jake's eyes as he walked her home. Spending the day organizing a closet and deep cleaning her kitchen helped to distract her, until she finally collapsed on the couch in exhaustion late afternoon. Minutes later the doorbell rang, and she hoped it was a delivery and not Christine looking for information she wasn't ready to share yet.

Instead, it was Jake standing on her doorstep, clutching a bouquet of wildflowers, and looking far more clear headed than she felt. He offered her the flowers as she gestured for him to come in. "Thank you, they are beautiful."

"From Stella's garden. She's a sucker for any romance, and apology flowers are important, she says." He leaned forward as though to kiss her, then hesitated and pulled back.

"You don't have anything to apologize for."

"I think I do. Can we talk?"

She nodded and gestured to the couch while she stepped into the kitchen to place the flowers in a vase. Coming out with two cans of soda, she found him pacing in front of her fireplace rather than sitting. "Did you come to end things with me? Because I'm exhausted and emotionally not able to handle that."

"What?" His head whipped around. "No, why would you think that?"

"You're acting strange, and I don't know if it's because of me, or what happened with me and Bob. But you were off even before we saw him last night." She struggled to control her emotions as she spoke, which made her sound shaky even to her own ear.

"I know. And I'm sorry." He came to sit next to her, grabbing her hand and holding it tight. "I want to explore this, whatever it is. There's just a lot going on in my head right now that I'm trying to work through."

"Maybe we could work through some of it together? It does involve both of us." She stared into his eyes, wanting to forget everything and just enjoy his presence, but knowing she couldn't do that.

He gazed at her, and she forced herself to sit quietly while he thought. "You're right, it does. I told you some of it last night. It's really messing with my head to be getting feelings for someone in the same place where I fell in love with Jenna. Does that make sense? If I had met you in Virginia or New York, anywhere but here, I think this would be easier."

"I get that." She nodded. "I wish I had known you in some other way as well, but we can't change that."

"No, we can't. I just need to be able to move past it, stop feeling guilty."

Shea forced herself to ask the question that had been on her mind all night. "Jake, have you been with other women since Jenna died?"

"Yes," His response was so quiet, she had to strain to hear it.

"Did you feel like you were cheating on her then? Did you have any of these emotional struggles?"

He looked into space for a minute before turning back to her. "No, and I get your point. I do. This is different though."

"What is different?" She pressed. "We are attracted to each other and want to see what happens. I assume that is what happened before?"

"No," he admitted. "I haven't been in a relationship since Jenna. Everyone has had a short shelf life, you could say. You are the first person that I wake up thinking about and want to end my nights with. It just feels strange, because when I see you, I think of Jenna. And no other woman has both made me think of her and made me want to get more involved than a sexual relationship."

"I feel a little weird about how we connected as well, and question if my friend would be happy to see me with you now or be mad. I just can't see Jenna being mad." She looked at him, and he nodded. "Not with how she lived her life, wanting everyone around her to be happy. I can't see that woman being upset that her friend and one of the people she loved the most have a chance to be happy together." Her voice was gentle, and she could almost see Jenna's smile, agreeing with the words as she said them.

He stared at her fireplace for several minutes, looking lost in thought. "You are right about that. She did want everyone to be happy. Does it feel weird for you if I talk about her sometimes?"

"No! Absolutely not!" She took a breath. "I want to honor her and remember her along with you, and I hope if we get to a point where Charlie is spending time with us, you'd be comfortable sharing parts of her with both of us."

"What happens if I leave?" The words burst out so fast she had trouble processing what he was saying.

"You mean to go back to the Army? Or leave this room?"

"Back to the Army. To my job."

She wanted to ask him not to go, but knew they weren't there yet. "I don't know."

"Me neither. And that's a big part of this."

"Are you going back? Did you get orders to leave?" She feared the answer but had to know.

"No, nothing like that," He sighed. "It's closer to the opposite, the doctor is encouraging me to retire."

"Would you stay in Windsor Peak if you did?"

He looked around the room and then back at her. "I can't imagine living anywhere else."

"Worst case, you go back, and it's a few more years?" She shrugged. "I could handle that. We've already been long distance friends, there's no reason to change that." She hoped she was doing a better job of convincing him of that than she was of convincing herself that things would be fine.

"Long distance friends and long-distance relationships are very different," He pointed out. "I've seen it go wrong a hundred times over with the people I've served alongside and the partners they left behind. I couldn't ask you to wait for me."

"I don't need you to ask if it's something I want to do." She met his stare. "What else?"

"Charlie gave his blessing, so that's one thing to check off the list." He smiled at her. "The last is maybe the biggest. PTSD still has me in its grips, and nights like last night will keep happening. I can only control so much, and I'm going to have bad days. Some things might be worse than what you saw last night. I can only

226

promise you that I would never hurt you physically and will try my best not to scare you."

She moved closer to him on the couch while carefully considering her response. "I can't imagine the things you have seen in war. I'm willing to listen if you want to talk about them. I'm hoping to be someone that you can lean on, that you can lighten your load with. I know you would do that for me, so I hope you let me do it for you."

He leaned into her, then slid his arm behind her so she was suddenly crushed against his chest. "I'm a mess, and you are a crazy person for getting involved with me. But I appreciate you so much, and I really want to try and make this work."

"Calling me crazy is about the least romantic —" She got cut off as he lifted her face to press his lips to hers, and she suddenly agreed that they had done enough talking for one day.

Chapter 34

Watching the sunrise over the rapidly changing leaves Saturday morning, Jake couldn't help but think of the clock ticking in his mind. He had less than a week to figure out if he was going to medically retire or try to serve out his last years, and he was exhausted from thinking about it. He knew the doctor was leaning in that direction, and lately his counselor and physical therapist had been dropping hints that it would be a good idea. It seemed everyone knew what was best for him but his own heart.

The night before, he and Shea had joined Ryan and Christine for dinner and some card games, and he had spent his first night in Shea's house. Creeping out this morning had felt dirty, but she had understood that he didn't want Charlie to know he was out all night, at least until he had a chance to talk to him. Besides, it gave him an excuse to enjoy the sunrise with a cup of coffee from his favorite spot, and he would take those opportunities however they happened. Even if it meant leaving a sleepy, happy Shea with her tousled curls lying in the warm bed he had just left.

"Morning," his dad greeted him as he came out with his own coffee.

"Hey, Dad, how are you?"

"Creaky and old. You?"

"Same." They both laughed softly and settled into a comfortable silence as the sun finished emerging from behind the trees.

"Going to the Harvest Festival today?" Ben asked as he stood and picked up his empty coffee cup.

"Yes, I'm going to Shea's at ten, we can walk from there. Are you and Stella going?"

"Of course. I'm on the committee, couldn't miss it." Ben was a regular participant in all the town events, helping to draw tourists to support their small town. Having retired from his position as President of the local bank, he felt the need to stay busy and involved with the town in as many ways as possible.

"Do you think Patrick will dare the crowds?"

"Last I heard, he planned to go and try and stay out of sight. But the gossip rags have already outed him for being here, so I suspect we will be overrun with young women who are hoping to catch sight of him. Good for the town's economy at least, although I wish we could set him up in a booth and raise money for the animal rescue here in town," Ben mused aloud.

Jake laughed. "Did you ask him?"

"No, I don't suppose I did. Maybe I'll run it by him this morning." He ducked back into the house, passing Charlie as he emerged from the front door.

"Morning, Charlie."

"Hey." The teen looked half asleep and was still pulling on his hoodie as he came out the door.

"Hockey this morning?" Jake smiled as Reese and Trix bolted up the stairs to greet Charlie.

"Practice, then the team is doing a dunk booth at the festival to raise some money."

"Oh, what time is your slot on the dunk board? I'm going to have to stop by."

Charlie smirked at him. "Guess you'll have to figure that out."

A truck pulled in, and Jake recognized Charlie's coach, who waved out the window at them. "You know, I'm happy to drive you to practice."

Charlie fiddled with the strings hanging down from his hoodie. "I just don't want to change things up while you're here, if that's alright. Easier to keep things the norm."

Jake felt his throat constrict a bit, so he just nodded and waved as his son loped across the yard to grab his gear from the garage. Losing the years with Charlie had seemed easier from a distance, now being at home, losing even the five minutes he would spend driving to the rink hurt. The sooner he decided about his future, the better for everyone in his life.

****

The weekend of Harvest Festival officially kicked off the tourist season in Windsor Peak, with a lot of the same crowd coming from Boston and New York to enjoy the activities year after year. The Inn was always filled, and many families made room in their homes to rent out spaces on Airbnb to supplement their incomes. The prime autumn leaf peeping season gave way to the ski season, so rooms would remain filled until mud season started in March.

Jake hadn't made it home for a Harvest Festival in fifteen years, and he couldn't believe the changes as he drove slowly through town towards Shea's house. Huge tents were erected over the town green, tables took up most of the sidewalks in front of local businesses, and lines were formed outside anywhere that served breakfast. It was easy to distinguish between the locals and the visitors just based on their clothing, and Jake laughed as he saw the back door of the coffee shop open to hand out coffees to locals. This town looked out for its own, even when it just came to getting caffeine without waiting in line for an hour.

Shea opened the door as he pulled into her driveway, and her welcoming smile had his heart ricocheting around in his chest like he had just seen a live grenade. "Hi," he murmured, leaning down to kiss her once he reached the porch.

"Hi, yourself." She pointed to the door. "Do you want to come in? Or just start walking down?"

"We should probably head to town; it was already looking very busy, and the festival just kicked off a few minutes ago."

"Alright, I'm ready to go." She picked up her purse from the chair next to her and reached out for his hand.

"You'll be warm enough?" He looked at her jeans and sweater questioningly.

"Yes, I'll be fine. It will be crowded everywhere we go, and if I get chilly later you can warm me up." She waggled her eyebrows at him, and they both laughed as they set out down the sidewalk.

He told her about Charlie and the dunk tank, and she promised to try and use her teacher powers to find out what time he would be on duty. As they crossed to the center of town, the sound of music playing mixed with loud conversations, and the smells of all the food offerings wafted from the tent.

"I am going to eat my weight in fried dough and caramel apples," she promised, taking a deep whiff of the smells.

"No pie eating contest?" Jake teased her.

"I convinced a few new teachers to sign up instead, I need room for all these other delicious options." She waved to Christine and Ryan, who were a few tables away looking at maple candy. "Is that Patrick over there?"

Jake looked to where she pointed, and sure enough, Patrick was ensconced at a table near the edge of the tent, gamely signing autographs and taking pictures with the fans lined up down the street. "I can get you to the front of that line if you want."

"I think I'll pass, since I will see him at dinner tomorrow night. Is Dan here?"

"No, he said he was going to come, but texted me a few hours ago that he was still in New York. Some huge crisis that requires his full attention. He didn't even respond when I asked what was going on, and Patrick hadn't talked to him at all." He pulled his phone out and checked again, still no response from his brother. Not completely unusual, since he got so caught up in his work, but several hours had passed without so much as a thumbs up on the text saying he would be missed.

Distracted by his phone, he didn't notice someone approaching until he was almost toe to toe with him. Stopping short, his eyes rose to find a young man who had served under him for several years, who he hadn't heard from in almost as much time.

"Sarge! It's so good to see you! I knew you said you were from around here, but never expected to see you." The young man stuck out his hand to shake, then grabbed him a rough hug. "Sorry, I should say First Sergeant."

"It's Jake, you aren't serving anymore so you can call me by my name. Man, it's good to see you. How have you been?" He gestured to Shea beside him. "Matt, meet Shea; Shea, this is Matt, he served with me for about six years."

"Best leader I ever had, Ma'am." He shook her hand politely. "I know it's been a while since we talked. I took your advice and got my life together, took a little longer than I'd like. But now I'm divorced, dating a new girl who's real sweet. I see my daughter regularly and am able to help support her. We actually brought her up here to see the leaves and enjoy the festival. I'm living in New Hampshire, working towards my masters now so I can work as a counselor for people like me."

"That's amazing, Matt. I'm proud of you."

"It's all because of you, sir. If it weren't for you, I'd be hooked on who knows what, living on the streets probably. Have no daughter, nothing to live for. You saved my life." The young man looked around the tent anxiously. "I want you to meet my girls, I don't see them anywhere."

"Tell you what, meet us over by my brother Patrick's table. You can get a picture with him, and we can meet them." Jake pointed in the direction of where the biggest crowd was.

"No way! That would be amazing. Okay, I'll be right there, I'll just find them really quick." He raced off, and Jake squeezed Shea's hand.

"That was quite a moment," she said quietly.

"He came home from Afghanistan, had a new baby at home and a lot of changes to deal with in addition to just getting used to civilian life. He started drinking more rather than dealing with any of it, and when someone offered something stronger, he tried that. I got a call one night from a police station in New Hampshire, he had given them my number to call. I flew up the next morning, dragged him to rehab, helped him get his head on straight." He looked at her, seeing the look of awe on her face. "I don't just sign up to lead them in battle. I tell them I will always be there for them, and I mean it."

"Jake Burrows, I just think you are amazing." She stood on her toes to brush a kiss over his lips, and he smiled at her.

"Just doing my job, ma'am."

"Yeah, I don't know how crazy I am about the 'ma'am' thing. At what age do you cross from Miss to Ma'am?" She tucked her hand into his arm and walked closely beside him through the tent.

Patrick was busy with a group of women who were part of a bachelorette party when they approached, so they stood to the side laughing as he was dressed in a sash and tiara before a picture. As he finished with them, he held a hand up to the next group and asked them to give him a minute before he approached them. "Don't you two have anything better to do than stand here laughing at me? I'm trying to do a good deed, raising money for the animal shelter."

"You are doing a great job, Patrick, I'm sure the shelter is thrilled to have your help." Shea kissed him on the cheek and his brother pretended to swoon.

"Better watch out, Jake, or I'm going to come steal your girl."

"I know where you sleep, so I'd rethink that." Jake saw Matt approaching. "Before you get back to it, I wanted to introduce you to a friend I served with. This is Matt Davis, and I'll let him introduce his family."

Shea and Jake watched as Patrick took pictures with Matt and his family, then signed the little girl's shirt with his Sharpie before slipping back into his spot to greet his fans.

"That was amazing! Thank you so much!" Matt's girlfriend gushed as she shook Jake and Shea's hands. "Natalie wants to watch all his movies now; I think at ten she has her first crush. I know Matt wasn't planning on letting her date until thirty, so hopefully this will buy him a few years." The little girl was still gazing at Patrick with adoration, oblivious to the adults talking around her.

"We have a lunch reservation over at the Inn, would you like to join us?" Matt asked. "We didn't realize there would be so much good food here but feel bad blowing off the reservation we made."

"No, you go on ahead. Call or text me later, if we don't see you today maybe we can catch up for breakfast in the morning?" Jake suggested.

"That would be great! Nice to meet you, Shea!" They headed across the green, waving to Patrick again as they left.

"Such a sweet couple," Shea remarked. "How old did you say he was?"

"Not even thirty, he joined up right at eighteen and was done by twenty-five I think."

"Wow. So young to have gone through so much in his life."

"Happens with a lot of these kids. I try to encourage them to get into counseling, and to go right into school if they decide not to continue with the military. When they enlist right at eighteen, military life is a shock. Then when they get out and they feel out of touch with everyone around them, it's another huge change. Some listen, some don't." Jake shook his head. "It helps them so much to find a connection right away, the ones who don't, struggle."

"It must make the bonds you form in service even stronger," Shea remarked.

"You're right, I think it does. Those bonds are like brotherhood, I'd go anywhere and do anything if I knew it would help one of my guys out, same as I would for Dan or Patrick."

"And as they would do for you, I think," Shea assured him.

Patrick shot them a look from the table, where he was holding a baby in one arm and a dog in the other, wearing a Santa hat. "Looks like someone is getting their Christmas cards done early," Jake yelled over to the couple standing behind Patrick for the picture.

"Can't turn down the chance to have a superhero on our cards!" The young dad yelled back, smiling from ear to ear.

"Let's go find our superhero a snack, I think he's getting hangry." Jake pulled Shea by the hand toward a table the bakery had set up, where she considered every option for herself before settling on an almond croissant. Jake grabbed a bag of chocolate covered pretzels and a piece of Kringle for his brother, along with a large cup of coffee, which his brother accepted with a grateful smile.

"Need anything else?" Jake asked him quietly, and Patrick shook his head no.

"I'm done at 2, so I'll grab some lunch and wander around after. Thanks for this." He toasted him with the coffee cup. "I saw Dad and Stella a few minutes ago, and Charlie went by with some kids from his team."

Jake turned to Shea. "Let's go check out the dunk tank and see if we can sink my son."

They wandered to the end of the tent where the high school students were circled around the dunk tank, and Jake saw Charlie's friend PJ perched on the bench, shivering in his wet clothes. The teacher in Shea had her concerned about the boys in the cold weather, soaking wet in their clothes. "I should find out if they have towels, or how long they are doing this for. They are all going to catch pneumonia."

As she started to make her way over, PJ stepped down and into a warm towel held by a teammate next to the tank. He quickly grabbed a backpack from behind the tank and disappeared into a changing tent someone had popped up out of sight. "Looks like they have it under control," Jake commented, watching as another player took the empty bench to the cheers of his classmates.

Charlie saw them and waved from where he stood next to the tank, munching on a bag of popcorn. Before they could make their way over, Phil came to shake Jake's hand. "Nice to see you, Jake. And Shea, hope you are enjoying yourself!"

"Thanks, Phil. The town has gone all out this year," Shea responded.

"Charlie is going up soon," Phil confided quietly.

"Thanks for the heads up," Jake grinned. "We'll have to stick around for that."

They all stood and watched as two more players got dunked, before Charlie took his spot. He raised a hand as Jake started to step forward, yelling across to him. "Parents have to pay triple to throw!"

"Oh, it will be worth it!" Jake assured him as he pulled his wallet out. "Do you have dry clothes?"

"Nope, so you should probably miss," Charlie taunted him. "But I would expect you to anyway."

Shea laughed as Jake threw wildly the first ball, clunking off the glass in front of Charlie's face. His next throw missed the target by an inch. "Getting nervous?" he called to Charlie.

"Nah, you'll miss it for —"

The ball hit the center of the target before he could finish his sentence, plunging him into the water. He came up sputtering and laughing, trying to splash water out at his father. Jake looked delighted, teasing Charlie by taking his wallet out again and holding it up until the teen cried uncle.

"Uncle? You calling me?" Patrick appeared, causing the boys on the team to quiet down and look at each other with wonder on their faces. "Is it my turn?"

"No, Uncle Patrick, you don't need to do it." Charlie pointed behind Patrick. "I think that little kid might want a turn."

"Oh, he won't mind if I go first, I'm sure." He passed money to the team mom who was collecting the funds, who was blushing as she handed him the three baseballs. Patrick considered the target, threw, and hit immediately, sending Charlie back into the water. "On second thought, maybe I'll let him take the rest of my throws." He turned with a smile and handed the balls to the little boy behind him, then moved over to shake hands and take pictures with the team.

Jake leaned over to Shea. "I think we can get out of here if you want."

She nodded. "I have a bottle of red at home calling our names, if you are sure you don't want to stay here with Charlie."

They both watched as he ducked into the changing tent, and the next player took the spot on the bench.

"Let's just say bye to him, and then we can go, alright?" Jake suggested. They made their way over, saying their goodbyes to Jake's family and friends, and headed back to her house for the night. It had been one of the most perfect days in Jake's recent memory and ending it alone with Shea was the icing on the cake.

***

They settled onto her porch, watching as neighbors walked by on their way home from the festival. Many stopped to talk, others simply waved and carried on, pushing tired kids in strollers or leading dogs on leashes.

"What a great day," Jake reflected after Christine and Ryan had sleepily departed from the porch after sharing the wine with them.

"It really was." Shea rested her head on his shoulder, soaking in the warmth of him.

"I should get home," Jake murmured.

Shea held her breath for a second, then found the nerve to ask what she had been wondering all night. "Any chance you would stay?"

He studied her, and finally smiled. "I want to, very badly. But I don't want to have to run out on you at dawn, and I feel like I would have to for Charlie's sake."

"I can live with that." She stood and stretched, then crooked her finger at him. "If you have a countdown going, let's get inside and stop wasting time."

Chapter 35

Jake met Matt outside the Inn early on Sunday morning, as they had planned over text the night before. Watching the young man walk toward him, he was instantly taken back to the first day they had met. Matt was fresh out of high school, from a small town in New Hampshire. He had never flown on a plane before, nor been away from his parents. Jake had known that he threw himself into boot camp, training hard and showing potential for excellence. As they met that first time, Matt's exuberance and excitement for the unknown was palpable. Today, his movements were a little slower, he looked guarded, but he had that same brightness in his eyes when he saw Jake.

"Sir," Matt held out his hand. "Thanks for meeting up with me this morning, I was hoping we could spend some time together."

"Enough with the sir, please." Jake shook his hand. "I'm glad we have time to catch up. The girls aren't coming?"

"No, they decided to sleep in. Figured it might be for the best, otherwise I wouldn't get a word in edgewise." Matt stuck his hands in his pockets and looked around. "Looks like today will be another busy day, so I'm glad they are getting some rest."

"Let's head over to the diner, we can grab some breakfast before it gets crowded." Jake led the way, pointing out some of the other local businesses they passed.

"This is a real nice town," Matt observed.

Jake nodded as he opened the door to the diner. "Sure is. It was a great place to grow up, and my son is doing great here."

They selected a booth in the back corner, accepting menus and the offered coffee from the smiling waitress. "Fill me in on your life," Jake requested as the waitress walked away.

"Last time you saw me, I was drinking too much. My poor ex-wife was trying to hold it together, but Nat was a baby, and she was all alone in raising her." He sipped his coffee. "I made some really poor decisions. Calling you that day was the best one I made."

"I try to help when I can," Jake murmured.

"It was more than that. You were a voice of reason I couldn't ignore. I saw what I was doing to my ex, and it killed me. She didn't deserve that." He shook his head, looking at the table. "I never got physical with her or anything like that, but I didn't treat her well. And she was raising my baby."

"How is your relationship now?" Jake asked.

"Oh, it's so much better. I apologized to her; told her I was in counseling. I went a while where I only saw Nat if my mom was with me, and that was understandable. No one trusted me with her alone," He sighed. "That hurts like hell to admit, but it's true. I owe my ex a huge debt of gratitude, because she could have kept me away from Nat, but instead she gave me a reason to get better."

"Sounds like an incredible woman."

"She is. She remarried, had a couple more kids and we are good friends now. We got married so young, we didn't even know what life would be like, you know?"

They both turned to order, and Jake felt Matt's words reverberating in his head. Were he and Jenna any different than Matt and his ex? Would they have imploded once life got a hold of them? He shook his head, refusing to let the thought grow. Of course, they were different. They would still be together today, with a houseful of kids, if she were alive. He felt that deep in his heart, and he knew it was true.

"Anyway, you gave me hope back then. And a purpose. If you hadn't basically ordered me into counseling and to look at college options, I never would have gone." Matt met his gaze with unwavering eyes. "I owe you a debt of gratitude as well."

"That's not true, you don't owe me anything," Jake insisted. "Seeing you here, knowing how well you turned out, that's all I need. I tell you all when you get assigned to my unit that I will always be there for you, and I mean that. I'm glad I could help."

"Do you remember Frank Thorton?"

"Sure, of course." Jake nodded.

"I talk to him all the time too," Matt shared. "We both decided not to re-up at the same time, and we did boot camp together. It's nice to have someone to talk to who has had the same experiences as you, you know?"

"I do," Jake agreed.

"He's doing great. He went right back to South Carolina, got a job on the police force," Matt shared. "We go down and visit them every year, and he comes up to ski with his family. I asked him once how he is so normal, and he laughed."

"Normal is different to everyone, I think." Jake commented.

"Well, Sarge, you certainly seem to have it together. You seem incredibly normal for what you have seen."

Jake laughed. "That's a stretch, Matt."

"Do you mind me asking," Matt hesitated. "I was just wondering, are you going back when you're done with your convalescent leave?"

"I honestly don't know." Jake stared out the window at his hometown, which was just waking up and getting started for the second day of the festival. All his friends and neighbors saying good morning, helping each other. They would do this all again in a month or so for the Holiday Festival and found a reason to celebrate as a town regularly. Despite being away for so many years, this town had sucked him right back in, accepting him just as he was. "This is a hard place to leave once it gets its hooks into you."

"I feel a little bad for the troops who won't get a chance to be led by you," Matt mused. "I know there are plenty of good leaders, but man, you are just the best of the best."

Jake felt his smile dim, thinking of the young men and women who had just started in his unit. The ones who were still in boot camp and headed his way, who had no idea what their future held. The people here in this town, they had each other to get through the hard times. These young kids who had just enlisted, they only had him, and what happened if he didn't go back to them? At the same time, if he went back to war, what would happen to the people who relied on him after they finished their years of service?

For days he had been leaning towards retiring, letting the town draw him in and the idea that he could be there for Charlie for the rest of his high school years. Suddenly the idea of staying was a little less bright. He only had a few more years left before he could retire, and Charlie did so well without him here. It wouldn't be fair to ask Shea to wait for him, but maybe his happiness was less important than the men and women who were sacrificing for their country.

The decision weighed heavily on him for the rest of his time with Matt, and as he walked back to the town square to find Shea in the book tent. It wasn't fair of him to continue to monopolize her time if he had any possibility of leaving in a few weeks, but he just couldn't bring himself to stay away. Maybe spending more time with her would help him make a decision, he told himself. Or maybe he was lying to himself to justify spending time with her. He pushed the thoughts out of his head, determined to at least enjoy this one weekend without the worries of the world on his shoulders.

Chapter 36

Sunday morning after Shea sent Jake off to breakfast with Matt, she went to work at the book tent at the festival. She spent a whirlwind couple of hours reading stories to young kids and helping them pick out the perfect book to bring home with them. Sharing the books that Vermont writers had published gave her a particular pride, and she loved seeing how many signed copies they had on hand.

As the Harvest Festival wound down, the residents of the town sleepily walked home, carrying tired kids and bags full of goodies from the vendors looking to offload the rest of their treats. Shea happily accepted a bag of maple flavored popcorn from a neighbor, offering some to Jake as they walked towards Main Street.

"This is delicious," he grabbed another handful from the bag as she pretended to hide it from him. "Want to go over to Windsor Peak Palace and wind down for the night? Big night for you, since there is no school tomorrow."

"Sure, that sounds perfect. And don't think you're fooling me, I know the Patriots are on tonight."

"Oh, is that right? Maybe we can catch the tail end." He pretended to check his watch as she laughed.

The bar was packed when they entered, with tables still full of families having a quick meal and the bar with those looking for a liquid dinner. As they stood in the doorway looking for a seat, Shea caught sight of Kendra waving to them from the kitchen doorway. "There, Kendra is trying to get our attention."

They pressed through the crowd, greeting Kendra when they made it to her side. "Come outside," she said, pointing through the side door. "I set up a fire pit, we have drinks and food. And the game on, of course."

Jake grinned. "You sure know your way to my heart."

"Yeah, yeah. Go on out, I'll be there in a minute."

They emerged from the building to find a small group laughing around a fire pit. The outdoor bar was lined with pizza boxes, and a TV hung behind the bar had the football game on at low volume. Patrick was already there, guitar propped up on his chair, sitting with the two women Shea recognized as Kendra's best friends. A few local business owners were clustered together on the other side of the fire. Christine and Ryan came out the door moments later, followed by Kendra.

"Hi." Christine hugged Shea and smiled at Jake. "Kendra just grabbed us and said to come out here. Okay if we are crashing?"

"Of course! We didn't know anything about this until now." Shea linked arms with Christine and followed the men to the bar, where they accepted glasses of wine. "It's so nice of Kendra to set this up."

Kendra overheard and smiled. "It's nice to have a little escape with friends after the craziness of this weekend. This always kicks off the busiest time for all of us, it's nice to kick back and soak it in while we can."

"For us teachers, it's craziness from September to June!" Christine exclaimed. "But at least we have the same kids to deal with. All of you who get the tourist traffic have it much harder."

"But it keeps us in business," Kendra sank into a seat next to her friends, sighing as she did.

"Where have you been, Patrick?" Jake asked as he pulled a seat closer to the one Shea had just claimed.

"I tried to go out to the tent today, and it got a little much. Kendra suggested I hide out back here until the crowd dispersed a little. I think word spread that I was doing the festival yesterday, and people came in droves." He sipped from the beer Jake had just handed him.

"Helped the local vendors a ton," Kendra's friend Tina chimed in. "They said business was double what it was yesterday."

"Happy to help." He looked at Jake and Shea. "What about you two? Have fun today?"

"We did," Shea replied. "Jake had breakfast this morning with a friend that he served with while I worked at the book table at the festival. Then we spent some time going through all the vendors inside. We had to run home for a few hours this afternoon to bring the dog home, she had her fill of people and other dogs after a visit to the festival."

"Took a few hours to get the dog home, did it?" Patrick teased, and Shea felt herself blushing.

"Easy," Jake growled.

"Yes, Patrick, take it easy. Wouldn't want Jake beating you up in front of the town," Kendra called out from her seat.

"Hey —" Jake objected.

She held up a hand. "I would have done it myself. Guy is charming when he's sober, but he's a bad drunk. I for one and glad you gave him a piece of your mind."

Kendra's friends nodded in unison and Christine nudged Shea. "Did he stop calling you?"

"He did, and the teacher who set us up apologized. She said she didn't know he could be so clingy."

"At least it had a good ending," Patrick stated. "I thought I was going to have to kick the guy's ass, and that would have been so embarrassing for Jake."

"I could have handled it myself, Patty."

"You have to stop calling me that. What if the tabloids hear?" He craned his neck, looking toward the fence that surrounded them.

"Dan started it, not me."

Kendra visibly stiffened at the sound of his name, and her friends seemed to huddle closer. "Is he back?"

"No," Patrick assured her. "I'm sorry, I shouldn't have mentioned him."

"He's your brother, it's not a problem." Kendra picked at her fingernail polish.

"I have a problem with him," inserted Julie, Kendra's other best friend, who was promptly shut down by a glare from Kendra.

"Is there anything we can do to help with that situation?" Jake asked. "Short of killing him or curing his idiocy."

Kendra shook her head. "It's all so long ago. There is no problem."

Patrick leaned toward Jake and whispered loudly enough to be heard for three blocks, "He's the worst."

Kendra hid her laughter with her wine glass and went back to chatting with her friends. The guys all got up to watch the final few minutes of the football game, so Christine pulled her chair even closer to Shea. "How are things going with you two?"

"So good," Shea admitted. "I'm afraid to wake up tomorrow and have it all be gone."

"Has he made any decision about his future?"

She shook her head. "Nothing yet. He has some appointments this week, so I'm sure it will be discussed."

"Are you going to be alright if he has to leave?"

Shea looked to where he stood, laughing with his brother and Ryan. "No, I don't think I will be," she admitted quietly.

Later that evening, Shea and Jake walked home with Christine and Ryan, warm from the wine and time around the fire. Jake was holding Shea's hand and feeling the most relaxed he had felt in years. If there was a way to stop time, he would be content to relive this very day over and over again for all of time.

"Thanks for tonight," Ryan said as they approached their houses. "It was a lot of fun. It's really great to get to know you better, Jake."

The two shook hands before the couples peeled off to their respective houses. Shea and Jake said their hellos to Muffin before letting her out into the fenced backyard, then settled on the couch waiting for her to come in.

"Will you stay over?" Shea pulled a blanket off the back of the couch and spread it over her legs.

"I'd like that," he said as he pulled half the blanket over onto himself. "Mind if I just watch the highlights quickly on ESPN?"

"Not at all, I'll read until you're ready to go up." She picked up her book and pretended to read while absorbing the normalcy of this night. It was shocking to her sometimes how comfortable she was with Jake, and yet just looking at him got her heart racing.

She peeked at him over her book, and he smiled at her. "Are you stuck on a word? I could help."

"What do you mean?"

"You've been staring at that page for a couple minutes now," he explained.

She laughed and put the book down. "You're right. I was just thinking about what a great weekend this was, and how much I'm enjoying being with you."

"Me too," he agreed. "It's like we've been together for years sometimes, it's weird."

"Yes! But then also exciting because it's new, and I like looking at your face."

"Just my face?" He teased her.

"Ok, there are some other decent parts of you too."

"We better let the dog in and go upstairs. If you think the rest of me is only decent, I'm clearly doing something wrong." He stood from the couch and offered her a hand, pulling her to her feet.

"You know what they say," she called as she went to the kitchen door. "Always room for improvement!"

"You are going to take that back before the night ends," he called back, and she shivered in anticipation.

253

"Jake! Jake!" He felt someone shaking him, pulling him back from the dust and blood of Afghanistan. As he came to, he realized he was on the ground, huddled on top of a pillow. Sweat poured down his face, running into his mouth so all he could taste was sweat. It took him a solid minute to realize it was Shea's voice, and her bedroom floor he was on.

"Are you okay?" He could see she was trembling, her face pale in the moonlight coming through the window.

"Yes. I'm sorry. I'll be right back." He stumbled to his feet and made his way to the bathroom, where he splashed cold water on his face and then sat down hard on the edge of the bathtub. *Fuck.*

When he left the bathroom, he saw the light was turned on in the living room, so he turned that way, finding Shea curled on the couch. She pointed at a bottle of water on the table, and although he wished it were something stronger, he grabbed it and chugged it down. Unsure of whether she wanted him close to her, he sat in the chair across the room and looked at her.

"I'm sorry."

"Please don't say that. This isn't your fault; you did nothing wrong. But it would help so much to understand what happened to you."

He sighed, hanging his head, and looking at his hands tightly clasped between his knees. "I don't know where to start. You can't imagine the horrors I've seen. But it would probably help if you knew what went wrong the last couple of months, which is where most of the nightmares are coming from."

"I just want to help you get better."

He met her eyes, seeing how much she cared about him. "About six months before I was shot, we were on a patrol mission. We did the same thing almost every day, the routes changed randomly but we covered the same area. Just different days, or going in a different way, so that we couldn't be ambushed. Or so we thought. We were headed into a small village; it was usually full of kids playing and women hanging the laundry. People were happy to see us, the kids especially. I was distracted, right before we left, I had a meeting with my commanding officer and I should have pushed it out of my head until we got back, but I didn't.

I missed that the kids weren't out, no one was running up to us to see if we had candy or toys in our pockets. A second too late the quiet hit me, and I called out to the team to hold. I heard the shots before anything else, and everyone dove for cover. But one kid, a nineteen-year-old from Iowa named Chris, went down. I grabbed him and dragged him to cover, giving orders to the unit so we wouldn't be surrounded. It turned out it was just three guys, holed up on the second floor of a widow's house, and my team took them out quickly.

I was calling over the radio for help while trying to hold pressure on his stomach, he was just gushing blood. He was a kid, and I watched him bleed out." He took a ragged breath. "It fucked me up. I have been in the same situation so many times, lost friends and so many soldiers, or seen people lose limbs. But something in this kid's eyes, I couldn't shake it. He was so full of joy, he seemed out of place with us, you know? He had enlisted because he wanted to see some of the world before he took over his dad's farm, and now I was sending him home in a casket."

Shea crossed the room and sat on his lap, wrapping her arms around him. "I'm so sorry."

"I couldn't shake it, and I think that led to me getting hurt. You have to be one hundred percent focused at all times when you are in a war zone, and I wasn't. My counselor asked me what I thought would go differently that morning if I had been paying attention. I know she wants me to realize that there was no way to prevent it, that it wasn't my fault."

"None of it was your fault, Jake."

"Chris was. He trusted me and I failed him."

"No, it wasn't." She pulled back to look him in the eye. "You didn't pull the trigger. You didn't even start this war. You didn't convince him to enlist. None of it was in your control."

"I talked to his parents last week," Jake said. "They called my commanding officer asking to speak to me, so he gave me their number. I always called the family after they were notified, but with Chris, I just couldn't bring myself to. Dan pointed out that it's because Chris reminded me of Jenna."

"How were they?"

"As good as you would expect, having lost their son. They said they don't blame me."

"No, and they shouldn't. It's not your fault, Jake."

"It should have been me instead," He whispered, then felt her grip tighten around him.

"I am so glad it wasn't. It's horrible that he's gone, and that his parents had to lose their son. But I am so, so glad you are here."

Jake woke the next morning, feeling like his eyes had grit in them and his head pounding. Shea was still asleep next to him, and he took the time to study her peaceful face. Her beauty was simpler than Jenna's, but warmer and more approachable, if he were being honest. How he had gotten so lucky to have found Shea, who saw past all his shortcomings, was beyond him.

Her eyelashes fluttered and she came awake with a sleepy smile. "How are you?"

"I'm good. Thank you for last night."

"There's nothing to thank me for," she insisted as she cuddled closer to him. "I feel like I understand you better now."

"Oh, yeah?"

"The whole back against the wall thing. I see why you are on edge all the time and need to see what's coming." She hugged him. "And I understand why you look so haunted sometimes."

"I'm trying to get better," his voice was gruff.

She half sat up and looked at him. "I'm not being critical. I want you to know that I will be here, and I'll fight alongside you, whatever the battle. I care about you, Jake. I want to see you happy and enjoying your life."

He smiled at her. "I'm enjoying my life right now."

"Well, that's a start." She leaned down to kiss him, helping him relax with her simple touch, which quickly turned into much more.

Chapter 38

"Open mike night tonight," Patrick announced as he poured himself a cup of coffee. "Get your guitar ready. Kendra has been marketing it as basically a Burrows show, so we should make sure we have enough ready."

"I am going to text you a list of songs, and you do the same. I'll listen on the way to Burlington if I don't know it." Jake picked up his phone and started typing. "I already mentioned it to Shea, so I'll pick her up and meet you there."

"I'm the third wheel? This is getting depressing." Patrick leaned against the counter, sipping from his mug.

"Get a date. Wouldn't be hard for you," Jake suggested, making Charlie laugh.

"Half the girls at my school have pictures of you as the backdrop on their phones," Charlie shared.

Patrick shook his head. "I'm a little old to date one of your classmates."

"Ewww," Charlie rolled his eyes. "Not what I was saying. At all."

"Any hot teachers?"

"Ms. Kerrigan, but I heard she has an annoying new boyfriend." Charlie finished filling up his water bottle and screwed the top on, smirking at Jake.

"Annoying is less insulting than you think," Jake tried. "At least you notice something that's annoying."

"Nice try," Charlie called as he headed down the hall.

"You aren't a third wheel," Jake said to Patrick as he stood from the kitchen table. "I have to run, but I'll see you over there later."

"Okay, if you run into any cute nurses, get their number!" Jake laughed at his brother's words as he ran upstairs to shower before heading out for the day.

Jake returned from the VA hours later, exhausted and thinking about a nap. The house was still, and it was the first time since he came home that he was alone in it, that he could recall. He checked his dad's office and yelled up the stairs, with no response. Odd, since both his dad and Stella's cars were in the driveway. He debated walking over to Stella's cottage and decided against it, using the quiet time to flop on the couch and put a movie on low. He fell asleep almost instantly and woke up to the sound of his dad and Stella coming in the back door.

"Jake! I didn't know you were home already." His dad came to stand in the doorway.

"Hey dad," he rubbed a hand across his eyes. "Didn't get a lot of sleep last night, so just catching a few winks. What are you up to?"

"Oh, nothing much." He glanced over at Stella, who was busying herself in the kitchen.

"Everything okay out back?"

"Hmm? What do you mean?" His dad looked confused.

"Were you out at Stella's?"

His dad pushed off the doorway. "Oh, that. Yeah, everything is fine. Go back to sleep, we'll stay quiet."

Jake stared after him for a minute, confused but not willing to leave the comfort of the couch to see why they were acting weird. He stretched and tried to figure out what was happening in the movie before giving up and closing his eyes again.

Shea finished grading the final essay and took her reading glasses off, then glanced at her watch and winced. She had less than a half hour before Jake came to get her, so she had to hurry. Going from being home every night doing schoolwork, to being with Jake almost constantly, had put her behind, so she had to get through this pile before her students revolted.

Rushing through makeup and hair while visualizing her outfit options saved her time, so she was ready when Jake knocked at seven. "Hi," she said as she opened the door, smiling at the sight of him. He was dressed casually in a black long sleeve t-shirt and a pair of jeans, and she let her eyes feast on him for a moment before stepping forward to kiss him. "How are you doing today?"

"I'm good. Had a good appointment at the VA, and then a long nap on the couch." He held the door open. "Are you ready to go? Patrick will freak out if I'm late."

"Yes, let me just grab my coat." She grabbed it from the coat closet and then locked the door behind them. "Are you driving over?"

"No, I'll just grab my guitar from the car. Didn't make sense to bring it up to your door. Give me one second." He disappeared to grab the case out of his SUV, then met her on the sidewalk. "All set."

They started walking toward town, seeing the sidewalks getting busier the closer they got to the Windsor Peak Palace. "I guess Kendra put out word that Patrick would be performing," Jake noted.

"I did see a post on Facebook hinting that Patrick would be putting on a show tonight."

"I'm second billing?"

She laughed with him. "If it makes you feel any better, you're first billing in my book."

"I'll see if I can do a song for you. Any requests?" He opened the door for her and gestured for her to go first.

"Not that I can think of, but if I come up with anything, you'll be the first to know."

Kendra was watching for them and pointed to a table with a reserved sign on it, the only empty one in the room. They made their way through the room, Jake pulling gently on her hand when she was stopped by people at other tables when she stopped for too long at a table to chat.

"Sorry about that," she said when they reached the table. "I can't believe how many people are here! And probably half of them aren't from Windsor Peak. Kendra must be thrilled."

"Did I hear my name?" Kendra snuck up behind them, carrying two bottles of beer and a glass of wine. "I took a guess on your drink of choice from last time, hope I'm right. Are your friends coming again tonight?"

"I think so, Ryan was running late from work, but Christine said they expected to be here." Shea looked around the crowded room but didn't see them.

"I'll keep an eye out," Kendra replied. "Anyone else coming?"

"Looking for anyone in particular?" Jake teased Kendra.

"Just wondering how many chairs you'll need," she replied quickly.

"Dan is back in the city, if that's what you're asking. Your friends are welcome to come sit over here if they want, rather than be crowded at the bar. That will make Patrick feel like he has a fan club." Jake waved to Kendra's friends Julie and Tina at the bar.

"Oh, I'll mention it to them. They usually sit there so we can chat, but I might be so busy tonight that I can't stop." She glanced over to where they sat. "They can come keep you company if Christine and Ryan don't get here by the time the boys go on stage, okay?"

"Thanks, Kendra." Shea settled into her seat as they watched her walk back towards the bar. "Oh, there's Patrick. You might need to help him."

They watched as Patrick was swarmed the second he walked into the bar, guitar case in hand. He smiled for pictures and signed autographs, barely making it five steps into the bar in as many minutes. Shea laughed when she saw Kendra march over, grab Patrick, and drag him to their table to drop him.

"Whew. It's crowded here!" Patrick sat down and grabbed the full beer on the table. "This mine?"

"It is now, since you just drank from it." Jake set his half full bottle down.

"You say that like I'm disgusting. My mouth is clean." He grinned at Jake as cameras clicked around them. "Some of these ladies might even —"

"Stop." Jake held up a hand. "I beg you, please stop where that was going. Shea is here too, try to have some manners."

"I was just going to say they might want to share a beer with me," Patrick winked at Shea as she laughed.

Kendra jumped on stage and the crowd quieted. "Welcome everyone to the Windsor Peak Palace! I'm thrilled you are all here. I'm sure most of you are here because you heard our resident celebrity might be singing tonight," she looked to Patrick, who waved. "And you would be right, Patrick Burrows and his equally talented brother will be doing some songs for us. If anyone else wants to perform, please sign up on the list to the side of the stage. If they are ready, I'll welcome Patrick and Jake to the stage!"

Jake leaned over to Shea. "Sorry to leave you alone."

"Don't worry, Christine just texted that they are almost here. And I see Kendra's friends making their way over." She gave him a gentle push. "Go!"

"Hey everyone," Patrick perched on one of the two barstools on the stage, holding his guitar. "It is so great to see you all, and I'm so glad you came out to support my friend Kendra's business. I hope that Jake and I can entertain you, and we are more than happy to share the stage if anyone else plans to perform tonight. We can also take some requests, as long as it's something we are familiar with. But first, let me introduce my big brother Jake. He's been away serving in the military, and we are so glad to have him home right now."

The crowd rose to their feet, cheering for Jake, and he raised his hand to thank them. Shea noticed his downcast eyes, and Patrick must have as well, because he quickly strummed on the guitar to bring the attention back to himself. "Let's get started with an old favorite, if you know it, feel free to sing along."

They settled into an easy rhythm together, Shea had no idea if they had practiced together or if it was just from years of loving music that had them so in sync. They switched between country, pop, oldies, and did a hysterical version of *Baby Got Back* that had the crowd going crazy. After almost an hour, they excused themselves from the stage, promising to come back after a break.

"That was amazing," Shea gushed as Jake sat back down next to her.

"It's crazy how it just comes right back to us. We have been playing most of those songs together for years, and just know who's taking the lead without even talking it over." Jake sipped from the beer Kendra dropped in front of him, toasting her with it before putting it back on the table.

Patrick excused himself from the table and made his way to the bar, while the rest of the table continued to praise Jake. Shea watched as Patrick had a conversation with a well-dressed man at the bar, before signing a packet of papers handed to him.

"Who is Patrick talking to?" She leaned over and asked Jake.

He glanced over. "Not sure, I've never seen him before. Maybe a fan?"

Patrick shook hands with the man and folded a piece of paper to put in his pocket before walking back to the table.

"Everything okay?" Shea asked him when he sat back down.

"Huh? Oh, yeah, great. Thanks." He turned to clap for the singer who had just finished a song on stage.

"Patrick, what was that about?" Jake poked at him. "You really shouldn't be signing anything without Dan looking at it, should you? What was that?"

"Nothing, what's the problem? It was already looked at by a lawyer, no big deal. Nothing to do with my career." Patrick wouldn't meet their eyes. "Ready to go back up there?"

Jake pushed back from the table, and they walked up to the stage, heads huddled together. As they stepped up to the microphones, Jake spoke first, surprising Shea. "As Patrick mentioned, I've been away from home for quite a long time. I never realized I missed it here until now, and I have one person who has made coming home so amazing. This song will go out to her."

Their guitars started strumming, and Shea recognized the song as "Home" by Michael Bublé. His eyes never left Shea as he sang about letters written and the desire to come home, and she felt her eyes misting while seeing the raw emotion on his face. When they finished, he placed his guitar down and ran over to her, kissing her before embracing her quickly as the crowd cheered. Patrick was already playing the notes to their next song as Jake jogged back to the stage.

They played several more songs, and Shea heard the buzz of conversation around her but couldn't get involved. When Jake started strumming the notes she recognized from the *Mamma Mia* play, she shook her head vigorously at him, met only by his smile growing. "I'm hoping we can get a couple friends to come up and sing this with us," he said into the microphone. "Shea, want to come up? And your friends?"

The traitors at the table jumped up instantly, Christine grabbing her wrist and dragging her along. Jake reached out when she got close and pulled her as close as the guitar would allow. "Don't kill me," he whispered to her.

"Oh, you'll pay for this," she promised. She tried to move as far away from the microphone as possible, but finally got caught up in the fun of the song and dancing along with her girlfriends, forgetting she was on stage in front of all those people. When the song ended Jake and Patrick thanked everyone again for letting them play, and they all left the stage together.

Jake sat first and pulled Shea onto his lap, wrapping his arms around her. "Don't be mad."

"I'll see if I can move past it," she sniffed. When he caught her eye, she had no choice but to laugh. "Okay, it was fun. Happy?"

"Yes," he admitted with a grin. "Music is a big part of my life; I want you to be able to share that and not worry about what you sound like."

"This will not be a regular thing. I'm happy to listen to you, but I think that's where it should end."

"Your voice is fine. We'll work on your confidence."

She shifted onto her chair, wanting to absorb the significance of the words. Although he hadn't promised he would be staying, or that they had a future, the simple reference to spending more time together had her heart skip a beat. The closer they got to him potentially leaving, the more she dreaded that day, so any hope that he would stay was worth clinging to.

Chapter 39

Shea had ten minutes to sit and enjoy her coffee before leaving for school when someone began banging on her door earnestly. She startled and spilled the hot beverage on her finger, her sharp intake of breath causing Muffin to panic more than she normally would have. Crossing to the door, she pulled it open to find Charlie puffing and red faced, his bike dropped on the sidewalk in front of her house.

"Charlie! What's wrong?" She felt the tension throughout her entire body, seeing the frantic look on his face.

"Is my dad here?" He was breathless and trying to look over her shoulder into the house.

"No, I haven't seen him today."

"Has he called you? Or anything?"

"No, I don't think so. Come inside so I can check my phone." She pulled him inside and directed him to the couch while she grabbed her phone, getting him a bottle of water at the same time.

"Anything?" he asked as she checked her text messages.

"No," she responded, seeing the panic rise in his eyes. "Why don't I call him?"

Charlie nodded, so she hit the button to call Jake. The call went immediately to voicemail. "I'll just text him, okay?"

"He left. I knew he would do this." Charlie stood and stalked to the front door.

"Please don't leave. Let's try and figure this out." She quickly sent a text to Jake, explaining that Charlie had just arrived and was upset, to please call as quickly as possible. "Come, sit."

He sat back on the edge of the couch, the bottle of water clenched so tightly in his hands she was surprised it didn't burst. "I woke up this morning and his door was open, he wasn't there. His car is gone. I thought maybe he was here, but he usually texts me if he won't be home at night." He cleared his throat. "Not that I have a problem with it."

"I appreciate that." She smiled at him gently, hoping he could calm down. No response from Jake, and between that and Charlie's nervous energy, she was starting to feel on edge. "Were his clothes still there? His guitar?"

Charlie stared off into space for a minute, then nodded. "Yes, the case was still next to his bed. And his laptop was open on the desk. I didn't check the closet for his clothes."

"Would he have left without the guitar and laptop?"

"No, I don't think so," Charlie sounded reluctant to believe that, but seemed to be calmer.

"Maybe we should give him the benefit of doubt here," She suggested. "We don't know what happened, maybe his phone is dead and he's just at appointments at the VA?"

"I guess so." Charlie stood and paced the room. "He does this, you know."

"Does what?"

"Just leaves. When things get hard."

"I talked to him just before I went to bed last night and everything seemed fine. Did anything happen last night?"

"No," Charlie considered her words. "You could be right."

"I bet I am," She declared, not feeling the same confidence she was trying to project. Where could Jake be? "You and I should both be getting to school; do you want to ride with me?"

"I left all my stuff at home, so I need to go grab it. I'll just be tardy; it will be okay."

Shea checked her watch, seeing she still had a few minutes to spare. "Let me grab my stuff, and we can race to your house for your bag and then go to school together. You can walk here after school and get your bike. Sound good?"

He agreed, so she directed him to go out and move his bike out by her garage, where it could stay for the day. She poured her coffee into a to-go mug, grabbed her lunch and work bag, and they headed out together. She refrained from checking her phone while in the car with Charlie, instead chattering on about school events.

As she parked, he glanced at her. "Will you tell me if you hear something from him? I texted him too, so if I hear back, I'll let you know."

"Absolutely, I will make sure to find you. I can pull your schedule up in the system, so I'll get you as soon as I hear anything. And if you need me during the day, please come find me." He gave her a half smile before turning to trot into the school. As soon as his back was turned, she grabbed her phone and checked, dismayed to see no response from Jake. Where could he be?

***

Charlie poked his head in her classroom between each class, looking more dejected every time she had to shake her head no.

271

It wasn't until the last class that she felt her phone buzz in her pocket and pulled it out surreptitiously to see it was a text from Jake.

I'm okay. And on my way home. Can you meet me at the house after school?

She sent back a quick message agreeing and asking if he had contacted Charlie but got no response. Quickly checking to see where Charlie was, she used the school phone to call the science lab and ask the teacher to send him down at the end of the class. He came immediately, so she excused herself and told her students to read quietly while she stepped out into the hall with Charlie.

"I just got a text from your dad, he's okay." She saw the relief flash in his eyes.

"Did he say where he was?"

"No, but he asked me to come to the house after school. Want to ride with me, we can get your bike later?"

"Yes, that sounds good. I'll meet you outside when school gets out. You sure he didn't say anything else?"

She pulled her phone out and checked, then shook her head. "Nothing, but he must be driving right now."

"He didn't answer me at all," Charlie muttered, and she could see the temper starting to rise in him.

"Let's give him the chance to explain before we jump to any conclusions," Shea pleaded with him, not wanting Jake to have a major setback in the relationship he was building with his son.

"I'll see you outside." He turned and jogged back in the direction of the science lab, and Shea felt her heartstrings tug at the sight of him walking away.

Chapter 40

Charlie's heart raced the entire way back to his house. He could hear Ms. Kerrigan – Shea – talking about the upcoming homecoming weekend, but his mind was too scattered to follow along. What was his dad going to tell them? Why did he need them both there? He was leaving for sure; it was the only possible explanation. Well, at least he had the balls to tell them to their faces instead of just vanishing. Was Ms. Kerrigan going to cry when he told them he was going back? He resolved to be emotionless, he wasn't going to let this bother him at all. Life goes on.

When they pulled in the driveway his dad was sitting in his usual spot on the porch, elbows on knees and head hanging low. His head rose as they parked, and he stood as if to walk over to them, then decided against it. As he got closer, Charlie could see that his dad looked exhausted.

"Thanks for bringing Charlie with you, Shea," His dad said, giving her a quick kiss on the cheek. He patted Charlie on the shoulder as he made his way past them to sit in the furthest seat, leaving one empty between him and his dad. Shea looked worried as she took the seat, and his dad wasn't helping things by staring off into the distance, not saying a word.

"Are you okay?" It burst out of his lips before he could stop it. "Where were you?"

"I got a call late last night; it was from a friend that I have served with for years. We did a few tours together and have seen some things together that we wish we could forget. I haven't seen him in a year or two. He was stationed in Georgia the last I had heard, I lost touch with him for a bit. Apparently, he got moved again, and is now in New York, a couple hours from here, luckily." Jake looked between both of them and shifted in his chair.

"Is this something you're comfortable sharing?" Shea asked. "I can leave if you would rather talk to Charlie alone."

"No, I want you both to hear this, and it will be easier to only say it once." He grabbed her hand briefly before continuing. "He came back home three weeks ago, found out his wife had packed up their kids and left him while he was gone. She didn't want to distract him while he was overseas, but she was done."

Shea made a noise and they both looked at her. "I'm sorry. That's really awful, to do that to him, especially while he is at war."

Charlie nodded, thinking the same.

"Unfortunately, it happens a lot," Jake said wearily. "The toll that deployments take isn't just on the soldiers, the spouses must do the work of two people suddenly. Kids miss a parent and then act out when that parent comes home. It's just as hard to come home as it is to leave, I hear it all the time from my soldiers."

Charlie relaxed a little, realizing that his dad didn't want to tell them he was leaving. If anything, maybe this would make him want to stay. He shut down the thought before they could set roots as hope, not wanting to set himself up for disappointment later.

Jake ran a hand through his hair. "Anyway, he got back, empty house, no one to distract him from the nightmares. Started drinking, doing whatever he could to dull the pain and block out the bad memories. When he called me last night to say goodbye, that he was going to kill himself, I convinced him to not do anything until I got there. I just jumped in my car and drove, made him stay on the phone with me the whole time."

"Oh, Jake." Shea reached over and grabbed his dad's hand, and suddenly Charlie wished he had taken that chair. He couldn't imagine getting that kind of call from one of his friends.

"I made it in time. He had just gotten to the bottom of the bottle and had planned to end things when he finished it. Fortunately, he came with me willingly, I really didn't want to call the military police to come help. I was able to get him into my car and to a VA hospital, where they admitted him. He can detox and get the help he needs there." Jake let out a raggedy breath, sagging a little in the chair.

"I'm sorry," Charlie heard himself whispering.

"You don't have anything to be sorry for, Charlie." Jake perked up a little, looking at him. "I knew you would think I had just up and left, but I worried if I tried to text you or anyone else that he would hang up on me. I had to focus on getting him to someplace safe, and I'm sorry that it scared both of you that I was gone. Once I got there, I was helping fill out the paperwork, and there was no cell signal, so I gave up trying to message either of you."

"What kind of —" Charlie suddenly wished he had some water; his throat was dry. "Umm. You have nightmares. And he maybe did too? What does that come from?"

"I told you a little, and Shea knows more. Some things are just so dark, Charlie, that I can't share them with you guys. It's not because I don't love you or trust you, but I can't burden you with those kinds of things. That's why I have a therapist. Things like death and people losing limbs, or seeing innocent people get caught in a war they don't want. That is all heavy, and ugly. And

I don't want that in your mind. I hope you understand that it has nothing to do with our relationship."

"I do. I just —"

"He's wondering what makes you different from your friend," Shea inserted gently.

"Charlie. You make me different. And I know that sounds crazy because my friend has kids too, but it's true. I know I'm all you have left for parents, and I'm not leaving you without a fight. My demons will appear sometimes, and I need you both to understand what that looks like. If I get worse than losing my temper or having a nightmare, I'll find more help than I'm already getting. You have my word on that." His gaze was even, and Charlie saw the raw honesty in his eyes. "People that have no one to welcome them home, or who come home to a battle in their own home, they have it much harder than I do."

"I shouldn't have assumed the worst. Shea told me that you probably had a good reason, and she was right." Charlie gulped past the lump in his throat. "I'm glad you could be there for your friend."

"I'm incredibly blessed, and I know that. I know way too many soldiers who come home and have no one to lean on, and the opposite is true for me. I almost have too many people." His dad shot him a smile, and Charlie felt himself relaxing.

"Will your friend be alright? Can you check on him?" Shea asked.

"I hope so. He can't have his cell phone while he's there, but I talked with his wife for my whole drive back here and she said she would keep me in the loop. She's struggling too, I think. I thought it would be a quick call to update her and then I could call you guys, and it turned into three hours of listening to her.

278

Home alone with three kids for years at a time, then adjusting to life when he comes back. I hear it all the time, families adjust to the soldier being gone, and then they come back, and they have to adjust all over again." His dad met his eye again. "I'm sure you can relate, Charlie. It's not easy."

"It helps a lot to know what you're going through." Charlie stood up, wanting to leave before anyone got emotional. "I'm going to go grab a snack. I'm glad you are back."

His dad grabbed him before he could go into the house, pulling him in for a fast, tight embrace. "Thanks for giving me something to live for all these years."

Charlie pushed him away halfheartedly. "You aren't so bad. I like having you around."

"Just not when curfew comes?"

Charlie laughed as he headed out of the kitchen. "Yeah, other than that."

Chapter 41

Shea watched Charlie disappear into the house and was happy to sit holding Jake's hand while he was lost in thought. She tried to push thoughts of the PTSD episodes that she had witnessed out of her mind, knowing that Jake wasn't up for discussing anything that heavy. He had offered reassurance just now, and she would hang on to that, while still watching him carefully for any signs of distress.

"I'm so glad you are here," Jake said, squeezing her hand.

She smiled at him. "I'm glad too, I was worried about you all day. Charlie was in a full tailspin this morning."

"Tell me what happened," Jake requested.

"He came banging on my door just as I was pouring my coffee. I thought something had happened to you, but he told me he was looking for you." She thought back to the panic on his face. "He was really worried, Jake. That boy does love you, and he wants you to stick around. I know that's hard for you to hear, but it's true."

Jake made a noise deep in his throat, but he wasn't pulling away from her, so she waited to see if he would respond. When he didn't, she continued on. "He came into my class between every single period today, even when he was on the other side of the building. I wouldn't be surprised to find out he was late to every class, because he was so intent on finding out where you were."

"I wish I had thought to leave him a note," Jake groaned. "He's probably already upstairs thinking about how this could have been avoided if only I had thought of anyone but myself."

"Jake," she said gently, "you were. You were thinking of your friend and keeping him alive. That's important. And I think Charlie is proud of you for that."

"I appreciate your completely unbiased support," he smiled at her. "But I should be a little more focused on those around me. I knew all day that Charlie would be freaking out, and I should have made more of an effort. If I'm going to be around more, I should be more in tune to what people need from me."

"Tell me more about your conversation with his wife," Shea prodded.

Jake sighed. "The good news is, I don't think she's completely given up on him. She was frustrated and she didn't know how to get through to him. He came home after the last tour and struggled but refused to get any kind of help. This time she had asked him several times to promise he would go to counseling, and he wouldn't agree. She felt like she had to get the kids out of there rather than expose them to what he was going through, and I don't disagree with her."

"Do you think he was a danger to them?"

"No," Jake considered his answer. "No, I really don't. But that doesn't mean kids can't be scared by him yelling or having flashbacks. Look what happened with me, I scared both you and Charlie with my nightmares."

"That would be scary for little kids."

"She just thought if she went to her parents' house, he would be motivated to get help. But he blocked her cell phone and unplugged the house phone, so she had no way of telling him that it was not a permanent decision. He was just beyond thinking clearly," Jake admitted.

"That's a relief though, that they could fix things. Hopefully the hospital will help get them both into counseling."

"That's the hope," Jake stated. "I was thinking about you on the drive back."

"Really?"

"If it gets to be too much for you, just tell me. I will understand if you need a break from my issues."

Shea got up and moved to sit on his lap, pressing her face into his neck. "I will never get tired of your issues, and I want to be here for you, always. Whether it's here or from a distance, I hope that I can be the person you turn to when you need someone to talk to."

He studied her for a beat. "You have been, for many, many years. You and my family are the reason I can even sit here and have a normal conversation."

"I should head home," Shea said, leaning in to kiss him. "Let you go check on Charlie."

"You sure? Stella will be cooking, why don't you stick around?"

"Twist my arm," she laughed, and then stood. "But go check on Charlie one more time before we relax. I'll sit here and enjoy the view."

Chapter 42

Jake arrived at the VA a half hour before his appointment with the doctor, which would decide his fate. He wished that he had come here with a firm decision about his future, but in either scenario, he was turning his back on people who needed him. Soldiers like Matt relied on him to lead them through battle, and to offer guidance for when they returned. What if the new first sergeant didn't look out for them the way he did?

On the other hand, he had missed so much of Charlie's life already. They were finally in a good place, and he felt closer to him than ever. His dad and Stella weren't getting any younger, and he was losing years with them as well. And the way he felt about Shea right now, he couldn't imagine leaving her behind. Choosing between two groups who depended on him for very different things, there was no good decision to make.

"Nice to see you again, Jake. How have you been?" The doctor entered the room, looking up from his paperwork to shake hands.

"Good, thanks."

"Physical therapy has been going well, I hear?"

"Yes, sir."

"They reported that your measurements for range of motion remain unchanged from last week." The doctor looked up from his notes. "How is your pain?"

"Some days I barely notice it." Jake lifted his arm as high as he could, feeling the twinge in his shoulder as he did. The doctor's expression showed he wasn't thrilled with the movement, or the look on Jake's face.

"Hopefully those days will become more common as we move away from the surgeries. Can you feel it here?" The doctor pressed on several spots on his arm and shoulder, asking the same question. "The nerve damage is what we expected, based on where the bullet touched and the surgeries. That will impact your ability to feel in some areas, which for most people wouldn't be noticed. For someone who could potentially have to carry a heavy pack or even a person, that is a factor."

"Yes, sir."

"You were already at sixty percent with your disability ranking, we talked about that last time." The doctor settled into the chair behind his desk, leaning forward with his elbows on the desk. "My assessment is going to put you at one hundred. I'm sorry if that's not what you were hoping to hear today. I can't risk sending you back out there."

"I understand." Jake started to stand, then sat back down. "And thank you. I had already realized this was going to happen, and the more I thought about it, the more I came to like the idea. You're giving me five years with my son that I wouldn't have given myself. If you had offered me the chance to go back, I would have felt obligated, and I would have been half the soldier I need to be. So, thank you."

The doctor cleared his throat twice, then stood to shake Jake's hand. "It's been an honor to get to know you. I hope you will continue to come and see me. I want to see you live a full, happy life."

Jake walked out of the office, and then from the medical building, feeling lighter than he had in years. The weight of the decision over his future was gone, now he just had to share the news with his family and Shea. And decide what to do with the rest of his life.

***

Sitting across from his therapist an hour later, he smiled at her for what was likely the first time since they had begun their sessions together. "The doctor just told me that it's time to retire."

"And you're happy with that?"

"I am. I wasn't sure how I felt, but hearing the words from him I knew instantly it was the right decision."

"Would you have come to the same decision on your own?" She tapped a pen on her lips, unwilling to let Jake off the hook easily.

He shrugged. "I can't say. I hope so. I told you about the incident with my friend, getting him to the hospital. That really got through to me, that I was only thinking of myself. Yes, I am worried about the soldiers overseas, but my place is here with Charlie. And Shea."

"Things are progressing with both of them?"

"Yes. Charlie and I get closer every day. He still holds me at a distance, but I'm hoping that will change when I tell him I'm retiring. And Shea," he smiled, thinking of her. "I got lucky. Jenna was amazing and I felt like I could never meet anyone else who knocked out my senses again, you know? But Shea does that. I wake up and think about her, I go to sleep thinking of her. She's been a rock for me through this, but more importantly, she's helped me find my smile again."

"Excellent." The doctor made a note in a small notebook. "Now let's talk about the nightmares."

They settled into their session, delving deeper into the memories that floated into Jake's subconsciousness when he wasn't careful. Somehow, facing them all here, in the bright office, with the kind doctor across from him, made them hurt less. He hoped the more he revisited them, the easier it would get.

Chapter 43

Charlie was walking up the driveway from school when he heard a car approaching and was surprised to see that it was his Uncle Dan's SUV pulling up. "Hey, welcome back," He yelled as Dan got out of the driver's seat.

"Thanks, bud. How are things here?" He popped open the back of the SUV. "Want to help me?"

Charlie trotted over to see the back was full of suitcases and cardboard boxes. "What's going on?"

"Just having a bit of a work crisis, and decided mountain air might be the best solution," Dan answered as he busied himself pulling out two suitcases. "Here, just these ones for now, we can each take one."

"I can help you get the rest?" Charlie asked as he closed the door.

"No, that's okay. Let's keep that between us for now, okay?"

"Sure," he agreed reluctantly.

"Fill me in on what I've missed," Dan asked as they went in the front door.

"I'm sure Stella will have more to tell you, but it's been pretty good. Things with my dad have improved a lot. He's dating Shea and they seem happy. Patrick has been busy working out and riding the horses, and Grandpa has been keeping busy," Charlie shrugged. "Pretty quiet overall, I guess."

They entered the kitchen at the same time Stella came in from the back door, rushing over to hug Dan. "Welcome home, Dan."

"Thanks, it's good to be back. My stomach in particular is glad to be back, it's missed your cooking."

She swatted his arm. "You boys always know how to charm me. I'm working on dinner now, why don't you unpack and settle in? How long are you staying?"

Charlie noticed him hesitating. "Not sure. Little bit."

He vanished up the stairs, and Charlie and Stella exchanged a look. "It's good to know that no matter how old my boys get, they always come home when trouble strikes," Stella remarked.

"How do you know it's trouble?"

"He's here, isn't he?" She laughed and opened the refrigerator, humming as she pulled out ingredients.

***

Jake and Patrick got home from the gym, shocked to find Dan's car in the driveway and their brother on the porch. "What's going on?" Jake asked as they greeted him and fell into their usual seats.

"I can't just come home to see my family?"

"You sound defensive," Patrick declared. "Doesn't he sound defensive?"

Jake nodded. "He does."

Dan sighed. "Can you keep this between the three of us?"

They both nodded. Dan glared at them. Jake glared back as Patrick reassured him they were serious.

"I left my job."

"You what?" Jake was dumbfounded.

"It was an amicable parting."

Patrick snorted. "Is that like conscious uncoupling? You sound very Hollywood."

"Something like that." Dan took a sip of the beer he had been holding.

"And you wanted this?" Jake asked, not buying his brother's casual act.

Dan picked at the label on the bottle. "More or less. I think this is going to give me a chance to reset, see what I really want to do with my life."

"I can see why a high rise in Manhattan would be tough to live with," Patrick said drolly.

"You'd be surprised," Dan replied cryptically, leaving his brothers to stare at each other.

"Anything we should know?" Jake finally dared to ask.

"When there is, I'll tell you." Dan met his gaze. "In the meantime, want to fill me in on what's happening here?"

"Well, Jake is madly in love," Patrick started.

Jake interjected. "We aren't discussing my love life."

"Things are going well, though?" Dan asked.

"Very." Jake wasn't giving them information Shea didn't have yet, it was only fair that he talked to her first. "One thing I've noticed, and I wonder if you guys have. Dad and Stella seem tighter than usual?"

Patrick grimaced. "I didn't want to say anything because it just feels wrong, but I did see Dad coming in from the cottage very early one morning."

"Now that you mention it, they came in together one afternoon when I was napping on the couch," Jake recalled. "I thought it was weird but didn't wake up enough to ask questions."

"Hold up." Dan held his hands up to his face. "Are you guys saying what I think you're saying?"

"I think so." Patrick looked at Jake. "What have you noticed?"

"A lot of little things. They just seem to be spending a lot of time together, and I was wondering if romance was in the air." He pointed at Patick. "You should ask."

"I'm so sick of you guys trying to make me the point guy for every uncomfortable conversation," Patrick sighed. "Besides, we can make Charlie do it. Everyone likes him the best anyway."

"Or we could let them have their privacy and tell us when they are ready," Dan suggested.

"That." Jake pointed at Dan. "That's my vote. Let's keep Dad and Stella's sex life - or potential sex life - out of our heads."

Chapter 44

Jake was sitting on her steps when she returned from her nightly walk with Muffin, and the sight of him caused both her and the puppy to pick up their pace. "Hey, you," she greeted him as she walked up.

He stood and opened his arms, folding her in while reaching down to pet Muffin's head. "How are my girls?"

"Much better now that you're here." She opened the door. "Come inside, it's getting chilly. Want me to open a bottle of wine?"

"I'm good with water, unless you want some."

"No, water is fine for me as well. Let me just fill her bowl and get us each a bottle, you relax." She busied herself in the kitchen for a minute, filling the dog's bowl and grabbing two waters and a bowl of nuts to bring to the living room. "How was your day?"

"It was interesting." He accepted the water from her and took a long swig. "How was yours?"

"Probably boring in comparison to yours. Kids are getting worked up about Halloween, hopefully the store is putting a limit on who can buy toilet paper this week." They both laughed, thinking back to their own teen years. "Tell me about yours."

"Well, first, Dan is back." He waited while she exclaimed her surprise. "Out of nowhere, he shows up and tells us he quit his job. Dan hasn't taken significant time off work since he was sixteen, so something is up, but he won't tell us."

"He will when he's ready," Shea guessed.

"And we all spent some time speculating about my dad and Stella's relationship, but then decided we didn't want to think about it."

"Probably for the best," Shea advised. "I've seen them enough to think there is something happening there, but if they wanted you to know, you would know."

"Exactly. And who wants to think about their parent's love life?" Jake mused. "I mean, Stella isn't our mom, but she basically is. It's a shift if they move from what we thought were just platonic friends to something else, but I'll wait until that is announced before I really think about it."

"Has either one of them ever dated?" Shea asked. "I mean someone other than each other."

Jake thought, trying to remember back to when they were kids. "Now that you mention it, no. I can't remember either of them ever going on a date."

"And none of you randy boys thought that was weird?" Shea teased.

Jake shuddered. "We have to stop talking about this."

Shea laughed. "Okay, what else?"

He took a deep breath, looking into her eyes. "I love you. I have loved you for so long, I don't even know when it started, but sometime when we started really opening up in our messages. I love the compassion you have shown me, the kindness you show everyone around you. I love how you stand by me even when I do something stupid. I love that you have helped me navigate this rocky road with Charlie, and I love how you are with him. I have been wanting to say this for so long, and I'm sure I'm fumbling here, but…"

"I love you too." She told him tearfully, leaning forward to kiss him.

He held back from sweeping her off the couch and to her bedroom, despite her wrapping herself around him. "Shea, there's more."

"Oh," she sat back, looking adorably flustered and pink cheeked.

"I saw my doctor today, at the VA," He explained. "I am going to medically retire. The doctor started the paperwork today for my disability to increase to one hundred, so I can't go back to active duty in the capacity I was in. I have been talking to my counselor about it a lot and thinking about my future. The more time I have spent with you and Charlie, the more I knew that I couldn't leave. You're stuck with me for the long haul."

She openly cried now, grabbing him, and holding on tight. "I can't tell you how relieved I am. I wouldn't have stopped you from going, but I am so incredibly happy to know you will be staying."

He kissed her again. "It's only been a few weeks, so I won't rush you to move in together or talk about getting married —"

"A few weeks? This has been happening for years, pal. You better believe I'm keeping you forever." She laughed through her tears. "I don't care where we are, or anything else, as long as we are together."

"No more tears, please." He wiped them away before kissing her. "I haven't told anyone else my plans yet. Or how I feel about you, and I need to have that conversation with Charlie to see what he thinks."

"I don't think he will be surprised."

"No, I don't either. But if you and I decide to live together in a few months, would he want to be with us?" Jake wondered. "Things like that, I need to talk to him and see where his head is."

Shea nodded. "I get it. We need to make sure he's comfortable, he's been living at your house his entire life, basically. Uprooting him to move might make things difficult when you're finally getting your fresh start."

"Exactly. So, if you don't mind not having me all the time, we can figure this out together."

"Of course. Charlie is the most important part of this," She smiled at him. "I hope one day we will be a family, and he is one-third of that equation, so we need him to feel good about it. What did he think when you told him about your retirement?"

"I didn't tell him yet," Jake admitted. "He had hockey practice and a team dinner, so he won't be home until around ten. I want to make sure I'm there when he gets home, so I can tell him right away."

"Did you tell your family?"

"Not yet. It didn't seem fair to tell them before you and Charlie. This impacts you two the most, so you should be the first to know."

"I think they'll be thrilled."

"Me too. Speaking of family, any news on Christine and Ryan's pregnancy hopes?" It was an abrupt turn, but she was touched that he knew how much she had been worrying about her friend.

"She hasn't said anything to me yet. I'm hoping their weekend in Montreal did the trick." She held up her hands, both with fingers crossed.

"We should probably talk about whether we want to add a built-in best friend for their baby." Jake looked thoughtful, and her heart felt it might explode.

"I would like that very much, but you need some time to adjust to being home and a regular member of society before we go down that path. Speaking of, do you have any thoughts on what the future holds for you?"

"I was thinking retirement and being a kept man might be a good idea?"

She laughed. "You'd be bored in ten minutes."

"You're right," he nodded. "I might try to go back to school, see what interests me. I've always been a big proponent of my troops doing that, and I'd be a hypocrite not to do the same. Careerwise, I'm a little torn. Part of me wants to be a counselor, helping people like me. The other part knows it's all too close to home, and hearing everyone else's stories is going to bring up my own. I can't help people if I'm a mess myself."

"No, that might be a little dark." She tapped her lip, thinking. "Maybe a guidance counselor? Or some other job in the Veteran world, help people find the tools they need to succeed?"

"I think we've discussed my distant future enough. Let's focus on our immediate gratification for a while," he suggested, reaching for her. She was more than happy to focus on any future that included him in her arms.

Chapter 45

Charlie got home from practice and walked in on his father scowling at a laptop sitting on the kitchen counter. As he got closer, he saw it was an airline website open, and his heart fell.

"Hey, pal." His dad closed the laptop and turned to him.

"Hi," he grabbed an apple from the basket on the counter and tried to keep walking to the stairs.

"I need to talk to you; can we sit down?" His dad was already pushing back the chairs at the table, pointing to one for him.

"I really have a lot of homework to get to."

"Charlie, this is important. And it won't take long."

He sighed, going back to lean on the doorframe in the kitchen. "What is it?"

"You don't want to sit?"

He just shrugged, feeling the weight of the backpack on his shoulder.

"I had my physical at the VA this morning. Today was to determine if I could go back to active duty, if I wanted to," His dad cleared his throat. "Before I get to that, I want to say how much this time together has meant to me. I feel like we are in a good place, and I hope it will stay that way."

"Sure," he bit into the apple to give himself something to do.

"I was just booking a flight to go back to Virginia —"

"Great. Happy for you." He turned to flee for the stairs then heard his dad call his name again.

"I'm not done."

"I am. You're going to give me some excuse about how you need to go back, but it's only a few more years, and everything will be fine." He hitched the backpack up higher. "Only in five years, I'll be in college, and I honestly don't think I'll have time to hang out then. Hope you enjoy your time in Virginia, I'll see you around."

"Charlie," his dad stood up at the table. "I'm not leaving for good."

His step faltered. "You aren't?"

"No," he shook his head. "I need to go sign some paperwork, pack up my place, turn in my equipment. I will be gone for a couple days, at most. I was going to ask if you wanted to come with me."

"What papers do you need to sign?"

"Retirement. I had already decided that it was time, and the doctor confirmed it today," He cleared his throat. "I plan to move back here. Spend time with you. And with Shea. I hope that's alright with you."

"Yeah, whatever. I like her." He finally dropped the backpack on the floor. "Are you sure about this?"

"Very. This is what I want."

"Okay, good." Charlie suddenly didn't know what to do with his hands. "I'm glad. And sure, I'd like to go with you, if you mean that."

"You won't mind missing a few days of school?"

Charlie laughed. "Can we make it a week?"

Patrick and Dan came in the back door, looking at both of them standing stupidly in the kitchen laughing. "What's up?"

"I'm retiring," Jake announced. "Charlie and I are going to fly down to finalize everything. Then I'm moving back here for good."

"Need us to fly down with you?" Dan asked.

Jake looked at Charlie and then shook his head. "I think we'll be okay."

"Wouldn't mind a private plane, if that's in the cards," Charlie suggested to Patrick.

"I can probably make that happen if you're serious." Patrick stuck his head in the fridge.

"For real?" Charlie felt his eyes bugging.

"Sure. For my brother's retirement? All the bells and whistles. Just let me know when you want to leave and for how long, I'll get my people to set it up." Patrick unscrewed the top of a water bottle, taking a long sip from it.

"His people…" Jake and Dan howled with laughter.

Ben emerged from his office with Stella, entering the kitchen amid all the laughter. "What's happening?"

"I'm retiring, Patrick's got people, and Dan has nothing going on," Jake answered. "Although the Dan part is just sad."

"I'm fine, thanks," Dan sniped.

"Oh, I'm so happy for you, Jake." Stella crossed to embrace him. "And you too, Charlie."

"Hope you don't mind me moving back in," Jake looked to his dad.

"About that." Ben crossed to where Stella stood and put his arm around her. "Since we are all sharing good news, we have some to share. Stella and I are getting married next week. I'll be moving out back with her into the cottage, so you boys can have the run of the house."

All four of them stood in silence, staring at Ben and Stella. Stella was blushing, looking at all of them and elbowing Ben in the side. "You could have asked me first."

"Wait, you didn't ask her?" Jake looked stunned.

"We've been together for long enough; I didn't think I needed to." He turned to Stella. "Do you need me down on one knee?"

"Don't be silly, you old fool. Of course, I'll marry you. But I expect a big ring and all four of these boys to be there to give me away." She dabbed at her eyes.

Patrick stepped forward to hug her. "This is blowing my mind, and I have a lot of questions I'm not going to ask. But I'm happy for you."

"We all are," Dan and Jake stepped forward, gesturing to Charlie to join the family hug. He wasn't quite sure when he had gotten used to having all five of his relatives here wanting to hug him all the time, but he was okay with this one more time.

Chapter 46

Jake straightened his tie, then turned to do the same for Charlie. Stella had planned the wedding in a week's time, telling anyone who would listen that she had waited this long for Ben Burrows to make her an honest woman, she wouldn't wait one minute longer than necessary. His dad had opted to have four best men, although Stella also wanted all four of them to walk her down the aisle. Patrick and Dan were ready to go, hollering up the stairs every thirty seconds for Jake and Charlie to hurry up.

"If Stella heard you yelling like that," Jake said to his brothers as he came down the stairs. "She would have your heads."

"Good thing she's already at the church with Shea, getting ready." Patrick smirked. "You two ready? Dad's been outside chomping at the bit to get there."

The five of them climbed into Dan's SUV and headed toward town, with Ben tapping on his knee nervously the entire way.

"Dad, you worried she won't turn up?" Dan asked as he turned onto Main Street.

"I've been waiting a long time for this day," Ben responded. "Ready to have it over with and finally claim Stella as my own forever."

"Well, if that's not romance, I don't know what is." Patrick clapped his hands together.

"Hey, smart ass, keep your funny business out of the wedding!" Ben snapped.

Patrick reached forward and squeezed his dad's shoulder. "I'm only teasing you, Dad. We are all thrilled for you. And couldn't ask for a better mother, even if we are well past the diaper stage."

Jake stifled a laugh as Ben pretended to try and swing at Patrick and unbuckled as they pulled into the parking lot of the church. They would have a quick ceremony here, followed by a small reception that Kendra had insisted on hosting at the Palace. Most of the town would be in attendance, although no invitations had gone out, everyone had heard about it and made it known they would be there.

"I'll go make sure they are ready," Jake told them as he turned to walk into the church. "Oh, Patrick, look alive. Looks like the paparazzi figured out where you were hiding out."

He pointed to where a small collection of photographers were stationed, cameras pointed at the SUV. "I knew that would happen when Deux Moi posted that picture of me last week." Patrick shook his head. "Guess you'll get some extra wedding pictures, Pops."

Dan was offering to speak to them as Jake jogged off, knowing the cameramen would ignore him. He ducked into the church and let his eyes adjust to the light, realizing suddenly that Shea was standing just inside the vestibule smiling at him. "Hey, you." He stared at her, a vision in a short black strapless dress and sky-high heels. "You look amazing."

"I'm a little uncomfortable and kind of want to go put a sweater on, but Christine is adamant that I show some skin." She fidgeted with the top of the dress.

"I always knew I liked her," he framed her face with his hands. "Will I mess up your lipstick if I kiss you?"

"It will be worth it," she responded, meeting him halfway.

They both turned at the sound of a loud throat clearing, to find the reverend standing behind them. "Unless you two want to make this a double ceremony, I would suggest you separate and get a move on." He winked at them and waved his hand, shooing them off to their tasks.

"I'll be in my seat," Shea whispered as she disappeared through the church door.

Jake knocked on the door to the bridal suite, and heard Stella call out for him to enter. He stopped just inside the doorway, his breath taken for the second time since he had entered the church. Stella was in a simple, dove gray dress with flowers embroidered along the bodice and down the sheer sleeves. The dress cinched at her waist and fell to the floor, hiding her shoes. Someone had pinned her hair up and added a few small flowers, matching those she held in her hands. He blinked away some tears and crossed to kiss her on the cheek. "You look stunning."

"Are you sure I don't look like an old fool? Patrick had a designer ship in a bunch of dresses and had a seamstress come to help me pick one. I would have been happy with something I had in the closet." She fussed with the dress as she spoke, but he could see the delight in her eyes.

"You look perfect. Exactly as you should on your wedding day. My dad won't know what hit him." Jake heard the church door open and quickly closed the suite door halfway. "That's him now, let us get him to the front of the church and then we will be right back to walk you down the aisle."

The four of them jostled for position the entire way down the aisle, each wanting to be the one who was right by her side. She solved the problem by stopping halfway, trading Dan and Patrick's arms for Jake and Charlie's to finish her journey down the aisle. The four of them slid into the pew, where Shea sat waiting for Jake, in the front of the church. He grabbed her hand and held on as they watched Ben and Stella exchange their sweet, simple vows.

"Maybe one day soon, this could be us," He leaned over and whispered in her ear.

"If that's your idea of a proposal, we have some work to do," she responded, squeezing his hand.

"You know how I love a challenge," he smiled down at her, until Charlie elbowed him and told him to quiet down.

They emerged from the church to the perfect crisp autumn day, surrounded by well-wishers who would follow them across the park to the Palace. The local wedding photographer grouped them for some family shots in the park, and the entire family agreed to one shot with Patrick's paparazzi photographers if they would agree to leave them alone for the rest of the day. Jake pulled Shea into that picture, knowing she would get a kick out of seeing herself in a magazine the following week.

Kendra had decorated the Windsor Peak Palace with autumn colors, fresh flowers on each table adorned with maple leaves, and pictures of Ben and Stella over the years. A band was playing on the stage, and a dance floor was set for the first dance. They all entered to cheers from the townspeople, who were happily sipping the champagne Patrick had ordered and enjoying the appetizers Kendra was putting out.

The band leader announced Ben and Stella, who beamed as they started their first dance, appropriately to Etta James' song *At Last*. When the band suggested other couples from the family join them, Jake pulled Shea onto the dance floor and was shocked when Kendra allowed Dan to lead her out to dance. Patrick and Charlie stayed on the edge of the dance floor; Patrick's arm draped over his nephew's shoulder as they swayed to the song.

"This is a pretty perfect day," Jake murmured in Shea's ear.

"It really is," she smiled at Kendra as they passed the other couple.

"To think, it just took me getting shot for all of this to happen," he mused.

She rested her head on his injured shoulder lightly. "Let's consider that a one and done, okay? No more bullets for this family."

"Deal," he kissed the top of her head and then pulled her from the dance floor as their neighbors swarmed to dance. Kendra and Dan soon followed, and Jake saw a whispered conversation happening between them at the opposite end of the bar.

"I wonder if he's making any progress?" Shea wondered.

He watched as Kendra walked away from Dan, who had a frustrated look on his face. "It doesn't look like it, but who knows. I'm sure they will figure it out."

Late that evening, he stood in a corner at Windsor Peak Palace with Shea at his side, smiling and laughing with his son and brothers, and watching his dad kiss his new wife. He realized he was full of happiness and peace; even knowing that he had to stand here against the wall, and that the nightmares would come again. Knowing the grief of losing Jenna so young would never leave him, he found comfort in knowing that ache could make way for happiness in his heart when he thought of her. This was what he had been searching for all these years, and he had finally found it by coming home.

Acknowledgements

This book would not have been possible without some amazing cheerleaders behind me. My parents, Jim and Arlene Giddings, have taught me from day one that I can do anything I set my mind to. They encouraged me to write, they supported me and my neurotic insecurity as I worked through drafts, and they were my first readers. I love you and am so grateful for you both.

Jeff and Danielle, thank you for always being there, always being ready to listen, and just being my amazing family. Brendan, Conor, Timmy, Tessa and Emmy – I love you all and am so excited to share this with you.

My friend from childhood on was lost on 9/11 when we were in our early twenties. I think of Jen constantly, and we say that she fixed up my husband and I from heaven. She was a beautiful person inside and out, and everyone who knew her feels her loss. I encourage you to get to know her and the good things her family has done in her memory by visiting her website (https://jenniferlynnkane.com/).

My friends, who were early readers and some of whom asked to be in the book, so you may recognize their names! Tina, Julie, Kelly and Matt – your excitement over me doing this helped motivate me. There are too many other friends to list, and I'm afraid I would forget someone – but I'm lucky to have you all in my life!

Book Designs by Shae (on IG at@bookdesignsbyshae), who created the cover art for me and put up with my changes. My critique partners, Tessa, Rachel, Meredith, Justine, and James. I can't wait to read your books when they are published!

Last but certainly not least - my husband, Tom, and our two sons, Cam and Calum. My husband is Retired U.S. Army, and although Jake is not based on him, the experiences we have had played a role in the idea behind this story. Tom retired from the Army after having served in Iraq in 2003 and Afghanistan in 2010, where he was awarded a Bronze Star. Our Veterans are so important and should always receive the care they need, from physical to mental and everything in between. I'm thankful for all our service members, for all they do for us.

Find me on Instagram (@DeniseLathamWrites), Amazon or Goodreads to be alerted when the next book will be released! Please remember to leave a review and share this book if you enjoyed it. I'm also happy to join book club discussions about this book, you can reach me via my website www.deniselatham.com

Turn the page to find out what happens next for Dan and Kendra in:

Staying Home

Windsor Peak book 2

Chapter 1

Dan Burrows had last felt sane on the night of his father's wedding, when he held his ex-girlfriend in his arms during the first dance. The moment had been far too brief, and the weeks since his world had completely come apart. Granted, it had started to come undone weeks before the wedding, when he had to walk away from his high-powered job in Manhattan, but things had gotten considerably worse.

He had lost the ability to have a coherent thought, he was so fixated on getting Kendra back into his arms again. The work situation needed to be resolved as well, and after spending the last few weeks talking to clients and evaluating, he was getting close to deciding his approach. Being betrayed by a person he considered a close friend stung, so the distraction of his ex-girlfriend came at a good time.

With that thought in mind, he pulled open the heavy door into Kendra's restaurant, The Windsor Peak Palace. It was midday, so there were only a handful of people inside when he entered. He saw a few of his dad's friends playing pool in the back, and a small group of women were playing mahjong at a table. Kendra Knight stood behind the bar, her back to the door, talking to a woman eating a salad. She turned to see who had entered, and her smile disappeared quickly when she saw it was him. Not one to be pushed off easily, he slid onto a barstool and waited for her to cross.

"Hi," she said as she slapped a napkin on the bar in front of him. "Want a drink?"

"Just a Pepsi is fine, thanks." He smiled at her. "How are you?"

"Great." She placed a cup in front of him. "This all?"

"No, I'm a little hungry so I think I'll look over the menu."

"Dan," she said quietly. "You must have it memorized by now. We have been doing this same thing for weeks."

"You could just agree to go to dinner with me, and then we wouldn't have to keep this up." Dan shrugged. "Otherwise, I'll just have to come sit here every afternoon and try to make you realize how much you miss me."

"I've seen you every day for weeks now. I couldn't possibly miss you, because you won't go away."

"Does that mean we're on for dinner tomorrow?"

"No, Dan." She rolled her eyes at him. "We're not going down this path again."

The door opened, and Dan turned to see his brother Jake walk into the restaurant. He crossed and slid onto the barstool to Dan's right, smiling at Kendra as he did. "What's going on? Day drinking for the unemployed?"

"Hey, Jake," Kendra greeted him.

"I'm not drinking," Dan said, pointing at his soda. "Just having a soda and trying to convince Kendra that she should give me another chance."

"She's way too smart for that." Jake grinned at her, and Kendra laughed in return as she agreed. "Stella wanted me to ask you to come to dinner at the house. She and our dad want to thank you for all you did for their wedding."

"That's really nice of them, but unnecessary. I wanted to help," Kendra replied.

"They spend a lot of time trying to figure out how to thank you, so don't be surprised if they do something crazy if you play hard to get." Jake pointed at Dan. "Just like this guy."

"Shouldn't you be in class?" Dan asked, trying to hurry his brother along. Jake had recently begun taking classes at Windsor Peak College, working towards his contractor's license.

"I'm done by one most days, so just killing some time until Shea and Charlie are done with school. We're going to Burlington to get Charlie some new skates. Kid grows too fast; his feet are bigger than mine now." Jake's son was about to turn fifteen after the holidays and was already taller than his father and two uncles. "Want to come with us? We're going to grab a bite to eat on the way back."

"No, thanks." He glanced at where Kendra was busy with customers at the end of the bar. "I'm going to stick around here for a while."

"Not a good look to beg, you know." Jake glanced at his watch. "Maybe she needs a little space?"

"I gave her all these years, didn't I?"

"Not on purpose. Or at least, I don't think it was on purpose. Did you ghost her so that you could come back all this time later and win her back?"

"Go away, Jake." Dan pointed at the door.

"Just stating facts, my brother. You're the older, wiser one, after all." Jake stood and slapped a hand on Dan's shoulder. "Try something different, that's all I'm saying. This isn't working."

Dan nodded and watched his brother leave, thinking about what he had said. So far, he had tried sending her flowers and candy, which didn't work. He tried to talk to her at social events where they were together, but she moved away as quickly as possible. Sitting at the bar every day was clearly not getting him any points. Aside from the one dance at his father's wedding, he had struck out entirely.

Watching as she made her way down to his end of the bar, he considered his options. She expected him to disappear again, so he couldn't just drop out of sight and hope she understood that it was to get her attention. "You really should come for dinner at the house. Are you free tomorrow?" He blurted it out without thinking and was surprised when it looked like she was considering it.

"Maybe," she said slowly. "I haven't seen your dad and Stella since they got back from Aruba, so it would be nice to see them. And I don't want them to think I'm avoiding them."

His day brightened up immediately. "They would love it. Come at six, okay?"

Making a move to slide off the stool before she could change her mind, he was stopped by her voice. "One thing, Dan."

"Of course, what?"

"I'd have to bring Calle." Her six-year-old daughter, who Dan had only met briefly in town and while at the restaurant.

"Not a problem. Stella will love having you both."

"Just don't start thinking this will turn into something, okay? I'm just coming to have dinner with the family, not as a date."

"Not a date, got it." Dan zipped up his jacket as he nodded.

"Dan," she waited until he looked up. "I'm serious. Especially in front of Calle, I can't have you trying to be my boyfriend. She has never seen me with anyone, and I don't want to spend the next three months answering questions. We're friends, that's it."

"Friends who also would maybe have a date in the future?"

"Dan. Don't make me regret this."

"I will be on my best behavior; you have my word." He turned to leave. "Six, tomorrow. See you then."

He drove home, tapping to the beat of the song on the radio, with a smile on his face. Finally, a tiny step in the right direction. However small, he would take it and run with it. He made the biggest mistake of his life at eighteen years old, and that included the huge error that had cost him his job. Putting his life together piece by piece would take time, and he needed to be patient, no matter how hard it was. He needed to figure out the next baby step he could take with Kendra, and he knew just who to turn to for help with it.

****

The smell of baking bread hit his nose as he entered his childhood home, where he had been living the last few months since leaving New York. His father and Stella, both of his brothers, and his nephew Charlie all lived there as well, but the house was large and had plenty of room to escape each other. In addition to the main house, there was a small guest cottage out back where Stella had lived for years, a barn and a stable.

Stella, now his stepmother, but really his mom in so many ways, was at the stove stirring a pot. He crossed the kitchen to kiss her on the head and grab a cup of coffee before sitting at the kitchen island.

"Hi, honey," she smiled at him. "What's up?"

"I just came from seeing Kendra, she's going to come to dinner tomorrow night," he told her. "She's bringing Calle as well."

"Oh, that's wonderful. I've barely seen her since we got back from the honeymoon."

"I wondered—" Hesitation to spill his emotions on the kitchen floor held his tongue.

"Wondered what?"

"If you had any advice for me. About that."

"Dinner, or Kendra?"

"I think I can manage to eat dinner okay," he smiled. "But I can't seem to get through to Kendra. She doesn't want to talk to me, won't even give me a chance to apologize to her."

"What do you need to apologize for?"

"You were here, you know."

"I do know that," she gazed at him. "But do you know what hurt her? That's something important you should be thinking about, because when the time comes if you're not sincere or don't hit what hurt her, you wasted your time."

"Do you think she'll ever give me another chance?"

"I don't know," Stella admitted. "She loved you deeply and was very hurt. But I hope she'll come to realize that you were

318

children, and you were bound to make mistakes. The experiences and lives you have led in the time apart can help you to build a better, stronger relationship now, if you both want that."

"I hope so."

"Dan, look at me." When he complied, she continued. "She wants to be strong, but she's fragile. I love you, and I want nothing more than for you to find happiness. I also suspect that your unresolved feelings for Kendra have kept you from finding that with someone else. But I don't want you to hurt her in order to resolve your feelings. If you only want to clear the air, or be forgiven, then there are other ways to make yourself feel better about things. If you want to really consider building a life with Kendra, you also have to be committed to being here. Being a stepdad. Those are things that will not change in her life."

He nodded, taking her advice to heart. It did sting to see Kendra so friendly with his brothers while ignoring him, and it was important that he wanted her for more than his ego. If she would give him a chance, spend some time with him, maybe they could both find out if they were even still compatible. Then he could figure out the rest.

Chapter 2

Kendra parked in the driveway and took a deep breath, looking at the house she had spent so much time in as a teenager. The white farmhouse seemed to glow in the night, with light beaming out the windows and from lamps along the long front porch. The nights got dark early this time of year, and the Burrows family seemed to accommodate the darkness by turning on every light in the house.

"Mama, let me out!" Calle demanded from the backseat, plucking at the buckles on her booster seat. Kendra knew she was overprotective to still have her six-year-old strapped in, at least according to the moms in the drop-off line at school, but Calle was all she had. She wasn't risking anything happening to her so she could save thirty seconds in the school parking lot.

"I'm coming, hold on." She gathered her purse, and the gifts she had brought along, before getting out to open the rear car door. Unbuckling Calle, she then handed her a small bouquet of flowers to carry. "These are for Ms. Stella. Or Mrs. Burrows now, I suppose."

"Okay, let's go!" Calle raced up the porch steps, no regard for the snow or ice that carpeted the pathway. Fortunately, she made it safely and was ringing the doorbell as Kendra climbed the stairs slowly. They both heard dogs bark from inside the house, and Calle's wide eyes met hers. "Mama, dogs!"

"Yes, honey, you know—" She was cut off by the door opening, showing a grinning Dan in the entryway holding two Labrador retrievers by their collars.

"Hi," he said, looking from Kendra to Calle. "I'm Dan. This is Twix and this is Reese."

"I love them," Calle declared, lunging forward for the kisses the dogs were waiting to disperse. She shoved the flowers into Dan's hands as she fell to the floor, giggling and surrounded by happy dogs.

"If only your mom was so easily swayed." Dan cocked an eyebrow in Kendra's direction.

"You promised," she whispered in what she hoped was a menacing way.

"I did, and I'll stick with it. Let me take your coats."

She handed him the bottle of wine she carried first. "I brought this for Stella and your dad."

"I'll pass it along. Thanks for coming."

They stared at each other for a long moment, and she let herself get washed back in time. Years ago, standing in this same spot, ready to go to prom. Her first kiss in the barn out back. Playing games with his family at the table they would sit at shortly, watching movies cuddled on the couch with him. Forcing herself to look away, she pushed the memories aside and focused on the present.

The thud of footsteps coming down the stairs preceded Dan's nephew Charlie appearing, and Kendra gave him a quick hug. Calle had grown up idolizing Charlie, the closest thing she had to a brother or cousin. Stella had made sure they saw each other regularly, so Calle had grown up seeing him play hockey and having him as an occasional babysitter, making their bond strong. She ran to him and threw herself at his legs, squealing with delight at seeing him. He picked her up and swung her around quickly before placing her safely on the ground. "Hey squirt, how are you?"

"I love your dogs. Will you read to me?" She gazed up at him adoringly.

He grabbed the small backpack she had dropped on the floor. "Sure, let's go on the couch. But I'm not doing Princess voices."

They argued as they made their way to the family room, and Dan led her into the kitchen, where Stella was behind the stove. Ben Burrows, Dan's father, sat at the island with a glass of whiskey in front of him. Kendra greeted both with a kiss on the cheek and pointed to the wine Dan held. "I brought a bottle of red, and Calle brought you flowers, but she dropped everything for Charlie and the dogs."

"I would do the same if I were her," Stella smiled. "Have a seat, or you two can grab a drink and go sit by the fire. Jake just went to pick up Shea, they should be here any minute."

Kendra hesitated, looking at Dan. He answered for them, holding up the wine he held. "Let's open this and sit by the fire to warm up while we wait for Jake and Shea." He quickly opened the bottle and poured two glasses, handing her one before leading her to the living room off the kitchen where a fire roared.

"I've always loved this room," Kendra mused as she walked around the large space. The room spanned the entire length of the house, and the wall with the fireplace was covered in pictures of the boys as they grew up. The wood beams in the ceiling and the stone going up the wall over the fire gave the room a cozy feeling despite being so large. A piano sat in one corner, a small bar set up in another, and a large seating area was in front of the fire.

"I appreciate it more as an adult than I did as a kid," Dan admitted. "We weren't allowed in here much when we were younger. I guess we just tracked mud everywhere and Stella wasn't having it in here."

"You three were pretty wild," Kendra agreed as she walked to look at the pictures on the wall, pausing when she came to one of Charlie as an infant with his mom, Jenna. Jenna had been tragically killed in a bombing when Charlie was only three months old, and Jake had shocked everyone when he enlisted in the Army and virtually disappeared for the next fourteen years. He had come home after being shot in Afghanistan a few months ago and decided to stay. "How is Charlie doing with Jake here full time now?"

"He's adjusting. I think it helps that he didn't have to move anywhere. Since my dad and Stella got married, they have been living out in the cottage out back where Stella has lived all these years. Stella keeps saying they will come to the main house when the honeymoon phase is over, which we all prefer to block from our brains." Dan pretended to shudder, and Kendra laughed. "Jake is thinking of building a house on a clearing just past the barn, that way when he and Shea are ready to live together, Charlie could still stay here but be around all the time, if he wanted."

"That's a great idea. Are Shea and Jake ready to move in so quick?"

"Well, remember, they wrote to each other for years. So even though the relationship is new, it's moving a lot faster than two strangers getting together."

She saw the look in his eye and held her hand up. "Don't start."

"I didn't say a word," Dan insisted as Patrick came into the room.

"Hey, Kendra." Patrick hugged her quickly before sitting on the couch. Kendra quickly sat next to him, leaving Dan the other couch or the chairs as his options for sitting.

"How are you, Patrick?"

"Great, staying busy. I just got back to Vermont yesterday, I had to fly over to Japan to do a commercial shoot." He yawned and covered his mouth with his hand. "Sorry, I'm still adjusting."

"That's a long flight to shoot a commercial. You must be exhausted."

Patrick shrugged. "You get used to it. And it's not like they have me flying coach, so I can sleep on the plane. I should have stuck around a few extra days or gone to Australia or Hawaii to break it up, but I just wanted to get back here. I'm so used to being home now, it's getting harder to leave."

"When do you have to travel again?" Kendra asked, leaning back on the couch.

"Not until after the holidays. I fly out in January to do some costume fittings, then we start filming in February in Georgia. I'll get home in between the two, I hope. The script is top secret, so I might need to relocate sooner than I thought to start working on that."

"Do you have lines? I thought you just flexed and beat people up?" Dan teased him with a grin.

"Yes, Daniel, I have lines." Patrick rolled his eyes at his brother. "These movies are no joke. We work long days, it's hard physically and we have to memorize a lot of dialogue. Some of it isn't even real words, since they introduced so many aliens and other planets. It's more than just fun."

"I know, I'm just kidding. I see all the paperwork you need to sign." Dan looked at his brother suddenly with a quizzical look on his face. "Speaking of, you never told me what the paperwork was that you signed at the Palace that night. What was that?"

"It was nothing, why do you keep bringing it up?" Patrick sounded irritated to Kendra's ear.

"As your lawyer, I should read everything before you sign it."

"You don't read the autographs I sign," Patrick pointed out.

Dan shot him a look. "Big difference between an autograph and what looked like legal documents."

"I bought some land, if you must know. And I had a real estate attorney check everything over, so you don't have to worry." With a huff, Patrick stood up from the couch. "If you'll excuse me, I'm going to find a beer."

They both watched as he left the room, and Kendra turned to Dan once he was gone. "You could cut him some slack. He is an adult. And a very rich, successful adult at that."

He sighed. "I know. It's hard, he lived with me as a teenager when I was in law school, and I was responsible for him. It's hard to stop thinking of him as my kid brother who needs looking after."

"He's pretty well grown by now," Kendra pointed out. "I think you owe him an apology."

"I will, later tonight. I promise." Dan placed his glass on the table in front of them and leaned toward her with a serious look on his face. "Kendra, I know- "

The noise level suddenly rose as Jake and Shea entered the kitchen, and the sound of all the voices and dogs barking broke up whatever Dan had been about to say. Kendra stood, wanting to break the tension between them. "Let's go say hi to them."

Dan stepped forward suddenly, putting himself between the door and Kendra. "Before we go out there, I just need to say one thing. I'm sorry. I know I owe you a million apologies, and it will never be enough, but I wanted to say it sincerely. I don't know how to explain what went wrong with me back then, and I don't know why I haven't fixed it until now. I'd really like the chance to try and explain to you. I plan to keep trying to convince you to let me, so you should get used to the idea."

She stared at him for a long moment, feeling frozen. "I appreciate the apology," she finally managed to say.

He stepped aside and waved an arm, indicating for her to walk through the door in front of him. She did so, feeling a little caught off guard. Yes, he had been hitting on her for weeks now, and trying to talk to her, but this was the first time she could ever remember him issuing an apology to her. Dan was not one to ever admit he was wrong, and hearing the words from his mouth shook her more than she wanted to reveal.

Pushing the emotions that rose to the surface aside, she entered the kitchen, determined to just enjoy the night with friends. Tonight, when she was alone in her bed, she could question what it was she was feeling for Dan at this moment.